THE EXPERIMENTAL

BUG

BOOK I: BRILLIANCE

By Jelani-Akin Parham

Printed in the United States of America

Akinink Publishing, 2017
ISBN 9-7800999-7339050-0
www.jelani-akin.com

Cover Illustrations by Ron Edwards
Twitter: @KirMett
Web: redwardart.carbonmade.com

Edited by Justin Poroszok

In memory of B.K.,
and my grandfather, William.

I

She clipped her student ID badge to her pleated skirt. The sound of the metal clip snapping shut was a gentle reminder that now, she had to be normal. At the very least, she had to play the part enough that no one bothered her. The brown-skinned girl tilted the badge into her view a bit.

Pilar Sans, she thought. *They managed to spell my last name wrong this time. That's new.*

It had been three years since the day Pilar's father vanished. And while her brother, Seth, tried to get her to move on, she continued hunting down as much information as she could. She truly couldn't help it; every night, she had the same nightmare of the monster that attacked him in his lab.

Until she found answers, that nightmare meant less and less sleep.

Seth didn't like her newfound obsession, especially as of late, and often made it known. There was little she could do about his interfering in her life though since he was her legal guardian. For her, staying with Seth was simply a means to an end. After all, she couldn't just live in the loft at her father's old lab by herself. That would require money, a resource she was quite short on.

Seth had expected Pilar to be unprepared for the aptitude tests from his school. To his surprise, she wasn't just ready for them, she aced them. She scored near-perfect in math and was only a point or two away from perfect in every other category. Her score on the math section was absolutely unheard-of, especially for the advanced placement exams. She'd scored higher than most of the advanced students.

So, at the age of sixteen, Pilar would be attending college. She knew in the back of her mind that it was the last thing that Seth had expected. And yet, for her there was a new level of insecurity building. She wasn't ready for it herself.

Her schedule at Rock City University consisted of all advanced classes except for History and English. Nonetheless, it was a pretty tough place to study. And yet she'd already convinced herself that it wouldn't provide much of a challenge at all. The challenge would be dealing with the thousands of other students there that she didn't care to meet.

She walked into the living room, still straightening her black, pleated skirt and violet blouse before she sat down in front of the television. The thirty-six-inch flat-screen provided a vivid picture, something her brother tended to ignore. She figured that his special talent in life was rarely knowing how to enjoy the things he got—even the things he actually earned.

The television was a gift from an uncle in Toronto. Pilar and Seth assumed he'd sent it as an apology for ducking away from looking after Pilar when their dad disappeared. Regardless of who had sent it and why, she was going to enjoy that TV while it was there.

Outside of a few uncles and aunts, they didn't have a long list of family members who kept in contact with them regularly. The last aunt who Pilar could have legally stayed with lived in Cairo, and Pilar wasn't very enthusiastic about moving to Egypt. She was far too well adjusted to American life to move to another country.

The first thing that popped on to the screen was the local *Channel 8 News. Since when does Seth watch or even care about the news?* She was prepared to switch to something more mind-numbing—reality television was a weakness of hers—when her attention was captured by the news story at hand:

". . . this masked vigilante has not been caught yet, but she has been spotted in the Shopping District in Downtown Rock City on at least three separate occasions within the past three weeks. Both the RCPD and Aegis Security have no leads they are willing to share as of yet . . ."

A small grin made its way to her face as she listened to the confused and conflicted reports from citizens and police officials alike. That same grin became a twisted frown when the next person who appeared was an older man who claimed that the vigilante was of little consequence.

"We are currently cooperating with the RCPD on a much larger issue plaguing the city, which I am not at liberty to speak of," he spoke through his smoky vocal chords. "The vigilante is far from our largest concern right now." He slid his brown-tinted shades from their firm place in his silver hair, back on his face. "That is all I can share at the moment on this matter. The RCPD hired us to provide extra security to this city. We will do so by focusing on actual problems, not someone playing dress-up."

"So what is expected to occur if this vigilante interferes with this . . . major issue that the RCPD and Aegis are working to resolve?" The reporter was not going to drop the subject. Pilar was oddly impressed seeing that.

"That ongoing issue, as detailed by our director a few weeks ago, is suspected to be terrorism-related and we are not at liberty to share more than that. What I can guarantee you, is that the vigilante has no part in it, and while we are actively investigating, our resources are focused elsewhere." He gave the reporter a curt little glance. "Don't worry. When we refocus on capturing whoever is in that suit, you'll be the first to know."

Pilar's scowl turned a little less fierce. Hearing that lie pleased her. *Of course they will.*

Pilar grabbed an apple from the kitchen table and rinsed it off in the kitchen sink. She was unlucky enough to not be in a "comfortable" walking distance to the school. She could walk there if she really felt like it, but of course that would mean she had to actually want to go to school. It wasn't that she didn't like school; it was more that she felt she was beyond school at that point. What could she really learn that she couldn't teach herself? She'd finished high school at the age of fourteen. There wasn't much that anyone there could teach her. She'd tried pointing this out to her brother on many occasions, to no avail.

That day, there was a sliver of hope that things could go her way . . . *He has to be dead tired after working yet another full night. Maybe, just maybe, he won't want to get up so early. Right?* She was still eyeing the television from the kitchenette. When she saw the footage of the night before, she nearly choked on the bit of apple she'd started chewing.

She could see it very, very easily, too. There she was, as the much-vaunted vigilante, "The Bug," shielding her eyes from the spotlight above that shone down from the news helicopter. And as she could clearly recall, there she was, aiming her palm at the helicopter, utilizing the power of her "Bug Suit" to overload the camera itself. But just behind her, in that same shot, she could see another figure in the shadows of the roof's entryway! She was taller, and wearing all black as well. Pilar couldn't make out any distinctive details other than her feminine body shape; her suit was skin-tight. She blended in to the shadows far too well. "I was followed?" she frantically uttered under her breath. "How? Who is she? Why didn't I see her? What could she—"

Before her thoughts could finish, Seth's raspy voice made her leap in the air at least an inch off the ground. She fumbled to turn the television off, nearly dropping the remote.

Seth's stare was incredulous. "You ready?" His eyes were bloodshot and drooping, and his voice sounded like a frog's croak at best.

Pilar's brow raised. "Um, are you?" She asked right back before biting into the apple.

Seth straightened his jacket, then his black cargo pants. His skin was as dark as Pilar's own, but at that moment he looked as though not a drop of blood was running through his body. He walked to the table and grabbed a plum from the same fruit bowl she'd pillaged a few moments ago. "I'm fine."

"You know," she continued between moments of chewing, "I don't really have to go to school today. I mean, you look completely exhausted, and I wouldn't dare put anything more on your plate."

He looked to her from the corners of his eyes. "Pilar . . . you still don't get why I'm sending you to school, do you?"

She took another bite of the apple.

"No, of course you don't," he answered in her stead. He then bit into the plum he was holding, and pointed at the front door of the apartment. "School. Let's go."

If there was one thing that Pilar admired about Seth, it was that when he said he was going to do something, he did it, no matter what the consequences. A breath of heated air left Pilar's chest. After she exhaled, she made sure he realized how miserable she was, slouching her way out of the front door of the apartment.

ᒲ

She didn't want to admit it, but she already felt lost.

Pilar didn't expect RCU to have such an enormous campus. The outside garden of the main building was comparable to a large mansion. In the back of her mind, she wondered if Seth was so tired that he'd dropped her off at some celebrity's home by accident. The flight of stairs leading to the doors was awe-inspiring. There was a statuesque fountain right at the entrance of a dolphin in mid-leap, spraying water from its mouth back into the fountain's pool.

Once inside, the sheer size of the school was even more intimidating. The arched hallways of the main building were something to behold; the softly lit halls gave off a warm, welcoming feel. As Pilar walked by each doorway, she could tell that most of the classes were in auditoriums. The paper in her hand was her "guide to the first week," as the enrollment counselor put it. Her first class of the week—on Tuesdays—would be World History II. *History, my worst subject . . . It had to be my first day, no less? Sign of things to come, I guess.* She grabbed her backpack strap a bit tighter, pressing onward to her horrid goal of surviving a history class without falling asleep.

The fears of looking awkward in her clothing choices were erased as her search for Room 251A continued. In fact, she might have been dressed more rationally than anyone there. After all, she couldn't stand out even with her large golden scarf around her neck when the boy adjacent to her had a blue Mohawk and jeans that looked as though they were sheared by a riding mower.

If there was one thing that she hated dearly about her previous schools, it was the uniform requirement. She hadn't grown much beyond five-foot-two since middle school, and that was after a growth spurt. Because she was so small in frame, she never needed to shop as much, as her clothing from even four years before still fit her. In fact, most of her wardrobe was just different skirts and blouses. Accordingly, her choice of attire wasn't terribly different than that: pleated skirts, casual blouse, and usually a long scarf. On days she felt particularly fancy, she'd wear a tie instead.

The odd stares around her were likely of students wondering what a sixteen-year-old was doing on a college campus, a question that Pilar had to admit wasn't unfair to ask.

After walking the halls for what seemed to be an hour, she paused in front of a smaller auditorium: Room 251A. Pilar sat in her seat, her lack of enthusiasm slowly joined by a lack of confidence. Looking about and seeing so many other people there was a bit of a shock to her. She was used to far smaller classes, and ending up as the center of attention in all of them. Here, she was nothing more than a younger student. Even her hair didn't seem to garner any of the shock value it did when she was in her last school. Perhaps that was the difference between a private school and a public school? Or perhaps, that was the difference between grade school and college. She'd never admit such a thing, though, as it could also prove that her brother was right:

She needed to experience society in full.

Pilar spent a lot of her time cooped up in her room, or visiting her father's lab. After he vanished, she was content to live out the rest of her life as a hermit if given the chance. At the very least, she considered the fact that as much as Seth needed time away from her, she needed time away from him. Maybe school would be her outlet. *At the very least, it could serve as a good excuse . . .*

As the professor began to call the class to order, another girl sat next to Pilar. She was Japanese, and gave her a friendly grin as she sat, as well as a polite "excuse me." Pilar, on the other hand, barely moved her arm out of the way.

The new girl didn't lose her smile. "Thanks, 'preciate that," she added.

"Uh, yeah. Sure."

Pilar's lean naturally went the opposite way, as she avoided any actual contact with her in the closely-knit auditorium seats. Meanwhile, Professor Nathan was busy going through roll call, and she seemed about as happy to be there as her students, if not less so.

She was an uptight, full-figured woman, and she was daring enough to present her entire lecture to the class via slides as she talked. Her monotone voice was not helpful in the least.

After twenty minutes of Professor Nathan's dry lecturing, Pilar found immediate comfort in her own folded arms, resting her head on the foldout desktop of her auditorium seat. The cold breeze filtering in from the roof on such a lukewarm day didn't help keep her alert. *Seriously, could they put the air on any colder in this place?* Pilar was more than happy to pass out on the first day, but instead of the blissful sleep she'd started to imagine taking over her mind, she instead felt a slight stinging pain as something flicked the back of her earlobe.

She shot up as if she'd been stung by ten wasps. Anger permeated every limb of her body. She fully expected the person who'd done it to try and hide.

She was stupefied right out of her anger when the culprit gave her a glowing little smile. Even more unnerving was that it was the girl sitting directly to her left, who only moments ago seemed so nice and friendly.

The girl herself wasn't aware she'd done anything wrong to Pilar; seeing the anger on her face, however, gave her a clue that she wasn't happy in the least. "Sorry about that," she whispered as low as her vocal chords would allow, "but Professor Nathan is really, really strict about people dozing off in her class. She's been eyeing you the whole time."

"Oh, I see. So, that's why you did that."

She grinned at Pilar, nodding to confirm her answer.

After a moment, Pilar tried to refocus back on to the lecture.

"You're . . . Pilar, right?"

Pilar tried not to answer; the professor seemed to be eyeing them as the girl continued onward.

"Zoe, by the way. Nice to meet you." She extended a hand in Pilar's direction, under their desks. Her ear-to-ear smile wasn't nearly as discreet, however.

Pilar returned that with a smile of her own. "Pilar," she reluctantly answered back; she didn't bother to hide her angst. Still, she shook hands with her. The moment she did so, Pilar's smile disappeared and her attention went immediately back to the professor's lecture.

"We should talk after class."

"For?" *What in the world would we have to talk about*?

"You're an interesting person." Zoe leaned forward a bit, smiling right at Pilar. "There aren't a lot of sixteen-year-old girls that attend a prestigious college who happen to have, um, pink hair."

"What does my hair color have to do with—"

"Ladies?"

The two of them jumped a bit, both looking particularly shocked and a bit frightened of their professor. She looked stern enough as it was, but at that moment, she looked as though she might physically harm them.

"Sorry, Professor Nathan," Zoe quickly answered. "Pilar just had a quick question on what you said about how important it is to have a worldwide view of history rather than a myopic view of certain events. I was, um . . . just repeating that back to her, so she could take notes. Yeah."

Pilar raised her pencil. "Yeah. Taking notes."

Professor Nathan scratched her head. "Well, for future reference? Pay attention and ask questions later. I don't like a lot of side-talk in my classroom. Zoe knows that."

Zoe nodded. "Sorry, I know."

"Good. Well, as I was saying, when we look at history . . ." With nothing more than that, she just went right back to her lecture.

"Thanks for covering," Zoe whispered to Pilar.

"Covering you? How did you get that impression? You covered my butt, not the other way around..." Pilar started to answer but decided not to pursue the issue further. *She is officially annoying the hell out of me.*

After enduring almost three more solid hours of lecturing and cold air, Pilar escaped History with no other trouble. Much to Pilar's dismay, however, Zoe was true to her word.

"Hey, you waited," Zoe cheerfully exclaimed to her, with no regard to the attention she drew to them both.

Pilar had hoped to duck by her right after class, perhaps sneak away from her line of sight. But before she could even calculate her escape route, Zoe was right there, smiling. Now that she actually took more time to observe Zoe, the girl didn't necessarily look weird or out of place. She was three inches taller than Pilar, her hair in a bun, and even her clothes were decidedly normal: a modest, pink, cropped top with a white blossom motif, and hipster black jeans. If anything, she looked decidedly average.

"So, is Pilar your real name?" Zoe asked.

Pilar's brow raised. What kind of *question—Whatever, fine. Small talk it is, I guess.* "Yes, of course that's my real name. Why wouldn't it be?"

"Well, why that name?"

Again, she humored her. "It's Spanish. It means 'pillar.' Probably means I'm strong, or something. I guess. I really don't know. Not like I named myself."

"Ah, well, yeah, that's obvious." Zoe seemed to realize how quickly that answer escaped, and immediately began to apologize. "No no, what I meant was, um, I didn't mean that the way it sounded. Which, probably sounded bad."

"Very."

"Let's just forget that happened then," Zoe laughed. "Either way, your name is more interesting than you give it credit for."

Pilar's eyes naturally rolled back at Zoe's answer. "According to your logic? Apparently so." Her hope was that Zoe would see just how agitated she was and leave her alone. Instead, Zoe only got more inquisitive with each agitated expression.

"So, your name's . . . Pilar Marie?"

"This is important because?"

"It isn't. I just think it's a cool name. Although your initials are kinda unfortunate, huh?"

Pilar moved her glance over to one of the emptying classrooms. "Just what did you want to talk to me about? I sincerely hope it wasn't just my name."

"Oh, right, yeah of course. All business." Zoe's right hand found its way to the left strap of her gray backpack. "I wondered if you had Professor Benson's Advanced Calculus class."

"And what makes you think I do?"

"Well . . . for starters, you're a sixteen-year-old attending college. From what I've heard, you're pretty sick with numbers."

"Sick with numbers? Really?" Pilar's scowl narrowed further. "What does that even mean?"

"It means you excel in math-related subjects."

Pilar found herself surprised at that. Even in just those few moments, Zoe didn't seem like the type who could answer in such a proper tone. She wasn't sure if Zoe was mocking her or genuinely answering.

Zoe continued. "You're a very, um, to-the-point person. It's like an impulse for you, ya know? That's why you don't like small talk, and really don't wanna deal with people. They introduce too much random stuff into what should otherwise be a perfect day."

Pilar's arms went to a stern, folded position as if it were second nature. "Really."

Despite the frustration Pilar clearly showed to her, Zoe just continued on rattling off facts. "And seeing as you don't like to leave things up to other people, you already have your necessary books for your classes. You wouldn't wait until the last minute like most people would."

Pilar's eyes widened a bit. She didn't want to sound impressed, but it did not keep her from looking as such. "Wait. How is that going to give you any clue as to whether or not I—"

"The only advanced math class that has its book available is the book for Advanced Calc—the book that's stuffed in that cramped backpack of yours."

A small, snide grin came to Pilar's face. "An amateur detective."

She nodded. "Well, gee, what gave that away?"

Pilar didn't share her joyful mood.

Zoe realized that Pilar wasn't exactly convinced of her skills at connecting the dots. "Forensics major, Graphic Design minor."

"Those two don't go together in the least." Pilar's first thoughts were self-serving. If Zoe were as good as she tried to make herself look, she might prove to be a valuable resource for information. It wasn't that Pilar was unsure of her own ability to draw conclusions. She was quite comfortable with that. But Zoe could prove valuable, even if only as a sounding board for her own theories. After all, Pilar wasn't a law major; she was a scientist. The only laws she studied with any concern pertained to how far she could go in testing theories before it crossed the legal line.

Having made peace with herself over her use for Zoe, Pilar decided to hear her out. "Okay, fine, yes I have the class. Why?"

Zoe laughed. "You sound like you're happy about that, just so you know."

Pilar let out a quick, dry chuckle. Her lips barely curled into a grin.

Zoe decided to move on, after clearing her throat. "Well, this is kinda odd for me, but I need a study partner, and I figured I'd ask you."

Pilar didn't make any attempt to hide her shock. "You have Advanced Calculus?"

"Well that didn't sound insulting. Nope, not at all." Despite saying that, Zoe's little chortle sounded almost as insulting, as if she were laughing at a curious child. "No, I don't have Calc. What I've got is Intro-level Algebra."

Pilar nearly laughed back in her face. She tried hide it as best she could. "Right. Guess that's rude of me."

"It's a joke, I know," Zoe whined, lazily falling back a slight bit and letting the wall catch her. "Anyway, my point is that math isn't one of my better subjects." She tapped the left side of her forehead with her knuckles. "One-hundred-percent right-brain user."

"You know that's been proven to not be a real thing, right?"

"Really?"

Pilar was exasperated. "Why me? Isn't there anyone else in this school you can bug aside from a sixteen-year-old freshman? Won't that look particularly bad for your reputation?"

Zoe looked about for a second, then returned her smile to Pilar. "I'm not the kinda person who cares about my rep more than my grades, if that's what you're thinking."

"I'm not."

"Oh."

Pilar sighed. "Look, I'm not up for this, okay? Find someone else to be your—"

Zoe's eyes lit up, as she snapped her fingers. "I knew your last name was familiar!"

"Come again?"

"Professor Sands . . . Are you . . . are you related to him?"

Pilar could feel her face drop. No amount of clever words and insults would hide it. The fact she brought it up so casually made Pilar's whole body tighten. "My dad, Zoe. He's my dad."

"Oh. Oh wow. I didn't mean to bring it up like that—"

Pilar knew she had to keep that conversation from happening. If there was anything she hated more than someone who was too nosy, it was someone who wanted to throw her a pity party, especially when he . . .

"Don't, okay?"

Zoe nodded. "Yeah. Boneheaded on my part. Right-brain. That's my excuse."

"Not a thing," Pilar reiterated.

"Right. I'll keep that in mind. Eventually."

"I'm sure you will." Pilar rubbed her forehead. "So, uh, you're not going to leave me alone about this if I don't help you, are you?"

They both looked about. Pilar noticed that the halls were starting to clear out again.

"Honestly? Probably not. Not too many math tutors who graduated high school before sixteen. And to be honest, I just want to help you adjust. Probably tough making an adjustment from high school to college after what, a year in? Especially when you're probably far removed from old friends, right?"

This girl has a horrific habit of bringing up painful moments, doesn't she? Still, the pestering would absolutely continue. And, at the very least, Zoe's honesty was refreshing.

But old friends? I don't have that to worry about.

Knowing that this "friendship" could benefit her in the long run, Pilar decided to take a chance. "Fine," she answered, adjusting her voice just enough to give it at least some level of authority. "We'll meet after school every Tuesday and Thursday, at five, at my house."

Zoe answered her with a thumbs-up. "Sounds awesome."

Pilar watched as the girl jogged off down the hall.

"Tuesday and Thursday at five, don't forget," Zoe yelled back to her.

Pilar just shook her head, mumbling to herself as she tightened her grip on the backpack dangling from her left shoulder. "Yeah, yeah. Totally looking forward to it."

The ride home was a quiet one.

Seth drove through the lower-west side of Downtown. It was considered by most to be the "Shopping District." All manner of stores lined each side of the street: clothing stores for men and for women, a furniture emporium, computer repair shops, and even small art galleries. Dotted along the strip were various outdoor markets as well. Some were selling fruits, some selling flowers, others selling cheap jewelry.

The most familiar locale for many of the students from the nearby RCU was the Southside Grill & Café, often referred to as the "South Café". It was a rather humble restaurant. Its patio was filled with small, clear tables covered by large blue-striped umbrellas. Meanwhile, the inside was more of a traditional setting with a bar area and a plethora of booths and tables.

It was where Pilar and Seth ate lunch on occasion. Years before, it was where Pilar often ate with her father.

Seth pulled the car up, and eventually managed to parallel-park after a dozen attempts.

"Not going to attempt to cook today either, I see." Pilar closed the passenger door after she stepped out of the car.

"Were you gonna cook? Because I wasn't." He made his way around to the parking meter, shuffling a couple of quarters out of his pocket and lazily sliding them in.

"I would if you didn't freak out about everything I cook."

"That's because you burn everything. I still don't know how."

"That is utterly untrue." She said the words, but neither Seth nor Pilar herself were convinced of that. Pilar cleared her throat. "Whatever. I'm just, you know, surprised we're here on a Tuesday."

Seth opened the door for his sister. "Here to pick up our new roommate."

"Are you joking? We can barely breathe in the space we have right now."

He held open the Café door for her. "You're being silly. We got three bedrooms in there."

"My bedroom is a closet. The middle bedroom is your studio space. So where will the newbie stay?"

"Don't need the den. Do need the extra income, though. And let's not call the new roommate a newbie, okay?"

He looked about once they were inside, bewildered. His eyes darted here, then there, then back again. "I'm pretty sure I told her five, right? She's in here somewhere."

Pilar looked about as well, awaiting the arrival of this grungy guy-friend of his to show up. She had met some of his fellow DJs, and she was not too fond of a lot of them.

Wait. He said "she" just now, didn't he?

"There you are, love!" A new voice exclaimed from the left. The slim cinnamon girl who stood up and greeted them was wearing clothing that looked more apt for Seth's usual party crowd. Black jeans, a loose violet blouse, thin frame glasses, black high-heeled boots, and her red unkempt hair swept up in a butterfly clip. Her British accent, while not very heavy, was strange to hear. Pilar had heard the accent before, but she couldn't recall anyone she knew personally who spoke with it.

The woman was positively radiant, and it showed in her wide smile. She hugged Seth as though she'd known him since birth, a bit giggly as she did so. Pilar could sense a mature air about her. She looked over to Pilar, standing a full hand taller than she did, and seemed just as surprised to see her. She acted far more familiar than Pilar had expected. "You've definitely grown up, haven't you?"

Pilar wasn't sure how to respond to that. After all, they'd never met before. "Excuse me?"

"You don't remember me?" Her smirk was playful. "I probably shouldn't be too surprised."

Pilar answered with a dubious little smirk of her own. "Um, no? Was I . . . supposed to remember you?"

She sighed, giving Seth a glance, and he just answered with a solemn, disappointed shake of his head. Still undeterred, the young woman reached out a dainty hand to greet Pilar properly.

"Bianca."

Pilar huffed, and barely tried to widen her minute smile. She made sure to put so little effort into their handshake that Bianca might as well have been grasping a wet rag and flopping it in the wind. "Pleasure to meet you," she mumbled.

Seth's eyes met Pilar's own. "I'm pretty sure mom gave you a name."

Pilar shrugged. "Yes."

"You gonna give it?" He hadn't raised his voice, but he'd certainly added a tinge of bass to it.

Pilar wouldn't admit that she was concerned with his tone. "Apparently she knows me, right?"

Bianca didn't look even the slightest bit cross. In fact, she seemed fine with the slight, answering the question completely unnerved. "Pilar Marie Sands, right? Nice to meet you for the second time."

Seth laughed. "I'd be careful if I were you. Feelings might get hurt."

Bianca looked to Seth, her amusement apparent. "I think she and I will get along just fine."

"Oh. I see. She's the roommate." Pilar folded her arms, and with a wicked little smirk, she jabbed her brother's side with her elbow. "I wonder why that is."

He slid his left hand down his face, not bothering to answer her innuendo.

Bianca, however, was more than happy to ignore that. After they'd all sat down, Bianca was quickly back to small talk, much to Pilar's frustration. "So how is everything?"

Pilar sat there, arms folded, looking out the window. For a moment, she acted as though she hadn't heard Bianca's question. Eventually, she peeked back at her. "It's okay, I guess. School sucks of course."

"It usually does. I imagine for you it's probably boring." She brushed a few strands of her red hair from her face. "You're in all the highest level classes, aren't you?"

"Except for History, yes."

Bianca opened the menu before her, glossing over it a bit anxiously. "Ah yes, History. Not the most enjoyable class, huh?"

"Wouldn't know, first day."

"Of course not. Can't expect you to be psychic, can we?" Bianca gave Pilar a slight laugh, but got back a frustrated scowl.

"I would appreciate not talking about school, right after school."

Pilar knew she'd overdone things when Seth was so quick to grab her arm that he might have yanked it out of her shoulder. He whispered as forcefully in her ear as he could. "The hell's your problem today? Got something you want to get off your chest?"

She hated this feeling. The few times it happened, she really did feel like a three-year-old. "It's been . . . a long day."

He'd let go of her arm but he was still half-whispering in her ear, and his eyes were sharp enough to cut steel on sight. "That does not give you the right to be an ass. So for once, try to be cool."

"Try to be cool. Got it."

Her eyes darted across the way to Bianca, then back to Seth. *Be cool with some random girl he's forcing into our life and forces me to hang out with while they go on a date. Let's be cool about that now.*

The silence at their booth was enough to drown out the noise around them. Each of them seemed to be trying to find the right thing to say to at least poke the tension, if not cut it. Pilar was glad that Bianca shifted the subject to food, the least arguable thing in the room at that moment.

"So, what's good here?" Bianca asked.

Seth leaned forward a bit. "Personally, I just get a cheeseburger and call it a day."

She smiled back. "It sounds like a cheeseburger for me."

He looked over to Pilar, still grinning. "What are you getting?"

"Just . . . fries are fine."

"You sure?"

Pilar nodded. "Yeah, Seth, I'm sure. Not really hungry."

Bianca was quick to joke with her again. "You're a rather energetic one, aren't you?"

"And you like to make witty commentary. I assume you're a comedian in your spare time?"

"I try to be sometimes. Probably should stick to being a nurse though, huh?" She didn't bother to peek up from the menu as she'd replied.

It was jarring to have someone flat-out ignoring her quips. Usually, when she did that with Seth, he played the Authority Figure card as soon as he got tired of her. Bianca was apparently comfortable enough to fling her quips away outright. And she did so with such a nonchalant attitude . . . before Pilar knew it, she was infuriated, and had to check herself very quickly.

"Ooh, a double cheeseburger sounds perfect right now!" Bianca's mature air was subdued by her childish reaction to food.

The tall, skinny black man who approached the table nodded to Pilar. They were fairly used to seeing each other, to the point he already knew what she wanted. "Seasoned fries basket, right?" His thin lips curled into a cool grin, as he held his note pad and scribbled down the order.

"Good job, Pete," she answered back, smirking.

"Told you I'd remember some day!"

She couldn't really say too much bad about Pete. He tended to be pretty good to them. Naturally, as he was dealing with their food, Pilar decided to go easy on her snarky comments. *It's amazing what respect the right position in life can afford you,* she thought.

"Strawberry Lime sounds absolutely perfect love. I'll have one of those." Bianca's smile was infectious, at least to Pete and Seth.

"Cutie with an accent! What are you doing here with this loser?" Pete pointed to Seth, who, surprisingly enough, laughed it off.

"Quite the lady-killer, huh?" Bianca glanced his way from behind her menu, still smiling.

"Not keeping a steady girlfriend isn't a good look. Something I'm looking to change." Pilar could tell what was going on. Easily. *Right, so this is a date, and she's moving in because you're looking to change that. Of course.* She couldn't roll her eyes back far enough.

"Well, good on you, brutha," Pete answered back. "Anyway, I'll stop buggin' you guys. Stop being strangers though! The only one I see a lot these days is homegirl." He nodded to Pilar, who tried her best to smile from the attention. Truthfully, she was too busy fuming.

After Pete walked away, Seth looked to his sister with his brow a bit furled. "How often do you come here without me?"

"Probably every other day. Neither of us can cook, remember?"

"I think that's where I come in, isn't it?" Bianca raised her hand. "I'm not going to be your maid though. When I'm done, you'll be master chefs." Her smile was cavity-inducing.

Pilar looked to Seth, then averted her eyes back out the window again. "Good luck with that."

4

"Is she involved? Any idea how deep her involvement might be?"

Zoe took a moment to breathe. How could she answer that? She'd only known the girl for maybe a couple of hours at most. There hadn't been a full conversation between them yet. It had taken her months to convince him she could handle it. She cuffed her hand over the phone and held its speaker closer to her mouth. "I'm not sure yet. Too soon to tell. She's obviously hurt by her dad's disappearance."

"That could mean anything. She could be trying to throw ya off."

She knew he couldn't see her through the phone, but she still shook her head vigorously. "I don't believe that for a second."

"Sounds like the answer to my first question is 'no,' then."

She looked around her for something to settle her eyes on. She was used to this place; it was her safe room. Above her head hung a variety of clothes—all hers—as she sat comfortably on the floor of her walk-in closet. Despite the darkness within that confined space, she was comfortable.

Of course, the real reason she stayed in that closet was to keep her conversation as quiet as she could. If her sister overheard her . . .

"I don't think she's involved. But I think she knows something."

"You just don't know what."

"Yeah. No idea what."

"Zoe—"

"Dad, just give me a couple weeks at the most. I promise, I'll figure out what's going on by then, okay? But you have to let me do this my way."

She could hear him huff right into the phone. "I shouldn't be letting you do this."

"You're not letting me do anything. I told you what I was gonna do, and did it. That simple."

"And as your dad, I shouldn't let you run around trying to find info that I shoulda got!"

"Dad, she didn't talk to you before. She wasn't going to talk to—"

"I know that. And I can't stop you from here. You'd start this 'investigation' of yours anyway. Just be careful. And don't blow anything up."

She smiled. "Come on, Dad. Since when have I—"

"Chemistry class, last year of high school. You decided to try and make smoke bombs in class."

The whir of the fan outside was all that echoed throughout the room.

"It was, um, good intentions?"

"Zoe."

"I promise, Dad. I'm being careful."

She knew he had no choice but to have faith in her. "All right. Just remember, that case isn't as important as you and your sister are."

"Love you too, Dad." She touched the screen, and its light quickly vanished. Even in that dark room, she knew exactly where everything was, without looking. She'd have no problem making her way to bed from the small closet space, even without a drop of light to shine.

Her heart nearly exploded when she noticed the deep, gold light pouring underneath the closet door.

Before she could stand up, the closet door flung open. Zoe fell backward into her own clothing, wide-eyed and dazed as she looked towards the mirror image of herself. She rubbed her bum a bit, her own shoes having broken her fall in the worst of places.

"This room isn't soundproof." She looked like she could be Zoe's twin, save the shoulder-length, brown-streaked hair and slimmer figure.

Zoe grinned like a child with her hand firmly in the cookie jar. "Well, um, howdy! What brings you into my room tonight sis—"

"Really?" She turned about face and marched out of her little sister's room. "Next time you talk to Dad, tell him to maybe call and talk to me, instead of sneaking around giving you some secret mission."

Just as fast as she'd stormed in, her sister stormed right back out.

When Zoe heard her slam the door, she exhaled. "Wow. Tess must be in a good mood tonight." She scrambled out of the closet, managing to finally stand up and get to her bed. Her eyes found their way to the opened window on her left.

"Okay then. I guess that's my task. Gotta figure this girl out."

She grabbed the remote from the nightstand, flashing through channel after channel. When she stopped flicking on *Channel 8 News*, she smirked at the top story. "Of course."

5

Pilar still could not fathom the change that was happening.

She was amazed that Seth was willing to give up his den to let Bianca stay there. It was where he kept all his equipment, and where he often had everyone pile into on the rare occasions he had company, whether to game, or to have a jam session, or whatever the case might be.

Seeing him casually move all of his records and things out of the room was a bit shocking to say the least. In particular, it agitated Pilar because she'd asked for that room long ago, to which he'd staunchly replied no.

Hypocrite.

Still, she had to admit that it was a much better solution than the one he'd originally tried to suggest: Pilar and Bianca sharing Pilar's room.

He wasn't happy to give up the den, but for whatever reason he'd come up with, Bianca moving into it was the better "situation" rather than Pilar taking that space for herself.

Their apartment was fairly humble. Seth had decided, once he'd taken Pilar in three years before, that it would be best to get a three-bedroom apartment just in case, and to use the third room as his own spot of refuge until further notice. He'd gotten help from other members of their family who apparently weren't keen on taking in another teenager, or lived too far out of the city to be of any help otherwise.

As luck would have it, Bianca didn't have much to move in. Aside from two suitcases of clothes, some "emergency" medical supplies were her only baggage.

"Pilar, I'm sorry, love, would you be a dear and put this in the medicine cabinet in the bathroom?" She asked that while giving that warm, motherly smile. Clearly, Pilar had no choice in the matter. "I appreciate it, love!" Bianca hollered after her.

Pilar made sure the entire apartment complex could hear her marching into the bathroom. At the very least, everyone else could share her frustration, even if only for those few stomps. When her brother yelled at her from the other side of the apartment, her moral victory was secured.

As she returned to the den, she noticed Bianca slipping something back into her purse. *A picture?* She couldn't make it out from the distance.

"Doesn't need to see this yet," she heard Bianca mutter.

"Doesn't need to see what?" Pilar realized she'd actually managed to catch her off guard when Bianca nearly leapt off the floor.

"Holy heavens, girl! Don't sneak up on me like that!"

"I didn't sneak up on you."

"Right. Right. Of course you didn't."

"Still didn't answer my question." Pilar's arms folded. "What don't I need to see yet?"

Bianca stood, extending the handle on her suitcase and dragging it to the closet. "Nothing. Just old stuff."

Knowing she wasn't going to get much out of Bianca without a lot of bartering, Pilar huffed her frustration out, then left her room. "If you need anything else, let Seth know. I'm going to bed soon. Wasn't joking about being tired."

Pilar returned to her own room, slamming the door behind her to let everyone know she wasn't in the mood to be bothered. Her eyes darted from spot to spot, trying to see what went where, and what wasn't there to begin with. On the floor next to her bed, she realized that there was something showing that absolutely should not have been.

My helmet! When did I—

The knock against the door was almost inaudible, but she still jumped back at least three feet from the sound of it. Instinctively, she slid the helmet completely under her bed, and out of sight.

"Come in," she finally answered the knock. She lay on the bed haphazardly, staring at the ceiling, pretending as best she could to be aloof.

"Hey there, you." Bianca gently opened the door, and eased her way into the room. "I hope we didn't get off on the wrong foot."

"Of course not," Pilar answered. "But let's not push the issue. You're here as a roommate to help Seth out."

Bianca sat on the foot of the twin-sized bed, and stared at Pilar with a sad glare. "I still can't believe you don't remember me at all."

"No clue."

"Well, I won't stretch that out to be a big deal." She stood up, and made her way back to the door. "Maybe we can chat later, love?"

"Not likely," Pilar answered back. "Why are you so intent on talking anyway?"

"Contrary to what you may think, I'm not here for just Seth. I moved back here for my own reasons, including you."

"What's that supposed to mean?"

Bianca sighed. "I used to babysit you when you were a toddler. Which . . . you don't remember at all, do you?"

Pilar's bewildered glare answered for her.

"Figures." Bianca's eyes trailed for a second, but she soon brought her gaze back to Pilar, smiling happily. "It's okay. I'm not surprised. We'll just, uh, start over I guess?"

Pilar sat up. "Yeah. I guess we could." She honestly wasn't sure what she wanted to say, but she almost felt compelled to tell her something: about her search for her father, about her family's break-up, about Seth's disdain for her . . .

Even if Pilar might have been too young to keep a solid memory, Bianca did seem familiar to her—just not enough so to trust her words immediately.

"Well consider talking to me at some point, okay? I'm not your enemy." Bianca gave her that smile again.

"Yeah. I know."

"Well, not gonna sit here and ramble." Bianca stepped out of the doorway. "I tend to be good at that."

"I can tell." Pilar's lips made an honorable attempt at a genuine grin. It wasn't the best she could muster, but it was something.

"Obvious, huh? Well, we've all got things to work on." Eventually she got around to closing the door to Pilar's room. And after a moment, to ensure she was gone, Pilar hurried to the door to lock it.

She rested against the door, looking back to the space under her bed.

6

She had to find any clues she could about his whereabouts. After almost two years of sneaking around and researching everything she could about her father's work before he disappeared, Pilar had finally found a good hint. Still, she couldn't begin to search for him without some sort of assistance.

That was where the Bug Suit came into play.

Professor Sands's last great work before he vanished was a pair of suits that would not only nearly double a human's strength and endurance, but also grant the person who wore it the ability to control machines through two strange "Virus Gauntlets."

Pilar would need to take more time to use them properly, if at all. There was something about them that made her fearful of them, something that made her afraid to utilize them. But as much research as she'd done, and as much work as she'd finished on the suit on her father's behalf, she still could not understand why. The only thing she was certain of was that she might be the only person left who could use them to their full ability.

In the interim, she'd designed a newer pair of gauntlets that allowed her to hack any machine's code. Until she could understand how the original Virus Gauntlets worked, her crude-yet-effective replacements would have to do.

With that portion of the Bug Suit completed and all the kinks seemingly worked out, Pilar had begun taking the suit on a few test runs. After a few months of reworking its design to suit her tastes, she'd begun doing various patrols and exercises to see just how efficient it was. This night was no different.

As "The Bug," she'd taken to the rooftops for most of her experimentation, to view the city from every possible angle and test the various viewing modes of the helmet's internal hardware. The Shopping District late at night seemed to be the perfect place for it; the bright lights of the malls would die down somewhat, so being spotted wouldn't be too much of an issue. What was inviting about it for Bug was that the buildings there weren't terribly tall outside of the central area. Theoretically, she could use that area to see just what the suit enhanced without risking her own safety.

Bug had to admit that there was a strange sense of enjoyment derived from the city's sudden fascination with her alter ego. In the news reports, she was known as "The Bug." And every morning she enjoyed seeing that name plastered over the footage of her escape.

Something else that was being widely reported intrigued her even more.

There had been reports for months of random bits of property destruction that looked impossible to have been caused by humans. Chunks of buildings seemed to be gnawed away, and multiple establishments in the downtown district robbed or outright vandalized. On the surface, it seemed like some petty crime ring the RCPD should've been handling just fine.

But they weren't. They seemed to have quietly hired the ASA—Aegis Security Agency—to crack down on these cases.

The same company that fired my dad years ago. Convenient.

She'd found a small group of their agents that splintered off, seemingly tracking someone or something on the ground. She, on the other hand, tracked that group on the rooftops.

What she didn't expect, was for yet another group of agents to be on the rooftops as well. She might have avoided them, if the suit's tracking disruption abilities hadn't decided to randomly fail right when she got close.

Good start to the night, she grumbled to herself.

Four men in black suits, and one dark-peach girl in black sweats and a hooded sweatshirt . . . The scene before her was more like something from an edgy pop-music video.

The hoodie-wearing girl stepped forward, twirling a baton in her right hand, holding its matching baton in her left at ease. Her blonde bangs blew across her face in the breeze.

Her smile was frighteningly cheerful. "Hey, you know, maybe you should just power that suit down and surrender, Bug Girl."

Ugh, really? Bug Girl? Pilar held in her groan. *I already don't like you. Can't risk getting my voice sampled though, which means I get to listen to her try to intimidate me, and nod at best. That sucks.*

"I don't want to tell ya stuff you already know, but," the girl looked about, eyeing all of her fellow agents, "you're pretty badly outnumbered. Won't get far."

Bug was barely paying attention. Her mind had already switched her top priority to "escape."

"Oh come on! Are you really going to ignore me and make this worse for yourself?" She moaned like a spoiled brat. "I mean, I can only hold these guys back for so long. They're kinda bored of desk work. Right interns?"

None of them looked thrilled with the perky girl's assessment of them.

"Okay, you guys took that way too seriously!"

She turned her focus back to Bug, waving a baton towards herself, taunting her.

Bug was unnerved by this girl, and even more annoyed that she would taunt her. Fighting hadn't really been her intention that night, but if that's what she needed to do, she would, if only to knock the smile off that girl's face.

"No choice, agents." The oldest agent amongst the four gave the cold command, drawing a sleek handgun from his waist.

"Wait, wait, hold on!" The girl stepped to his side, resting a hand on the barrel of the gun, then gently lowering his aim to ground. "I can handle her. No need for all of that, is there?"

The agent glared at Mars, then backed down. "All right, Agent Mars. She's yours. But if she causes you trouble, we're taking her down."

"Jesus, old man, chill a little, okay? You act like I'm not the lead on this to begin with."

Bug wasn't sure what to make of this girl. For someone threatening to take her down in moments, this "Agent Mars" talked like some hyper teenager.

When Mars's first swing just barely missed the tip of Bug's jaw, her perception of the quirky woman quickly changed.

Bug did not hesitate to draw her Powered Staff, but just as soon as she held the thing in her hands, Mars nearly knocked it lose. She grabbed each end of the staff, and planted her feet before shoving it right into Mars's batons.

Mars nearly fell over from just that.

Bug saw the chance to strike at Mars again, but found her staff easily repelled by Mars's batons this time. She knew there was a chance she'd be outclassed in a straight-up fight. What she had to rely on now was her battle suit allowing her to keep the advantage.

This Mars girl is obnoxious.

When Mars landed a hit right in her abdomen, she had her suit's strength confirmed. *Little bit of a tingle, but other than that…*

She got back to her feet quickly, tumbling away from Mars's next flurry of swings. Even if it didn't hurt much, she still didn't need the suit taking any unnecessary damage. After all, she'd have to repair it herself, and she couldn't even be sure there were enough raw materials to do so.

Bug caught a moment to whip her staff around, bouncing Mars back a few feet and finally giving herself some breathing room while Mars continued to tumble from the impact. Bug took off like a rocket, sprinting straight for Mars's legs. *If I can just knock her off her feet, just hit her legs hard enough to . . .*

She wasn't able to stop her momentum and went into a skid, realizing too late that she was back in Mars's range. Mars had already gotten back to her feet.

Need to do something fast!

Bug tumbled left, then ran at Mars again. The smack of Bug's staff colliding with Mars's thigh echoed through the air. She nearly fell on her bum as she tried to cope with this new pain.

Even with that convincing strike, Mars was back on her feet far faster than Bug would have liked.

Would you give me a break with this? Why are you standing already?

A shot from Mars's baton collided with Bug's left forearm, causing the disembodied voice in her computerized helmet to ring out, "Suit damage minimal," multiple times.

Mars followed with three more shots to Bug's calves and right hand. Of all the areas of the battle suit, those in particular were weak areas, where the armor and the cloth underneath it were not nearly as well protected.

How the hell would she know that? Lucky guesses?

Bug nearly dropped her staff from the hand strikes. "Suit damage minimal. Gauntlet damage minimal."

"Minimal? You're not the one who actually felt that," Bug mumbled, trying to shake off the pain on her knuckles. She had to leap out of the way of Mars's next swing to give herself time to think. All she had was a second, and Mars's next swing was already coming too quick. However, her swing at Bug's helmet was so far off, even Bug was amazed.

Bug wasn't going to hesitate. She wasn't sure why Mars had missed, but that gave her the chance to whack her in the side with her staff, this time making sure the business end of it hit her fully. Bug wasn't ready for the impact herself, nearly spraining her own wrist.

Mars folded over and nearly collapsed in a heap, holding the left side of her gut. And yet, she still returned a cheeky little smirk at Bug.

The heck're you smirking at?

"All right. You had your fun, Mars." The older agent trained his weapon on Bug once again.

Mars pouted like a disappointed child, her left hand firmly rubbing her new injury. "Alright, alright," she whined. "But let's make sure we don't do too much damage, alright? Gotta keep the suit clean."

Bug was still smarting from her fight with Mars, trying to take a moment to catch her breath. This was, after all, her first actual fight in the Battle Suit.

This situation isn't improving the longer I stand here.

She let loose a puff of air. *Well, that fight was more than enough of a test. I think I can call this a success for now. Guess I do owe this Mars girl, in a weird way. That doesn't sit well with me.*

A neon-blue beam flared from the shaft of the older man's pistol, grazing the armor of Bug's left leg. Almost immediately, her body armor reacted with a flurry of "warnings" and "cautions" all over her visor's view. The round itself fizzled into the ground with barely a ripple, only leaving a few sparks in its death.

"That was your one and only warning," the older man continued, the three other agents following his lead and aiming their own guns at Bug. "Hands up."

She did as asked, realizing what she'd just witnessed. *What kind of weapon is that and why the hell is it interfering with my suit?*

Mars ran in front of her allies, arms outstretched. "Guys, hey, whoa! Do all of you need to draw your weapons? And didn't I say keep the suit clean?"

"Agent Mars. You're in the way."

Bug could see Mars's once jovial face sour as she looked to the other agents, then back to the man arguing her supposed authority. Even Bug had to admit, if that girl was the leader, she sure as hell didn't act like it.

At least, not until that moment.

"I'm also the lead here, right? So can you guys put your weapons down? It's one spy in body armor. I don't think we need to fry the suit. Which, by the way, is what we're supposed to try to confiscate, not fry. Two totally different words. And by the way? Frying the person wearing the suit isn't exactly our goal either."

"This isn't going to fry the person wearing the suit," he shot back. "And you're the same level of security I am, Mars. You're the lead but I have the right to supersede that, per the director. Now—"

"If I'm unable to perform," she shouted back. "I'm pretty sure I can do that just fine, thanks! So if you don't mind . . ."

Bug wasn't going to take their arguing for granted, whether Mars started that whole dispute on purpose or not.

"Flare," she whispered. Despite how quiet she was, the armor's CPU received the command without issue.

The light that erupted from the prongs on top of her helmet was like a miniature sun exploding right before their eyes. If not for the lenses of her helmet temporarily blocking her vision, she would have been just as blind as the agents surrounding her.

By the time the light faded, she'd already run to the western edge of the roof, going as fast as her feet—and the suit's mini-propulsion systems—could take her.

She didn't dare look back at the barrage of laser rounds following her, but she could tell the agents were all still disoriented as their rounds continued to zoom way overhead. One blue ray zipped past the left side of her head however, causing immediate interference. The gold, glowing "eyes" of her helmet were the only visual outlet to the world without deactivating the suit completely, so the static was a massive worry.

Well, that is certainly something that shouldn't be happening!

She flung her body across another rooftop as the four agents gave chase. They weren't as brave about leaping from roof to roof as she was, but then again, they didn't have the added bonus her armor's jet-propelled boots offered. She wasn't going to take off flying by any means, but leaping a few feet between those small alley gaps wasn't much of a chore.

Bug continued to make distance, realizing there was no way they could catch up with her. Who in their right mind would follow her in that manner without her gear?

Of course! That idiot would!

Mars was a few buildings behind, latching on to each edge with her batons—which apparently had claw attachments built-in for such an occasion—as she leapt.

Bug was at a loss seeing the girl chase after her! "Who the hell even thinks to do that," she yelled aloud, forgetting her lack of a voice changer in her shock. "Oh, I may need to leap across buildings one night! Better add freaking claws to these electric batons!"

Though Mars was barely making the leap at times, her determination put fear into Bug. Even Mars's fellow agents called her insane, pleading with her to give it up.

And yet she kept after her!

Bug knew there was only one way to lose her now—she had to jump a distance that was too far for that insane girl to even think about chasing her.

Main Street isn't too far. And if I'm going to test the gliding capabilities, no time like the present right? Bug veered left on the next rooftop. *Right.*

She kept as much control as she could as her momentum kept her running forward, then spread her arms, as though she were about to swan dive into the traffic below.

"Glide."

She could hear Mars far behind her, yelling for Bug to wait, to not jump. She wished she could've seen the look on Mars's face when her seemingly decorative scarf flared outward like enormous wings, carrying her along the skyline. Combined with the propulsion from the boots of the armor, Bug sailed through the air with amazing ease.

If that girl pulls out a hang glider and chases me, I'm gonna lose it.

After a moment of sailing and peering behind her to make sure the girl wasn't actually giving chase in her own hang glider she had somehow conveniently stashed in her hoodie, Bug finally took a deep breath, exhaling her anxieties out as she sailed further on. She still had another challenge to conquer, however:

Landing.

She couldn't just glide to the streets, as there was too much of a risk she'd either be seen, or land in traffic and probably be run over right after being seen. The next logical choice was to land on another building as she'd originally planned. But with her current momentum, she'd risk running right off the edge and careening off the building and likely to her death on the streets below—possibly also into traffic.

Of the two options, the roof landing had at least less chance of her dying.

Okay. Just need to hit the ground running. One step at a time.

She managed to land well enough, but she underestimated her momentum. The glider hadn't retracted, and now she was running too fast to safely stop. By the time her momentum seemed to die down enough, she'd leapt between two more buildings. She had to come to a stop soon or she was going to run out of buildings to leap across. "Retract Glider," she commanded verbally of her suit. It responded as expected, and at least now she could feel herself slowing down.

One foot at a time, one foot at a time, one foot at a time . . .

Her left foot caressed the ground again, then her right foot. Then her left again. Then her right. One clumsy step was all it took to take her airborne, sideways.

Crap crap crap crap crap crap . . . Every exclamation was a bump on the hard concrete roof as she tumbled sideways. The only thing that stopped her momentum this time was the guardrail on the roof.

If it wasn't for the protective layers of her battle suit, she probably would have sustained far more bruises and a broken bone or two. As it was, she was able to stand after a few moments to orient herself.

She let loose another breath of relief as she straightened the scarf out once more. "Well, considering that was my first time in my life ever hang gliding, and I did it in an experimental battle suit that probably doubled my weight, and using a transforming scarf to do it? Walking away is probably the best landing I could ask for. Suit's still in one piece, too."

She heard a popping noise in her ear, and immediately the helmet went dark. She could see, but just barely. It was as if she were wearing sunglasses at night. Worse yet, there was no way to check her surroundings without the helmet being powered on.

"Wonderful."

Her unexpected leaps across downtown had at least bought her more than enough time to try to fix the helmet. *The list of bug fixes is starting to get big again.*

With a few virtual keystrokes, the lights on the armor she wore dimmed further, then flashed red. She could hear the soft male voice of the computer within: "System Reset. Initiating."

Bug attempted to access the sensors of her helmet by pressing a hidden touch-sensitive button on the left side of it. The moment she did so, the display before her crashed. All the statistics in the helmet's HUD turned a bright crimson red, and anything that showed any alphanumeric information now simply read "ERR," further obscuring her view.

"Now? Seriously?" There wasn't exactly a good spot for that to happen, least of all that moment. The functions in the helmet were what kept Bug masked from Aegis's agents and any other electronic surveillance. The helmet contained most of the suit's control mechanisms, including the circuitry that jammed tracking devices and signals of all sorts nearby, and also including the camouflage technology that kept her out of sight. She couldn't use those functions without moderation already, as they sufficiently drained the power of her battle suit when active. Having them go down at that moment, while it saved some of that precious power, was not ideal. And, despite everything else in the suit having failed at least once before, the helmet had worked perfectly since the day she completed the first modifications to the suit.

The disrupters those agents fired. Of course. It's the only logical explanation.

As she continued to work on her seemingly temperamental helmet, someone approached her. Under the light of the neon sign, she wasn't able to get a clear look at this newcomer. At best, she could tell from the shapely shadow that it was likely a woman, and possibly wearing a form-fitting body suit.

"Nice to finally meet you," the newcomer said to her. Her walk oozed confidence. Her voice was smoky and smug.

"Who are you and why in the world are you here?"

The girl walked closer, finally becoming a bit more visible. She had three different belts on her body suit: one slung across her shoulder lined with small throwing daggers, and two belts hanging loosely on her waist. The larger of the two hip belts was a dark-violet color and had multiple pouches—it was her utility belt.

She adjusted the smaller belt slung across her shoulder as she approached. "Good question."

"You'd better have a good answer. Otherwise I'm going to have to assume you're a threat and act accordingly." Bug kept one hand on the staff she wore strapped to her back. While it had done well against that Mars woman, there was still a mode she needed to test to consider it fully complete, though that wasn't something she'd be thrilled to try on a human being.

"Act accordingly?" The woman seemed perplexed by that. "You're already threatening me?"

"And if I am?" Bug's grip on the staff tightened.

"I'm your ally, not your enemy. It'd be kinduva shame if we fought. Unless you work for Aegis. Then it wouldn't be a shame as much as it would be my duty, *Marie.*"

The woman stood there, arms folded. Bug could tell she had some sense of pride, just from knowing her middle name.

That alone was all Bug needed to hear to confirm just whom she was dealing with. The entire aura that she'd built up crumbled away. Bug's fears of who this woman might be turned into sheer aggravation because she now knew who she was. Her tense nature calmed, and she went right back to work on her helmet. "You done, *Shinomori?"* She couldn't have stressed that name any harder if she'd tried.

"Who?" Although she tried to act ignorant, she'd forgotten to keep her voice changed. The smoky, dark tone had disappeared, replaced by the surprised—and somehow still bright— college girl's voice. "Um, who is this Shinnoh-Maury person?"

Bug didn't bother to look up from her helmet. "No way you're actually trying that, Zoe."

Zoe shrugged. "Worth a shot."

"No, it wasn't. Is there a reason you're out here playing vigilante?"

Zoe relaxed her own grip on her shoulder belt. "That's an ironic question."

"What's that supposed to mean?" Now that Zoe had stepped much closer and wasn't nearly as obscured by the shadow of the sign, Bug could see that she was in her own homemade getup that must have cost her ten dollars to make, at most.

Still, the fact she'd snuck up on Bug so easily did raise a legitimate concern for her.

Zoe pulled up the lower half of her mask—just enough for Bug to see her lips—as she grinned and continued to talk. "It means nothing at all, Pilar. Nothing at all."

Pilar made an audible grunt at her. "It's Bug when I'm in this suit."

"Oh, right. Yeah, sorry 'bout that. I, as an expert vigilante, should know better."

"Uh, expert vigilante?" Bug finally got the helmet to reset properly despite the distraction, and hastily put it back on. "Whatever. It's fine." Upon the system rebooting, she was thankful to be greeted with all greens on every display; everything was normal again.

"You need to get out of here before you're seen," Bug implored her. "I was already running from Aegis. Chances are, they're still looking for me. You won't help my chances of getting away."

"Me? I haven't been caught yet. In fact, you're kinda the reason that it's been harder for me to do my own work. The media's caught your scent, not mine."

Bug tried the touch-button again, this time with success. "Yeah, well I'm sure that homemade suit of yours doesn't have anything built in to throw off their signals, so if you don't mind?" She stood at the edge of the building again, looking down to the street.

"I don't emit any signals that need to be thrown off."

Bug couldn't even try to write that off. *Touché.*

"So what exactly have you found out so far?" Zoe was on the opposite side of her, staring down into the street corner ten stories below. "Aside from the fact that Aegis agents have that FBI stereotype down to a science. That's obvious."

"I suppose we do agree on that, at least." Bug darted her glance at every sign of movement on the street, trying to find any hint of her pursuers. "And I've got nothing tonight. Except chased."

"I'm not surprised. Aegis is teeming all around this city right now." Zoe stood perched, as if she were a patient predator watching her prey. Yet, there was nothing below but concrete, cars and streetlights.

"Well, you go ahead and you look your way. I'll finish my test solo, if you don't mind—"

Before either of them could react, a brilliant light rained from above, causing Bug and Zoe both to shield their eyes. Bug took a moment to get a peek through the blaring searchlight; she could barely make out one of Aegis's helicopters lowering itself to the rooftop. The agents within were furious, to say the least.

It hovered downward until they were only a few feet above the roof, just enough to allow the agent to lean out of the cockpit and bellow at Bug and Zoe through his megaphone: "You two! Stay where you are and put your hands up!"

"This is your fault," Bug shot to Zoe under her breath.

"Doubt it," she shot back just as easily. "I would like to think you wouldn't just toss the blame on me when you know that's not the case." Zoe reached into a pocket on her utility belt, grabbing three silver globes from it in her right hand. "I can get us out of here."

"Oh?" Bug wasn't about to turn away her charity now, considering the situation. "I'd love to see how."

"You really can't help being snarky, can you?" Zoe still held the three globes tight in her grasp. "Gonna wait for the right spot."

Wind from the helicopter's blades began to blast by them; combined with the already strong draft on such a high rooftop, Bug could feel her balance waning. While she struggled to fight the gusts, the much-more-stout Zoe stood firm, and managed to pull a dagger from the belt full of them slung across her back. She tossed it right into the wind without fail, as it pierced the metal of the helicopter's nose just enough to remain lodged in it.

"Time to run!" After Zoe dropped the silver globe contraptions on the ground, she grabbed Bug by her left arm, yanking her towards the adjacent apartment building. She unbuckled the second belt on her waist, and it fell lazily behind them as they ran onward.

Before Bug could manage to actually see where they were headed, Zoe forced her to make a leap of faith across the chasm between two buildings. Just as they landed on the other side, still hearing the shouts and commands from the Aegis agents behind them, a bright light erupted.

It seemed as though daylight had returned for a brief moment. That light faded quickly, but anyone near the source of that flash with their eyes open was at the very least in phenomenal pain.

"What was that?" Bug asked.

Zoe urged Bug onward as they leapt across another set of close buildings. "The dagger was a flash bomb," she eventually answered, heaving as they continued to run. "I've been working on that for a while, good to see it works!"

"And those silver marble things?"

Those had started to explode as well. When Bug took a peek back, she found herself amazed at what Zoe had managed to do. The silver globes were in fact extremely potent smoke bombs. "Anyone who breathes it in directly will feel like they're peeling hundreds of onions inside a dirty chimney."

"What?"

"It really, really, sucks."

"And you think that'll hold them off long enough?"

"If not, the belt I dropped will be the only clue they have, and I purposely left false information in there."

She said it with such confidence that Bug could only imagine she'd spent hours testing those smoke bombs. And somehow she found a way to create and even test a flash bomb she'd fashioned into a throwing knife. Regardless of how odd her methods were however, thus far they'd managed to escape without a hitch.

Once they had jumped to about their seventh building, Zoe quickly changed their course. Now they were heading down the fire escape of the current stable structure until they were at street level. Bug started to see some of the skills that this girl brought to the table.

It took them just under a minute to get to the alley floor. Once there, Zoe ran to what looked like a large obtrusive object covered by a dark brown tarp. She then proceeded to fling the tarp off. What was underneath the tarp was likely the most impressive thing Bug saw that night, her own armor aside. There was Zoe's getaway vehicle, nice and well stashed away: a sleek, black motorcycle, fully fueled and ready to go. She quickly turned to Bug, and offered a hand. "C'mon. Can't hang around here much longer, Bug."

This girl makes flash bombs for fun, tosses throwing daggers around like a circus performer and makes smoke bombs out of metal globes. Okay, Bug, gotta admit it. Zoe could actually prove to be very useful.

Emphasis on the word, 'could.'

Bug hesitated. She wasn't sure she could trust the hand she was about to grasp.

"You're overthinking this," Zoe added. "Think too long and we'll be caught."

Bug realized that Zoe likely planned for this moment, too. Even so, for the moment, none of that mattered. And seeing as there wasn't a better plan tapping her on the shoulder, Bug reluctantly jumped on.

"All right partner, let's jet!" Zoe yelled above the roar of the bike's engine.

"'Let's jet'? That's what you're going with?" Bug could feel her eyes widen as she realized the more important part of her sentence. "Wait. 'Partner'? Since when did I say I wanted a partner?"

"But you kinda need one right now, don't you?"

Bug grunted under her breath.

"I'll take that grumbling as a resounding yes."

Zoe revved the bike to life. Bug grabbed on to her waist as tightly as she could. In mere seconds, they were shooting out of the alleyway like a fully armed missile. Bug couldn't deny that Zoe would be a great asset, no matter how much teaming up with someone else unnerved her. At the very least, it was a bit of a relief to have someone who seemed to distrust Aegis as much as she did.

Zoe's trap left the Aegis agents busy above and scrambling to figure out just where the two shadows had crept off to. Zoe kept heading toward the east, but stopped abruptly on the corner of East 12th and Warner. Bug began to ask why she had stopped, but one good look at the surroundings answered that for her.

⌐

It had been a massacre. There were over a dozen Aegis agents strewn about like pieces of discarded toys. Not one had been spared, and many were left mutilated. Someone monstrous had been through there.

Zoe immediately checked the pulses of a few agents who were, at least, in one piece. Once she'd checked the third solid body, she looked to Bug, shaking her head.

Bug looked to her left, seeing more bodies strewn about. One in particular didn't look more than four years older than herself, wearing the usual skirt and blouse uniform she'd seen female agents wear. Seeing her was a startling moment. Bug couldn't shake it off.

"This is . . ." She could feel herself getting nauseous from the smell of it, let alone the sight of it.

Zoe was trying just as hard to keep her own composure; it wasn't an easy sight to take in.

Bug could see her holding her stomach tight. "You okay?"

Zoe gave a weak nod. "Just a moment. Need a moment."

Bug gave a slight nod, and continued to observe the bodies herself. *Claws? Claws this big?* The body of a middle-aged white male lay a bit ahead. His wounds furthered her fears. "This is like . . ."

She could see the monster from her nightmare vividly. Rare was the occasion that she could when she was wide awake. Behind her, she could hear a straining voice, followed by the sound of liquid forcefully splattering upon the ground. *I don't think I can blame her for that.* Another minute later, Zoe was back at her side again, examining bodies as though nothing happened.

"Definitely not done by a human," she mumbled, "but definitely not wounds like any other animal I know of."

Bug sighed. "Yeah. Aegis has a lot of tech on their side. To be slaughtered like this would take something well beyond their pay grade." She touched the left side of her helmet, tapping it as though it were a touch screen. And in response, the color of light from the helmet's eyes changed accordingly: first from yellow to red, then from red to green with the second tap.

Zoe stood up from the body she was looking over. "I don't know what you just did, but it looks very damn cool."

Bug could see Zoe watching her survey the area with unrestrained awe. For her it wasn't a big deal, but she had to remind herself that Zoe likely hadn't seen that sort of tech before.

"I'm trying to find traces of anything foreign or just . . . unexpected."

As if to answer her, the helmet's HUD flashed brilliant lights all to her left, pointing to a massive gathering of an unknown substance. Bug pointed Zoe's attention towards that direction. "You see anything there?"

"Not a thing."

"Then this is really not good."

"What's not good?" Almost as soon as Zoe asked that, she jumped to her feet, her hand at the pouch on her waist. "Uh, Bug? I can see the not-good-thing now."

Bug turned off her visor's settings, and now she too could see the monster very clearly. What frightened her more was that he made no attempt to hide. He simply walked towards them, grinning all the while. The figure had gotten so close that Bug could see his face in the mixture of moonlight and street lamps. He pulled back his hood, and flashed them a bright, toothy grin. He was ugly, to say the least, His rough face was long and thin. His head was bald, save for two long and bushy red sideburns that stretched to his jaw. His red eyes were fixated on them with an unreserved hunger.

His pace quickened a bit. "Aegis is certainly good about feeding its enemies, aren't they?"

"Okay. I don't know what this guy's deal is, but I have one useable weapon on hand," Bug whispered to Zoe. "You?"

"I have these," she whispered back, pointing to the numerous daggers still on her waist belt.

Bug nodded. "Good. We might have a chance against him then." She drew the staff that she'd held onto for so long, twirling it once before holding it in front of her.

"An electric staff? Impressive," Zoe commented.

"Not quite." Bug twisted the mid-section of the violet, metal staff. The top of the staff soon expanded outward, continually unfolding and transforming its upper end. The *whir* of machines within the staff became increasingly louder, until the top of the staff had become an enormous head of a hammer. "Well it expanded properly. That's a good sign."

"Holy hell that is amazing," Zoe uttered.

"Just hoping it doesn't goof up like the helmet did," Bug added.

The stranger raised his left arm, and the duo realized that his sleeves were far too long and baggy. They draped over his limbs like a child in his father's sweater. They soon saw why however, as his sleeve suddenly began to fill. A large, jet-black tendril with an impressively large maw at its front erupted from his sleeve. It was still dripping with blood, searching out more flesh to consume. Soon another tentacle erupted from the same sleeve, and more followed, until at least four crowded each sleeve, all drooling as they watched their new prey.

Before he could move towards them however, another intruder appeared. This one—who looked and sounded like a woman—was under a cloak as well, her face completely obscured.

"What a mess." Her voice was sultry, and very condescending. "Is there a reason you did all this? Aside from drawing attention to us?"

He held up his left arm, allowing the living ink-like leeches to ooze from the sleeve. "Can't help it if they need to be fed. Besides, they weren't exactly forthcoming with the information we needed."

"And they're so very forthcoming now, aren't they?" She looked to the costumed girls before her, curling her lips. "And you are?"

"We're here to stop you." Zoe said this, but even Bug could tell she didn't actually believe it. Not that she could sound any more convincing, considering what they were facing.

"Cute," the woman answered back. Her eyes glowed red as she glared at them, and now they could see that she had far more than two eyes on her face. There were at least four more on her forehead. Her smile was murderous. "Exactly how do you plan to do that?"

Bug's first instinct was just to get out of there as soon as possible. She had no idea who these two monsters were. She couldn't even tell for certain *what* they were. What purpose would fighting them serve, aside from getting them nearly killed?

She realized just as quickly, however, that these two monsters might have information to give as well. And even as indifferent as she was about Aegis, she couldn't let these two escape after their slaughter, especially after realizing how similar the leech-armed beast was eerily similar to the monster from her nightmare. *This is an actual lead.*

She whipped her hammer around once, then rested the gigantic weapon on her shoulders. "I want information. And you're going to give me that information."

This woman didn't even bother to look in their direction again. "We've wasted too much time here and drawn too much attention. Let's go."

The man glared at her as if he might devour her whole. "I'm not finished here," he barked. One of his tentacles shot from his left sleeve, cutting through the air like a knife. Bug whipped her hammer before her, holding it in front of her face, unable to react in time to do much else. There was a blood-curdling scream from in front of her. She wasn't certain when it happened, but Zoe had leapt between her and the detached leech, knives in both hands. Just seeing her there, and having heard that scream . . .

Zoe!

The tendril dropped to the ground a few feet away from Zoe, still screaming its primordial heart out before becoming a lifeless wad of black gunk. Bug was at Zoe's side again, realizing that she hadn't been hit at all. Instead, the six-eyed woman had simply grabbed the leech at its root, and crushed it within her claws.

This woman proved her high rank in nearly a second, dashing right into the monster's face, snarling a little as she stared him down. "Do you recall why I'm here?"

He grunted as he held his now-injured arm of monsters. "Because you're Mantis's little pet. He sent you to check on me."

Even though the woman was at least five inches shorter, she stood in his face without the slightest bit of hesitation, or any sign of intimidation, glaring up into his eyes as though her stare alone could slash his limbs from his body. "Get out of here. Now."

He looked like he might put up a fight. For a moment, he stood even prouder, chest out as he glared down at her.

The sounds of sirens started to permeate the air.

"That's not good," Zoe said under her breath, just audible enough for Bug's ears. "If that one psycho-monster did this to Aegis agents who were pretty well armed . . ."

Bug could feel the hard air rising in her throat. "If they decide to stay and fight the police, we'll have to stay and protect them. And I'm pretty sure my suit isn't ready for that."

The monster smirked. "Lucky you." He retracted his leech-like limbs back under his sleeves.

The woman looked to them, and let a snide little grin escape her lips. "You two are fortunate. The only reason I didn't let him consume you, is to irritate him. Part of me wants to consume you myself." She licked her hand, sopping up bits of the destroyed leech that still dripped from her fingers. "But this mess will attract too much attention as it is. For now, you're providing a very nice diversion." She pulled her hood forward, obscuring her face entirely. "I'd advise you to drop the vigilante act, for your own sake. You've got nothing to gain by interfering with us but an early grave."

"Who the hell are you people?" Bug yelled after her.

The woman leapt upward, ascending a nearby edifice with alarming ease before vanishing into the skies in a puff of black smoke. The tentacle-wielding fiend made his way to a nearby sewer cap, and his body seemed to quickly melt into a thick, black substance. It soon splashed about like black oil and slimed its way into the sewers, leaving a trail of the liquid and blood on the ground.

Bug was still standing there, fascinated by it all. It took Zoe yanking her by the arm to get her to move.

"We've gotta go, Bug!"

Both started to make their way back to Zoe's motorcycle, but Bug had to make a momentary stop to scoop up a sample of the creature's remains. With a small vial from her own utility belt, she took a sample of the black sludge that the severed leech had left behind.

This will definitely need further study.

The darkened street of West 33rd was nearly silent. It wasn't the worst looking neighborhood in Rock City by far, but there was an air of danger that blanketed the few blocks on that particular street. Most of the larger buildings were warehouses, and a few had been converted into clubs. As such, most of the area was a breeding ground for local DJs and MCs.

It was for that reason that Seth often found himself on that street, usually at a multitude of clubs, perfecting his craft and earning the extra money he needed to cover rent.

Not once had it occurred to him that he'd be running through the alleys of West 33rd, fearing for his life.

The beast that hunted him down had an amazing ability to keep pace with him, despite Seth's almost encyclopedic knowledge of the area. The monstrous shadow continued to spawn long, black blades attached to very lanky arms from its back.

What worried Seth even more was how insanely fast those blades jutted out.

He made a sharp turn into another alley, onto North 40th; the beast was still right behind him, firing away with those blades. Seth hopped one, then swayed away from another. The third blade in the set finally managed to slash his abdomen.

He screamed, holding in as much of the pain as he could through gritted teeth. He tumbled to the ground, glaring upwards as the shadow closed in.

I've already done this once. The last time I did, I nearly ripped the guy in half. Maybe one more will do it.

Seth aimed his right palm towards the beast. *Maybe.*

As if it were nothing more than flexing a muscle, Seth commanded a powerful orange flame to shoot from his hand. It was just fast enough that the monster could not avoid it. Instead, it braced itself with its arms, taking the powerful release of energy head-on.

When the flame dissipated, the monster lay on the ground a few feet away from Seth. Both of them began to stand, fighting their wounds to regain their stability, and hopefully the upper hand. When the monster stood completely upright, Seth was already prepared with his next attack. He wasted no time, blasting away again, and again, and again. Four times in succession, Seth blasted it backwards, until it could just barely stand on its own.

He could feel his sweat drenching his clothing. He was completely worn out. If this wasn't the end of that monster, he'd have nothing left to fight it with. When two more beings appeared, wearing the same cloak as the guy he'd just incinerated, Seth could feel the frustration hitting his brain. "You've got to be kidding me."

Although there was no chance he could take all three of them alone, he held himself upright. His fists were clenched and aglow as he continued to gather heat. Destruction of property wasn't a fear of his, all of that could be repaired. What he dreaded was dragging those witnesses in. What worried him even more was the idea that the monsters before him probably wouldn't mind dragging them in at all.

"Shall we take him?" The voice that spoke the question was female. Seth could tell that much.

His former pursuer had made it back to his feet, smiling wryly at Seth. His grin was just barely noticeable from under his hood. "No. He is still too powerful right now. He could likely kill us all. But," his attention turned back to Seth, "your power is getting weaker. The last time we fought, we were hardly a threat. But as we've continued to get powerful, you've continued to weaken, haven't you?"

I have gotten weaker. Not what I wanted to hear from this clown, though. Seth looked about, making sure he hadn't lost track of anyone. "Don't know what you want, but I can tell you right now, it's not happening."

"Mantis," the woman urged, "if we can't take his power, then we must return to Ninety-Nine. For now."

The one she'd called Mantis nodded. "I guess so. We'll just be patient then, huh? Next time we meet, after all, I'm sure his power will be low enough that we can retrieve it without much of a fight." He looked back to Seth, grinning like an innocent child. "Guess we'll be meeting again soon, huh?"

Seth didn't even bother to look behind him. There was no need to. He raised his hand just behind his head, opened his palm, and released all his energy into the slime-covered blade that Mantis had snuck behind him. It didn't just collapse however—it literally exploded into pieces.

"Get lost," Seth growled back.

Mantis flinched a bit from the injury to his extended limb as he withdrew it back into the shadows. "It was worth a try, right?" The bright, cheery smile gave Seth chills.

Mantis's smile didn't waver for a second. "Until next time."

Seth watched as they vanished, leaving an odd trail of black dust that lifted into the night skies before dissipating. As they faded away, he began making his way back to his car, blocks away from where he stood.

So they're after me again. He winced as he grasped his wounded waist. *All right. First things first. I have to keep Pilar out of this.*

Once inside his car, he looked about before he pulled his keys from his pocket. On the passenger seat, right under his stacks of records, sat her English book.

He winced from the pain in his abdomen, then shook his head as he started the Camaro. Finally hearing such a common sound as his car rumbling to life was oddly relaxing.

Keep her out of it. Yeah, Seth. Good luck with that.

9

At such an early morning hour, Aegis Security Agency was almost always utterly silent. She preferred that silence.

Inside the spire of steel and glass lay machines and research the world would be shocked to know existed. The hundreds of employees who made it all work were likely still asleep in their beds at home, dreading the sunrise that would come in a few minutes. And yet, there she sat, before dawn, somewhere close to the top of that majestic tower, staring out the glass wall at the city below.

I know it's her. She heaved a bit as she thought. *She's the only one he would have given that much power to.*

Now, she thought as she looked to the empty shot glass on her desk, *what is she doing with it? That part is more interesting.*

The sound of heavy footsteps was instantly familiar. The moment she heard them, she was already reaching for the bottle of scotch under her desk.

He was a dark, mountain of a man who was squeezed into a black suit. Even in the early morning darkness, he wore shades.

She started pouring a touch of scotch into the shot glass on her desk. "Good news?"

He didn't move an inch. As far as she could tell he might not have been breathing.

The sigh that left her chest was pure aggravation. She knew what that cold silence was. "Bad news it is, then."

"Agent Mars did as instructed. Maybe a little too much, considering she was up against that battle suit." He adjusted his sunglasses a bit. "There are snaps of her but it's just more shots of the suit."

"Well, I already know what that looks like." The bronze-skinned woman turned the chair to fully face him in the dim light, and moved some of her platinum hair from her face. A wry smile crossed her lips as she reached out a hand to him, gesturing to grab whatever he was holding onto. "Share?"

He handed her the manila folder he'd brought in with him. "All the photos of the incident we managed to get. Have to admit, surprised Mars hung with her, considering."

"Well, Mars is trained. Pilar is a girl with no experience using a suit she's likely just starting to understand at a basic level." The director rubbed her chin. "Told Mars not to engage the suit directly."

She took her time examining each shot. "It's the Bug Suit all right." Saying those words so easily wasn't something she'd expected. Internally, despite knowing who and what they were dealing with from the very beginning, she was still hoping to somehow be wrong.

There was a possibility, after all. This wasn't the first time some girl in a costume had been snooping around, trailing her agents from afar. However, this one . . . this one was the first one they could confirm was wearing that armor.

In her mind, she'd known this day would eventually come. She'd hoped to have a plan by then. And yet, here they were. Considering that she was the director of the company likely responsible for whatever had befallen the girl's father, it would be no easy process to approach her.

We don't even know for certain how he died. She looked to the photos again, and her eyes fixated on the helmet itself. She's the only one who could possibly know. The witness. And she doesn't remember.

"Something wrong?" He was closer to her desk now, and though he was still keeping his formal tone, it was obvious that some of the formality had dropped away. For at least that moment, she wasn't his boss.

"I'm fine, Abel. Just, thinking, I guess." She peeked back to him from the pictures, her eyes sharpened. "Any agents asking questions? The last thing I need is for them to know too much."

"Define 'too much.'"

She massaged her brow.

"I'm serious on this one, Director. A lot out there already."

She took one moment to think it through. "Anything beyond, 'it's some crazy girl in a suit following us around'?"

Abel shook his head. "Myself, Swords, Mars, and June. We're still the only agents who know all the details." He folded his arms. "Of the four of us? I'm reasonably sure we aren't leaking anything."

"I wouldn't expect you to," she answered.

Now it was his turn to huff in frustration as he prepared the rest of his report. "It's only a matter of time before the board gets more interested and more serious about her capture," the agent added. "Seems like they're less interested in the city attacks and more worried about the suit."

The director looked as though her entire world had crumbled. "They're idiots. They think threats to our own are less important than recovering tech that wasn't theirs to begin with."

"And Pilar is chasing down Aegis agents to find out what we're chasing." Abel made his way towards the windows. "It's definitely her, no mistake there either. Probably the only other person able to finish that suit, let alone use it."

"We've got to keep her away from what we're dealing with," the director added. "If she gets involved, things could get worse. But—"

"Eventually, we're going to need her help," Abel said, finishing her thought.

The director gave her favorite agent a nod. "Keep an eye on her. I don't want to engage her personally until I know what she's up to. And what they're up to."

"Already bugged," he replied, tapping the Bluetooth earpiece nestled in his left ear.

"Wow. He really was thinking ahead." She smirked a bit, then picked up the small shot glass from the desk, shaking it and watching the golden liquid within circle about. "Just like him to be that paranoid. Right up till his . . ."

The silence that fell between them was as loud as the largest explosion. Eventually, Abel found his voice again. "You really think she knows something?"

"Don't know, really. The police certainly weren't able to get anything from her, but I doubt they care at this point. Pretty sure some of the board members paid them under the table to stay out of it." She snuck a glance at him, her amber eyes softening a bit. "What do you think?"

His brow raised at that one. "I'm not the director."

Her smile was almost childlike in response. "Trade ya?"

Abel's brow couldn't have lowered any further if he'd tried. His stern grimace gave her the obvious answer.

After finally downing the alcohol she held in her grasp, she let out a "damn, that's strong," and slammed the emptied glass onto the desk before her. "We can't outright help her. Not with the other board members watching me so closely. We mess up, she could end up in jail, the suit could end up in their hands, and all the turds'll probably slam into the fan."

"Seems careless to just let her wander around freely tapping our communications, though." He put his left hand in his pocket, relaxing his stance a bit. "She's going to step into the wrong fight."

She nodded back. "Which is why I want you and your partner to watch her. Tail her night and day. You'll know when it's time to tell her more."

"And how will we know that?"

"Because I'll tell you when."

Abel's phone rang with a much different tone than either of them normally heard. It took him a moment to recognize his own ringtone and answer the call.

The silence as he listened told the director all she needed to know. This was not good news.

10

Pilar paid for having such a long night out.

Normally, her plan was to return home by no later than 1:00 a.m. That night, she didn't get back until after 3:00 a.m., and had to treat a few small bruises to be able to sleep. Said sleep lasted only three hours, and even then, she ran late due to oversleeping by a half hour.

She was ready to die by 11:00 a.m. Fortunately, the class ended early. By noon, when she met Zoe at the South Café, she was nearly dead. Every second between sentences of conversation, she rested her head on the table, hoping for some sort of quick nap.

"You look undead. I guess last night was a bit rougher on you than me." Zoe yawned. "Not that I'm exactly thrilled today."

Pilar raised her head from her folded arms, glared at Zoe for a moment, then put her head right back into her comfort zone. "I don't suppose you have some secret formula that keeps you from being as destroyed as I am?"

"Nope. I just exercise."

"Define 'exercise.'"

Zoe leaned back in her seat, taking a sip of the icy, unsweetened tea before her. "So you really don't have any formal training? You don't even work out a tiny bit?"

"You sound surprised."

"Considering how much running around that requires? Yeah, color me surprised. Somewhat impressed actually. For all the wrong reasons, but impressed either way."

Pilar shook her buried head. "Sorry I'm not as athletic as you are."

"Oh come on, I wasn't bringing this up to insult you." Zoe's worried smile irritated Pilar for some reason, and yet Zoe continued on as if she didn't notice the grimace on Pilar's face. "What I was trying to get at is I wouldn't mind helping you."

"Help with what?"

Zoe held her phone upright in front of Pilar's eyes. The most immediate thing in her view was a clip art graphic of some sort of ninja cutting through a wooden doorway with his sword. "Is that how much ninja training costs these days? Two ninety-nine?"

"Plus the subscription. So, thirty-two ninety-nine. Give or take."

Pilar's bloodshot eyes met hers and showed nothing but disbelief. "You're serious."

Zoe didn't back down. "It did wonders for me."

"I'll pass, thanks."

"Pilar. Holy hell. I'm kidding."

"You played it too straight."

"You really think I'm insane enough to parade around tailing security agents and preparing to fight off monsters using what I learned from the app store?"

Hearing it aloud, Pilar had to admit that was pretty unfair. "Okay, I get it. Sorry. Still, I don't need the help. My suit gives me more power than any training could."

"Or you just don't feel like exercising that much."

"How could you tell?" She rolled her eyes and buried her head in her arms again.

Zoe leaned in a bit. "But what about those situations where your suit isn't available to you? Depending on technology is pretty shortsighted."

Pilar rolled her eyes. "Why are you bugging me?"

"Bugging you? Was, that intentional?"

"Yes. Puns are how I get through annoying conversations," Pilar answered. "And still a valid question regardless."

"Not much to argue there, I guess." Zoe's eyes met hers. "I asked out of curiosity. And . . . out of concern."

That made Pilar uncomfortable. She knew exactly what sparked that concern. "I know."

"You made it sound like that hammer was still in testing, but your best reaction was to hold it up like a shield. Was letting one of those monsters try to cut through it really the best idea?"

"I didn't have a better one at the time." Pilar stared off into the café across the street.

"Exactly. Training, even a little bit, would help."

Pilar rested her chin on her folded arms. "Look . . . let's just focus on our current problem first, okay? We still haven't outlined all the parameters of our little partnership yet, and we still need to figure out just who that was last night."

Zoe finally relented. Still, she gave Pilar that same worried look. "Just promise you'll keep it in mind, okay? Any time, you let me know. I'd hate to have my first partner bite it because of something I could have easily prevented."

Zoe's concern was unnerving. The fact she'd even leapt to defend Pilar that night in the first place was already hanging on her mind. Because truthfully, Pilar wasn't so sure she could do the same. It was why she didn't want a partner, an associate, anyone, to help her. They were a liability, and she did not want to have another person in her life to worry about losing. That had happened two times too many already.

But, as much as Pilar may have wanted to say no, Zoe had real, tangible skills. She also knew more about the whole "vigilante" thing than Pilar could ever know. For now, Zoe was a necessary evil. A means to an end. Nothing more, nothing less.

That's what Pilar told herself. Repeatedly. It didn't seem to be working, but she'd keep saying it until it did.

"So what's the plan for tonight? Math study I hope?" Zoe eagerly asked.

"Please. Like you actually need help."

"What? Pilar, I do." Her glance became more curious. "You really thought I just made that up? For what?"

"To stalk me, maybe? You're the one going on about 'partner' this and 'partner' that."

Zoe slumped in her seat. "Wow. How trusting you are."

Even as brazen as she could be, Pilar couldn't help feeling at least somewhat guilty there. "So you're really serious about the tutori—"

"Oh my god, Pilar!" Zoe rolled her eyes, leaned back and laughed. "Yes! I was serious! And you agreed," Zoe sat up a bit, smirking as she looked Pilar right in her eyes, "so no excuses. You've gotta keep your word."

"Damn." Pilar buried her head right back in her arms. "Guess that means I actually have to tutor you tonight, doesn't it?"

Zoe sat back once more, arms still folded. Her smile had turned almost wistful after Pilar's tepid answer. "Geez, thank you for making me feel like such a huge burden," Zoe said with a laugh. "It's the starting assessment. So, if you want to skip studying, we can. I'd prefer not to look completely dumb on the first day, though. At least a refresher would be nice."

Pilar waved it off. "It's fine. I said I would help you, and I will. After that, though? I sleep," Pilar answered with a huff.

"No other plans?" Zoe couldn't be more obvious if she tried.

Pilar's brow raised. *She was thinking that to begin with, I bet. She's more manipulative than I give her credit for, that's for certain. Either way . . .* "None," she answered in a flat, low voice. "And besides that, I have no way to leave the house that late. My brother is home all night on Wednesdays. No way I can get around him and back in without some major issues cropping up, unless he gets called to do a show at the last minute."

"A show?" Zoe seemed to be connecting the dots in her head. In a few seconds, her eyes lit up. "Wait. You're DJ Shade's little sister, aren't you?"

Pilar nodded. "That guy. Yeah. Him." She could tell that Zoe picked up on her lack of enthusiasm.

"Um, wow, that must be fun, having your brother be a famous DJ."

Pilar shrugged. "According to him, he's not quite famous. But hey, you know, whatever works for you."

"You don't seem very happy with your brother for some reason."

That earned her a snide reply from Pilar. "No. I'm not. How could you tell?"

Zoe folded her arms, looking directly at Pilar. She didn't have to wait long for her to continue.

"So what do you want me to say? That it's all lovely, and peaches and cream, and gumdrops? I've been forced to live with him for over two years, out of the blue. Not happy about it."

Pete had returned with Zoe's food—grilled chicken fingers—and turned to Pilar. She could see the disappointment all over his face when her answer was a curt "no."

"Just the iced tea? Everything all right?"

"I'm fine, Pete. Just a little annoyed and not hungry."

"You do know that's not doing fine, right?" After a long, silent pause, he waved it off. "All right, all right. You'll figure it out on your own. I know." He snapped his fingers. "Speaking of your brother, who was that girl with him? If I knew he was hiding someone like that—"

Hearing about Bianca was the very last thing Pilar wanted. "I don't know Pete. Why don't you ask him?"

"I'm no idiot. That's his girl. Not hard to tell that." Pete did his best to look nonchalant about it. "Some guys have all the luck. But yeah, that's not important, and why am I even asking you that?"

"Desperation?" Pilar answered, a wry smile on her face.

Zoe's eyes widened. Pilar could damn-near sense her disbelief just from her look alone. "Really, Pilar?" she asked almost completely under her breath.

Pete laughed back. "See that's why I mess with you. Hilarious, kid." His laughter died down and his smile couldn't hide his worry. "Just don't take it out on your bro. I've known Seth for some years, man. He means well."

Pilar shrugged. "You tell me that every time we have this discussion."

Pete shrugged back. He walked away at a smooth, slow pace, trotting back indoors. "Because it's true." With that, he left them to talk again.

"He's interesting," Zoe added.

Pilar nodded. "You get used to him after a while."

"You make him sound annoying."

Pilar's gaze fell to her again. "I make everything sound annoying. Or so I've been told. Usually by that DJ Shade person."

"All that aside, You have to have some sort of plan, right? We can't be caught off guard if they decide to do something that atrocious again." Zoe's eyes fell to the cup of tea in front of her.

Her drop in demeanor was understandable. Pilar herself dreaded remembering the scene, and she wasn't the one who'd thrown up looking at it. "We won't be caught off guard. Trust me on that. It'll take some work on my part, but the next time they show up? It'll be tons easier to deal with them."

Zoe nodded. "Well, first things first, we need to come up with a plan to get you out of your house tonight."

"We?"

Zoe had just finished taking a quick sip of her tea. "Yes, 'we.' As in 'team.'"

"I told you—"

Zoe didn't let her finish. "I know what you said. And it's a lousy way to think. If we don't work as a team, we'll be at odds all the time, because neither one of us is going to back off of Aegis or these other cloak-wearing monsters, right?"

"You're mistaken if you think I care that much about them."

"They're your lead. I'm not sure to what, but you said so yourself."

"No, I didn't."

"'You've got information I want.' I'm pretty sure I didn't say that."

Pilar hadn't even realized she'd let that slip. "Okay. Color me officially impressed. Now, why are you so determined to help me?"

"Because we've got more in common than you think." Zoe took a sip of tea. "That, and I think we'll work well together. Which reminds me," Zoe's glee returned in all its odd glory, "I think I know what to call myself now."

Pilar couldn't wait to hear this one. There was really no telling what this girl was thinking. "And what did you come up with, exactly?"

"Brilliant Blazing Moth," she answered proudly. "Catchy, right?"

Pilar waited for her to laugh, for her to hand-wave the name away. When it didn't happen, she rested her palm right over her own face. A defeated "oy vey," was all she managed.

"What? Too much? I mean it's not as simple as Bug, but it works."

"Why a moth? I thought you already had an identity."

"Not really. I was just a stealthy vigilante. But this whole Bug thing? That could really work for us."

"You realize you chose something with the lifespan of about a day?" Pilar looked to the traffic passing by a few dozen feet away. "Besides, that's a mouthful to say. I'm not calling you that." She rested her right elbow on the table, and let her chin sit on her upturned palm. "I'll just call you Moth."

"Well, that's just dull." Despite saying that, Zoe gave her a wink. "Works for me."

▋▋

It was rare for anyone to set foot on that floor. The few who did were all likely to wield as much power within the company as she did. For her, that meant there was just as much of a chance that any of them could be spying on her.

She hated operating like that every day. The assumption that permeated her mind was that anyone, even the people she trusted, could be the leak from her office. Not even Abel could be fully trusted. Thinking of that cut her right to the core.

As she stepped off the elevator and into the darkened conference room, she realized the irony of her thinking. After all, she herself was lying to the seven people who kept her employed. Not that she cared much for her position. *I'm just the person they lay blame on. The public sponge. That should be my nickname. My own deception is the one thing the board can't take from me.*

There were seven monitors surrounding a gray, round table in the center of the room. Each monitor had a camera affixed to its top, and on each screen was an executive, sitting comfortable in their seat. Two of them weren't even in business attire, seemingly at some country home far off in some backwoods area that no one had probably heard of.

If Aegis's board of directors was anything, broke wasn't it. Chances were that the man in the country home probably owned it.

Must be nice, she thought. She had to catch herself a bit there, as she almost spoke the words right to his face as she looked at his monitor.

When she sat at her seat at the head of the table, the lights brightened just enough around her that the tan-skinned woman was perfectly displayed to the others. Crossing her legs, then straightening her hair was just her delaying the inevitably sour start of the meeting.

"So would you care to explain just what happened, Director Delacruz?"

Delacruz wasn't in much of a hurry to explain that. After all, it would include explaining how they'd ended up completely empty-handed as well. The agents who had lost their lives? Not so important to them. They were replaceable, after all. Plenty of college graduates who would love to be interns at the most prestigious technology and security firms in the city.

But the technology those fiends had access to? That was irreplaceable.

It was also something that had once belonged to Aegis. The board was fairly obsessed with keeping their toys to themselves, even ones they'd thrown away long ago.

These idiots sicken me.

"There was this little known project called Indigo that you might all remember?" The silence that permeated the room let her know she'd hit the right mark. "Right. As I was worried about long ago, it isn't exactly as dead and buried as we thought it was. I'd say it's actually worse than I personally feared."

The man who spoke up next had to be the oldest man she'd ever seen having a say in a company. A part of her wanted to venture a guess that he was well over a hundred years old. However, he was sharper than most of the twenty-somethings who walked into the company. "And the vigilante?"

Delacruz peeked over to him, smiling a bit. "As far as I know, the vigilante and her cohort were both gone from the area by the time our personnel arrived. We have nothing to report on that end."

"But the vigilante was in the area, correct?"

Delacruz looked about the monitors, hoping that at least one of them realized this line of question was pointless. As expected, not one of them sided with her. "From what my agents have reported? Yes, the vigilante was in the area."

"And from previous reports given to us, by you, no less, the armor this vigilante is using is our old tech that Emmanuel Sands developed, correct?"

She found a bit of relief in that piece of misinformation. *It's better they don't know what role I played in that thing's development. Last thing I need is more blame.*

Delacruz cleared her throat, then proceeded. "Right. The vigilante is using a very similar armor from what I can tell. What that has to do with so many of our agents getting murdered in one night, I'm not sure. So," she folded her arms and glared directly at his screen, "please elaborate on that for us."

"You know, for someone who is barely holding onto the position she's holding, you are doing a very good job of getting voted out of here," said the old woman on the far left. Delacruz was always tempted to make a personal attack on her at each one of these conference calls. But for the sake of her agents and her job, she managed to refrain from doing so pretty well.

"I'm quite comfortable dancing on the edge of the line," Delacruz answered back.

"The only reason you are still here is because there's currently no better candidate that knows the company better."

"I'm still here because *A*, my father ran the company before me so it looks good for you publicly, and *B*, I do a really good job of cleaning things up." She looked to each of the other monitors with a scowl. "So excuse me if I'm a little bit weary of you questioning my methods when I'm the one taking the heat for you."

"You haven't answered—"

"The vigilante is not our major concern. At best, said vigilante has done nothing outside of spying on random communications between our field agents, who have purposely offered up very little intel on my command. I'd like to think I don't have to remind this board that there is a group of mass murderers out there using our abandoned living armor, right?"

Delacruz glared at each person, waiting for any response. None came.

"Right. Like I said, unimportant." She huffed a bit, then continued. "I will keep a very small number of our eyes on the vigilante until we can determine her usefulness. Outside of that, my priority is dealing with these monsters that the RCPD is not equipped to deal with, and keeping more of our agents breathing."

"We will offer you leeway on this," said a much younger Chinese man on the panel. "That said, I have another question."

"Shoot."

"Have you gotten in to contact with Sands's daughter?"

She needed to keep as straight a face as possible when answering that. "I have not, but I am aware of where she is."

"That girl could be of great use to us as an agent."

"That girl hates us, considering what we as a company did to her father."

"Then convince her otherwise. She could be the only person who could understand his research."

Delacruz was fighting her every instinct. "She could not even have a clue."

"At least give me a bit of credit, Angela. I've researched her pedigree. If anything, Pilar Marie Sands could be even more intelligent than her father in his prime." He smiled. "Bring her on board."

She was extremely reluctant to do that, and yet, having their blessing to do so set off a new set of gears in her mind. "Very well. I'll see how she responds soon enough. For now, I'd like to keep her out of the loop until I know exactly what use she would be to us."

The young man gave her a nod. "Good. And keep in mind, there is nothing you can do that we cannot find out. Your agents report to us just as you do."

"I'm aware of that." The dismissive tone was more than Delacruz meant to expose. Still, if there was someone in that circle who would tolerate it, he would. It was hardly their first time having such a discussion, after all.

He laughed off her smug answer. "I didn't say that as a threat." The sound of three children yelling out to their father in glee drew his attention for a moment, and caught the eyes of everyone else in the conference. "If you'll excuse me, I have far more important business to attend to."

Without another word, his screen flashed, then died, leaving a black void where his face and the beautiful countryside had once sat. Seeing one of the only two people on the board she could tolerate for more than a minute ditch her, Delacruz wasn't exactly thrilled to stay longer than necessary. "If there's nothing else?"

"We're keeping you on a much shorter leash," the old woman snapped. Her smile looked as though it was going to crack her entire face apart. "I suggest not wandering too far from your pole, unless you like choking."

Before Delacruz could retaliate, all the monitors flickered off, and the room brightened back to its full gold-tinged glory.

If she could have punched that old woman's monitor, she would have. If it had been her actual face, that would have been far better.

Her steps out of the conference room seemed as though she'd leave holes in the ground, but despite her furious walk, the director kept her face utterly void of expression. When she arrived at the elevator door, she was greeted by another of her agents, this one a blonde woman who was just about as tall, far thinner in figure, and ten times more bubbly than Delacruz wanted to deal with. Still, this was one of her most trusted agents as well.

"Any news on my special project?" Delacruz asked the girl.

"Nothing as of yet, Angie. Still signing the paperwork!" The girl peeked at the director's pained grimace, and offered a bright smile and a thumbs-up.

Delacruz rolled her eyes. "Not 'Angie' today. Really poor mood. And could you be any more obvious?"

"Sorry! Still not used to this kind of responsibility, ya know?" She cleared her throat, and spoke as seriously as she could muster. "Your project requires more paperwork filing, Miss."

She could see the girl's lips quivering as she tried to hold in her chuckling. "Oh god, Madri, you can't be serious for even a few seconds, can you?"

"Hey, you didn't even call me 'Agent' that time!"

Delacruz's eyes looked as though they were moments away from firing a laser through Madri's face. "Agent Madriella Mars, keep your eyes on . . . the paperwork, if you don't mind. And have Agents Rose and Swords pick up the paperwork when ready."

Madri Mars's salute forced Delacruz, even in her annoyed mood, to smirk a bit and shake her head.

"See? Knew you needed to laugh."

As Delacruz exited the elevator and entered her office, she peered back at Madri over her left shoulder. "And that's why you're still employed."

"We've all got our talents, right? Works for me!"

Once the doors shut, she had to take a moment to straighten herself out. And, as much as she hated to think about it, she had to sort out who it was who could be giving the board all that information they claimed to have.

Mars, Swords, Rose, even my own daughter. If the board's plan was to get me paranoid of my own shadow, it's starting to work. And they want his daughter here, too. Actually, that's perfect. That's better than perfect. I can keep my eyes on everything this way, and keep my word. Good, good.

She sat at her desk, once again reaching for a shot glass, though this time she only poured a bit of soda into it. Her eyes caught the small bottle, and she smirked.

Better save that for later. Gonna need it when they get here.

12

By the time Pilar got home that afternoon, Bianca had been there for a couple of hours. She knew if she so much as greeted her, a long conversation would ensue, and Pilar just plain wasn't interested in that. She was far more interested in her bed than anything that woman had to say.

Still, she had to actually get to her room unnoticed. The door to their apartment was always creaky, echoing through the outside hallways as well as within the living room. There was literally no way she'd be able to open it and sneak in. The only reason she could do so at night was because her brother usually wasn't home by the time she got back, and if he was, he was dead asleep.

Normally, she'd have more than enough time when he left for work to fix any kinks in the Bug Suit. The plan was to leave it at the lab, but with as many emergency fixes as she needed to make, coming up with random excuses to get to said lab became more and more difficult by the day.

Hopping on her Vespa and then disappearing for a few hours wasn't as easy to do, though she'd managed it. Now that she thought about it, having someone like Zoe around did give her a good cover.

She still wasn't sure what to make of Zoe. That girl was just weird.

Her mind jumped back to the malfunctioning suit again, as she realized she had no choice but to keep the suit in the apartment, for now. It needed an extensive once-over, at the very least. If she ran into those monsters again, she wanted her suit to be at two hundred percent.

Bianca was going to hear Pilar when she entered. There was no way around it. As such, Pilar eventually decided not to sneak in, and wait to see how long it took before Bianca badgered her.

The smell of garlic and salt seemed to fill the apartment air. Surprisingly, the blinds in the living room were drawn back, the large window open about halfway. Whoever had put that garlic smell in the air—likely Bianca—was aware that it was too strong.

Sure enough, as Pilar approached the kitchen she saw Bianca standing over the stove, using it to sauté something unfamiliar to Pilar's eyes. Bianca noticed that Pilar was eyeing her, and smiled back to her curious look. "Perch," she said, raising a silver pan from the stove and tilting it just enough to show her its contents.

Fifteen seconds, Pilar mused to herself. "I hate fish," she mumbled back. She turned to the hallway leading to her room, and dragged herself inside. Her hand was firm with the door itself, slamming it closed.

Please get the hint, she silently pleaded to her roommate.

It took less than five minutes for a soft rap to hit Pilar's door. That rap was answered at first with a groan. When Bianca inevitably asked if she could enter, Pilar could only logically answer with "it's open."

Bianca opened the door at a pace that would anger a snail. Pilar didn't care about that, despite how annoying it was to hear that long creaking sound. What absolutely irked Pilar however, was that Bianca closed the door behind her. Pilar rolled her eyes when she heard the door shut and saw that Bianca was still in her room. Having dealt with Seth for the past couple of years, she knew full well what that meant.

Oh joy. "Therapy" time.

"You okay?" Bianca leaned against the door, arms folded. Though she held a stern look, her voice was soft.

Pilar's answer wasn't nearly as direct as she would have liked. "Been better," she said, despite her mind saying *kick rocks*.

"Pilar, hon." She paused for a breath. "Listen. I know you're not exactly happy to have someone else sharing your space, but I'm on your side."

"You're my brother's roommate," Pilar shot back.

Bianca's eyes widened a bit, but she suddenly narrowed them. "You've got a lot on your mind, I get that." She stood for a second, then looked to her left. "That helmet was pretty interesting, by the way."

Before Pilar could even begin to say anything, Bianca raised her hand. And clutched in that raised right hand, was Pilar's Bug helmet.

Pilar's anger was immediate. The downward curl in her eyebrows pointed directly to the bridge of her nose. "Oh. So now the roommate sneaks into my room while I'm gone?"

Bianca's chuckle was, at best, condescending. "No. The roommate happened to see this bloody thing on the kitchen counter before Seth got home. Sure you would have had a fine time explaining this to him though, wouldn't you?"

Pilar started to argue, but then realized the horrifying truth. She hadn't switched the helmet's display mode. Right in front of her, clear as day, was the helmet of her battle suit, in its "Bug" form. That should have never made it to the kitchen table, and even if it did, leaving it in that mode . . . She'd been completely careless. Pilar actually found herself at a loss for words.

Bianca tossed it on the bed. "So I'm sure you had a firsthand view of that massacre in the 10th precinct."

Pilar looked to her from the corners of her eyes. "What does it matter to you? And why didn't you just tell Seth? What exactly is your angle?"

Bianca's lips curled. Pilar smiled at the sight of it.

"Ah, I get it. Seth is your angle." She folded her arms, proud that she could make the stoic woman freeze. Bianca looked as though she wasn't sure if she should laugh at, cry for, or stab Pilar.

Pilar realized in that moment that if Bianca did the latter, she couldn't even blame her. After all, what had Bianca done to earn that shot? It wasn't something she could easily take back, and even if she could, she wasn't certain her pride would allow it. *Why did I say that?*

"You've had a tough time." Bianca's tone was still motherly. Only now it was the disciplinarian side that every child feared. "I understand that much. It's obvious. But perhaps you should take some of that anger and direct it at the monsters who deserve it, instead of sharing it with the people who genuinely care about you?"

"And how do I know you care about me? I've known you for a couple days at best, and maybe from preschool, right? You really expect me to remember you from that long ago?"

Try as she might, Bianca couldn't continue to hide her wearing patience, that much Pilar could see easily.

"You're right. Maybe I shouldn't have." Bianca took a long breath, then just sat next to Pilar on the bed, timidly propping herself upright. "Seth contacted me a month ago, asking me for advice on how to talk to you. What he didn't realize was I'd returned to the states a while ago."

Pilar folded her arms. "Why would he be asking you?"

"You were probably too young to remember me much, but I really was close with your family. Even after my aunt moved us to London, I've stayed in touch with Seth over the years." She leaned back a bit. "I have many reasons for coming back, but you should know that you're one of the primary reasons I did."

When Pilar realized what she was saying, her eyes lit up, fearful of just how much she actually knew. Before Pilar could even ask, she answered:

"I only put things together a week or so ago myself, Pilar."

"Just . . . how?"

"I've been to your dad's lab, Pilar. I told you, I used to babysit you until you were five."

"Which means," Pilar looked to the helmet, "you were there when this was being worked on. When he was still cementing it."

"Imagine seeing the thing I saw as a teen being built, showing up on the news almost a dozen years later. Weren't too many other conclusions for me to draw." Bianca placed a comforting hand on Pilar's shoulder. "Listen, I know I probably feel like a complete stranger to you. And in some ways, maybe I am. But I'm on your side in this. I just want to make sure you're okay. That you're safe."

Bianca reached into the pocket of her blue slacks, then handed Pilar a laminated picture.

"What's with this? Your just-in-case-of-snarky-kid emergency photo?"

"You . . . really do have to have a snippy comeback for everything, don't you?"

Pilar's glance to her was flat. "Yes."

Despite her quip, Pilar's curiosity led her eyes back to the picture in her hands. In that picture, she could see herself, much smaller and much younger, wearing a pretty pink dress and smiling. Her hair was still black then, too.

Kinda miss that sometimes.

Even Pilar had to admit that she hadn't smiled like that in years. But back then, her parents were together. Her brother had been her protector— and her friend. She'd looked up to him. He'd seemed to genuinely care about her. She hadn't been a burden.

Looking at herself in that dress, with that smile, started to hurt. She'd probably always been a burden to everyone back then, too.

In the picture, she was holding the hand of a teenage, peach-skinned girl with long cinnamon hair, thin glasses, and a nervous smile that showed her braces. She was certain that was Bianca. Next to her, she could see her brother. If there was nothing else that gave away how long ago that picture had been taken, the fact he was happy in their father's lab told her all she needed to know: Mom was still alive.

Her father was there, standing next to Bianca. He looked about as calm as she remembered. Same lab coat, same ponytailed hair, same big-rimmed glasses. Next to him, however, was an older teen who looked eerily similar to Bianca. And no matter how much she tried, she couldn't think of who this girl was at all. And the more she stared, the more her mind wanted to remember.

There was one last person in the photo. It was another, older man, who was dressed in a similar lab coat as her father. He was maybe a bit taller than Bianca, red hair slicked back, grinning with unmatched joy as he held the other girl's hand.

"My dad," Bianca answered before Pilar could even ask. "Different person back then. We all were."

"Why exactly are you showing me this?"

She felt Bianca's arm wrap around her. "Whatever happened that day, it didn't just affect your memories of your father's disappearance. When Seth and I talked, he was distraught. He told me that even in the few words you were saying in the days after your father . . ."

They both fell silent. Pilar could tell she was searching for how to bring it up. "My father disappeared?"

Bianca seemed shocked to hear Pilar say that, and yet, she cleared her throat. "Yes, yes. His disappearance."

The way Bianca said that didn't sit well with Pilar.

Still, Bianca went on. "Since his disappearance, your memory has been scattered at best. Some things were completely gone. You've come a long way since then."

"Then?" Pilar still wasn't fully understanding her point. She was well aware of her memory lapses, but as far as she knew, they were just of that period of time when her father . . .

. . . *when dad disappeared. Those three days, I don't remember anything about them.*

"Your memories of much more than that seem to be all over the place. Not gone, but, confused." Bianca added. "I didn't expect you to know exactly who I was, but to not even be familiar to you at all is worrying. I'm here to make sure things aren't going to get any worse. Seth thought that maybe having me around would help jog more of your memories, and that maybe I'd be able to diagnose what's wrong. Although," she chuckled a bit, and released Pilar's shoulder form her grasp, "I told him he's greatly overestimating my abilities. I'm fresh out of school myself."

So this was his doing, but, for me?

Pilar huffed. "Okay. Say I believe all of this. Why are you so adamant about being involved in my life?"

"Well, it goes deeper than that." Bianca tapped the older man in the picture. "I suspect that he is responsible for the monster that attacked the 10th District."

"Your father?"

Even without a word said for the next moment as Pilar studied the man's face, she could sense Bianca's anger.

"When my dad finally went mad, your father got my sister and me removed from his custody. We were eventually raised by relatives, but we were always fearful of dad's reach. He'd tried to contact us before, and we'd managed to stay away from him. Last we'd heard of him, he'd apparently vanished. Not even Aegis seemed to know what became of him."

Pilar nodded. "Of course they didn't. They never know anything. It's their motto."

"Yes. It's a worrying, tiring trend." Bianca's gaze seemed to be piercing right into the floor. "But there's something else."

"Something that made you think he's around."

She nodded back. "Around a year ago, before I left England to return here, I lost contact with my sister. The only guess I could make is that maybe, just maybe, she came back here, trying to seek him out for answers—answers I doubt that bastard would be willing to give freely."

"Do I . . . know him too?" Pilar's voice was so uneasy that even she could feel her fear. She didn't understand what she was looking at, but somehow that man's face, that eerie smile of his, and Bianca's words brought a dread within her that she'd only recalled in her nightmares.

"His name is Evandrake Hyde." Pilar watched as Bianca's lips curled inward, and her fists tightened in her own lap. "Sharing his last name . . . it sickens me."

Now Pilar wasn't sure where things would go. After all, if that was true, then Bianca was the daughter of a vile monster. There should have been no way for her to trust even one word from her mouth.

"Bianca Hyde," Pilar mumbled. "You never answered my question, you know." Pilar glanced over to her, a bit embarrassed by it all. "Why didn't you tell Seth about the Bug armor?"

"Because now that I know for sure that it's you under that armor, I'm almost certain no one else will be able to stop Hyde. Sands entrusted it to you for a reason." She leaned to Pilar a bit, resting her head against hers for a moment. "That, and would you really stop if I told Seth and he came down on you?" She chuckled at the thought of it. "At best, it would drive a wedge further between you two, and definitely put the Gulf of Mexico between you and me."

Pilar fidgeted, fairly uncomfortable with Bianca—or anyone, really—being anywhere near that close to her. Bianca didn't seem to notice that.

"Off, please."

Bianca nearly jumped up. "Oh! Sorry about that. Still learning everyone's boundaries."

"Yeah," She answered with a huff. "Anyway, If he finds out—"

Bianca was still sitting stiff and upright. "It won't be from me. I'll trust your judgment on when the time is right to tell him." Bianca jokingly tapped the helmet. "Or, heaven forbid, you accidentally let him find out."

Bianca stood, straightening her red locks. "I came back to help you and find my sister."

"And for Seth?"

She smiled. "I don't think that's any of your business. Not that there's really any to tell."

Somehow, Pilar felt strangely relieved to hear that. *Guess we relate there too, then. The workaholic doesn't have much time to acknowledge anything that isn't work.*

Still, she wasn't sure how to process what she'd heard. The memory loss didn't make sense, and it didn't explain how she'd lost something from that long ago. And even then, just how much more had she lost?

And of all things, why did she remember the lab—the place where all that horror actually took place somewhere in those three days—and the Bug armor, yet she couldn't remember what happened to her father?

Bianca made her way to the door. "Seth won't be home tonight. Said he had an all-nighter at some club. ROOM-E, I think it was? Lucky you, honestly. Had he not gotten that gig and had to go straight there after class, he'd've seen that helmet of yours long before I did."

Pilar's eyes bulged hearing that. Mostly because Bianca was right. He should have been home first, not her.

But then, how?

Bianca laughed a bit as she left. "Oh, and if you want something else for dinner, I can cook it, you know. No need to suffer through the fish if you don't like it. Just . . . talk to me sometime, okay? I'm really not that bad of a person to talk to."

She answered with a bit of a smirk. "Yeah. I guess not." *For now, anyway.*

With that, Bianca closed the door behind her, leaving Pilar to her own thoughts. And when she looked to her helmet again, only one thought came to her mind:

Guess I should give her a call. Bet she'll be happy. Not that I won't be.

They had no way of knowing who was setting a trap for whom.

"And she says that the guy in charge is named Hyde?" Moth seemed unsure what to make of it. After all, until that point, the only "bad guys" she'd followed were Aegis. But the slaughter the night before and the two perpetrators certainly fit with the explanation of a bigger monster at work, one who obviously had a deeper hatred for Aegis than Bug did, and was not apprehensive about showing it.

"Yes. And I still don't know what to make of it. Which is why I asked you if it was a familiar name. Apparently you're not going to be helpful there either." Bug looked about, using her helmet's zoom function to try and observe anything interesting in the distance.

Bug and Moth stood a few buildings away from the very explosion Moth had caused the night before. They were strictly observing at that point, but neither was exactly thrilled to jump into battle against the monster they'd managed to stare down the last time.

After all, it wasn't as though their authority and menacing eyes forced him to retreat. That award belonged to the other monster-woman who commanded him.

Regardless, despite their nervousness, Pilar was at least just as excited to try their newer weapons against the fiends. There was a lot that could go right this night.

What worried her was that essentially they'd have to protect Aegis. They had to predict their next move too if they were going to keep another massacre from happening.

"I have my uses. Of that much, I'm certain," Moth answered with a chuckle.

Bug was surprised she seemed to accept that so easily. "Well, yes. You do." Bug peeked back to Moth for a moment. "I insult you because it drives you to improve and be even more useful."

"What a wonderful empowerment method." Moth shook her head. "Anything so far?"

"Nothing." Bug wished she could give a different answer, but no matter how many times she looked about, not a blip jumped out at her. She started to wonder if her helmet was malfunctioning yet again. "Hey, Moth. Off the top of your head, where do you think they're likely to strike?"

Moth stood, then paused. "It's hard to say. It's not like we even know what they were after before."

"Is there something or someone nearby that's of any significance?"

Moth knelt near the edge of the rooftop. She looked about the world below them that continued to buzz. "There has to be some connection. But what?"

Moth almost made Bug jump backwards with how fast she shot upright.

"What?"

"Bug, they aren't after Aegis. Aegis is just getting in their way."

"That makes sense. Now we can maybe get more of an idea of what they're actually after."

"Yesterday wasn't supposed to happen, right?" Moth continued to glare at the streets surrounding their current perch. "That leech guy wasn't supposed to fight Aegis."

"Right, I got that."

Moth folded her arms. "They weren't after anything near here. These attacks are diversions."

Bug nodded. "Diversions? Okay, but then, what were they actually after?"

"Well that's not as easy to answer. I've got nothing to go on." Moth's glance returned to the streets below, watching as a flood of red and blue flashing lights poured through them. "Well, that's promising." She reached into her utility belt, revealing what looked like an old walkie-talkie. She pressed a small, white switch on its left side. "This will hopefully catch one of their frequencies," she added.

Bug nodded. "Cute. Not really effective, but cute."

"Well, it works."

"Let's try jumping into the twenty-first century, shall we?" Bug reached into her own utility belt, lifting a small, mechanical bee from its furthest-left pouch.

"A bee?"

Bug held the insect on her palm. "Not just a bee. It is, for all intents and purposes, a small camera and transceiver I can control with my gauntlets. It's barely noticeable, if at all, and even if it were eventually noticed, I can cause it to pop and melt into nothing but a lump of metal. I've created dozens of these. Pretty handy, if I say so myself."

"Less time admiring your work, more time putting it to work." Moth folded her arms and turned her gaze back to the cops below. "They're not going to be around here long."

"Yeah yeah."

She touched the back of the mechanical insect, and they watched as it flapped its wings. Without further notice than that, Bug pointed her finger towards the swarm of cop cars, and the Burst Bee shot after them like a tiny rocket.

In the HUD of Bug's helmet, there was now a small window in the upper right, displaying everything the Burst Bee captured on its own camera. And as Bug's right hand moved in various directions, so did the Bee.

"I need them to slow down." She continued to follow them, pointing in a new direction every time they made a turn or a swerve through traffic.

"Got it!" Pilar's right hand relaxed to her side. She stood on one knee again, her right hand tapping a touch-sensitive area of her helmet. It acted as a button to change her helmet's various functions—in this case, switching it to the view of the transceiver. Slowly, sounds began to filter into Bug's helmet, at first garbled, but slowly becoming clearer. Bug could see her partner still glaring in the direction the Bee was headed. "Okay, I want some of those."

Bug turned towards the direction she'd sent the Bee as well. "Got something." Again Bug pressed a button on the side of her helmet; almost instantly, sounds of frantic orders erupted from it:

"We've got multiple assailants in the East Downtown District! Location is East 1492 Stanley Drive! No shots fired, subject has multiple appendages! What the hell is—"

"I know that address," Moth quickly added. "It's the Emerald Club. People call it ROOM-E. Popular place for dubstep and Ecstacy, but not for something that a creature-feature like that guy would want."

"ROOM-E?" Before she knew it, Bug had quickly charged towards her, grabbing her by her arms. "How fast can you get uptown?"

"Pretty fast, I'm sure! You mind not shaking me to death?"

Bug let her go, and ran for the edge of the building. She leapt down, and the enormous scarf she wore on her suit now functioned as a glider, allowing her to safely swoop to ground level. "We've got to get there!"

Moth didn't hesitate, quickly following her off the side of the building. Unlike Bug, she had to rappel down utilizing rope to get to the ground safely. "Okay, no problem. But what are you—"

"I know what they're after! We've got to get over there! He's not gonna stand a chance!" Bug jumped on Moth's motorcycle before she herself could. She didn't bother to argue it, either, as Bug actually kicked it into gear, and within seconds peeled off, weaving through traffic, headed towards the east Downtown area.

"I didn't know you could drive a motorcycle," Moth yelled above traffic and the growling engine.

"I'll explain later!" Bug cut through another alley. "Maybe," she added under her breath.

Her traffic-weaving continued to get more and more erratic as her nerves worsened. *You're not getting to him before me*, she told herself. Even if Seth was a jerk, she wasn't going to lose the only person left in her immediate family. She would do whatever it took to keep him out of this. Racing through the city was the easy part.

14

When they arrived at the club, Bug didn't bother to stop. She wasn't going to wait for a chance to sneak in. Her goal was to save her brother—she would handle the consequences of her actions later.

Moth wasn't too thrilled with that idea. Not only had the RCPD arrived, but so had their primary target. "Bug, we can't just ride my bike in there!"

"I'll pay you back for the damages!"

"That's not my concern!" Moth hung on tight, realizing that at this point she was merely hanging on for the ride on her own vehicle.

The RCPD's barricade was not of importance to Bug—she plowed right through it, and shot the motorcycle right through the gaping hole in the brick wall. She was pretty sure that whatever was after her brother had made that hole to begin with.

Once inside, she leapt off the bike, looking in every direction for a hint of what had transpired. The scene was surreal. There were so many neon lights and colored spotlights everywhere that Bug's heads-up display was receiving garbled information. She'd quickly been reminded that the lenses were light sensitive; the setting they found themselves in wasn't something she'd had a chance to fully test.

A flash from a broken light bulb popped in her view. A message in red letters appeared in her vision, warning her that the lenses of the helmet were malfunctioning. *Wish I did have Moth's homemade mask right now*, she thought to herself. *Wouldn't be dealing with any of these stupid glitches, that's for sure.* She mentally added the lens issues to her long list of things that really, really needed to be fixed, ASAP.

Moth took notice of her strange flinches. "You okay, Bug?"

"Define 'okay.'" Bug continued to look about, trying to find any sign of her brother in the vacant club. When she finally caught a glimpse of him to her far left, all manner of fear set into her.

He stood hunched over, gasping for air. He was sweating terribly, and his face and arms were both fairly well bruised. And yet, despite that, there was no sign yet of their assumed targets.

Bug continued to scan the room, trying to see just what had created that gaping hole in the wall and run her brother to exhaustion. Her helmet's sensors hadn't picked up anything yet, but she desperately searched the room to and fro for any sign of something abnormal.

"Bug! Three o'clock!"

She heard Moth's yell a few steps away, and she quickly turned to her right—just barely recognizing the object speeding towards her—and tumbled to the ground face first. It stabbed into the wall behind her, barely missing a few members of the club crowd. The long, black tentacle was as sharp as a newly forged sword. Had Bug not lain down, she would have been cleaved clean in half.

She rolled away from her precarious spot. "Okay, I'd really not like to do that again," she moaned before standing. She could now finally see the beast who dared to threaten her life.

It was exactly whom she'd suspected.

"You two again, huh?" He slowly reeled his leech-like arm back into his sleeve. "I would've assumed you'd be smarter after getting away clean last time."

"I don't back down easily."

"You'll regret that soon enough." He looked to his right, giving the young man next to him a devilish smile. "You don't mind, right? Of course you don't. You don't mind anything, do you?"

Moth and Bug were side by side now, and gave the young man standing next to their familiar target a once-over. He didn't look particularly powerful, but as with the woman from the previous night, there was an aura about him that unsettled Bug. He wore a black cloak as she had; however, his had green trim along its edges, and an emblem of a large green scythe across the front. He stepped away from the wall he'd been leaning on, and pulled a bit of his waist-length black hair out of his face. His silver-green eyes had an astonishing emptiness to them.

Moth got chills just looking at him.

He looked to his ally, then to the two of them, and snickered.

Moth's entire body got chills just from hearing that. "Bug. This is bad."

"That's obvious."

"No. I mean because he laughed at all of us." Moth's hand moved to her utility belt quickly. Without another word, she drew two daggers, holding one in each hand. "A common comic trope. The guy sitting back giving orders with a carefree smile? Usually the guy who can kill everyone with his pinky finger."

Bug held her giant hammer before her, with its handle crossing in front of her body. "There's a more obvious, and logical reason I'm going to go with."

"Which is?"

"He's their leader. Of course he's more dangerous."

The man shrugged at their suggestion. "You're overreacting, you know," he said to them, brightening his smile even further. "Not much I can do right now. That human did a good job of repelling me earlier." He motioned with a quick nod towards Seth. "Of course, it's probably for the best, right? We still have a month before his power becomes useless to us."

He patted his underling on his shoulder. "Don't fail, Leech. You know how Master Hyde is about failure."

Leech looked back. "As if I care. I'm hungry."

"Well, I'm leaving this in your ever-so-capable hands then." Mantis flashed Moth a lighthearted grin. "It was nice meeting you. Unfortunate that our first and last meeting had to end this way." He gave them a smug little wave. The color of his skin and clothing became as black as his hair, until the only thing that could be seen of his figure was his glowing, green eyes. His figure then turned into a burst of black smoke, and faded as if his existence had become nothing.

Leech huffed, returning his attention to Seth. "Now that he's gone, I guess I get to force you to return with me, huh?"

Seth stood upright, inhaling deeply, then exhaling. "I've got more than enough left to smash your face in. I'll take a nap afterwards and get all recharged."

"Okay, maybe I'm missing something, Bug." Moth was speaking in a fairly low tone, just enough so Bug could hear her as they stood side by side. "If Mantis is their leader, and Leech was able to take out a mob of Aegis Agents without mercy . . ."

"How the hell did Seth hold off Mantis?" Bug finished.

"Yeah," Moth answered with a nod. "Not only that, but he's claiming to have enough left over for this demon?"

Bug nodded, then took a step towards Leech. "Hey you! You butt-ugly b-movie reject! What exactly is your beef with Se—"

She just barely caught herself. "I-I mean, uh . . . with this kid?"

"None of your concern," Leech answered back. "You two were lucky the other night. But you just had to come back and interfere, didn't you?"

"It's what we do." Bug held her hammer outward, aiming the head of it at Leech, holding it with one hand. "I don't know what you want with him, but it's not happening."

Leech's left tentacle shot directly at Seth, as if it were a living switchblade. Seth dodged with blinding speed, moving himself into Leech's range, and punching him so hard in his abdomen that Leech actually doubled over from the pain. Leech's tentacles reacted to his pain, as the one that he'd attacked with slumped to the ground like a mound of old meat.

Seth's fists were aglow with a fiery, red aura. It was as if his very hands were on fire.

Moth pointed to him, glaring at Bug. "Okay. Explain please."

Bug was at a loss for an explanation. There was no logical way to explain what she saw. The only thing that her helmet revealed to her was an unidentifiable violet-tinged steam that seemed to originate from his body, particularly from his hands. This power was completely new to her.

Seth wasn't done amazing them just yet.

The glow around his hands changed from crimson to a vibrant aqua-blue. The moment that change began to happen, Bug noticed the drop in temperature around them. With a touch of a button, her helmet soon displayed more information to her—in particular, the temperature within the club was now below forty degrees Fahrenheit.

"He can manipulate the air around him," Bug mumbled, not expecting Moth to hear her. "It's . . . incredible. How can he even do that? He's—"

"Human?" Moth finished her thought. "Exactly. But at least now, we can guess why they're after him."

Bug nodded. "His power." Things started to add up. Just how many of those "gigs" were actually gigs? How long had he been hiding this?

She knew that their answer wouldn't come until Leech was dealt with, at the very least.

"This should make your worms a little tame." The way Seth spoke to Leech was far beyond what Bug was used to seeing of her brother. The look in his eyes was a serious, violent stare. He might actually kill him.

Leech, with his free right arm, grabbed on to the ceiling, pulling himself out of Seth's range, smiling. Fully submerged in the shadows of the poorly lit roof, Leech cackled with glee. He had them exactly where he wanted them.

"Well, look at that! Not many options left for you, are there? Me, on the other hand? I can attack from any angle, any position, anywhere from up here. Like this, for example."

Had Bug not looked towards the ceiling to find Leech, she would not have seen the monstrous maw that swooped down at her. She rolled left, and the maw missed her by an inch, rebounding off the cement from its momentum. It looped back around, and she leapt away again, landing on all fours. Her gigantic hammer was still in the grip of her left hand, but she couldn't get a moment to actually use it.

She needed someone to bait him.

Moth looked to Bug and nodded. "Get ready."

Bug nodded back.

"Well, this is going to be easy. I didn't realize you were blind!" Moth looked directly to the ceiling, pointing a dagger upwards. When he didn't seem to respond, she turned her rear to the air, and patted it with her right hand, taunting him. "Right here! Come on ugly!"

Leech grinned.

His next shot went right for Seth instead.

Seth leapt back, avoiding the piercing arm completely. "Wow, you really are blind, aren't you? Pretty sure I'm not a chick in a costume."

Moth couldn't help smiling to herself. She didn't expect Seth to follow her lead.

Leech shot four tentacles down to the ground, and each one missed. Unlike before however, these remained in the ground like giant spires.

"Good to know you're an idiot," Bug snipped with a smile.

She slammed her hammer into the column nearest her. A thick, black ooze spewed out like pus from a sore.

Leech leapt down from the ceiling, cringing for a moment, trying to hide his pain. When Moth and Seth punctured two more of his arms, he erupted into a bloodcurdling scream. He retracted all of his ink-like limbs back into his body.

There he stood once more, his arms now submerged in his sleeves. He held his injured limb. "Stupid human scum. You will—"

Bug careened her hammer off of Leech's skull without hesitation. He fell to the ground with an awful thud. She didn't care if that beast was still alive or not, but she suspected that her hammer wouldn't be enough to do him in that quickly.

She was at least a bit thankful seeing him stumble to one knee. The left side of his forehead had cracked open, more of the black liquid oozing outward.

"How diplomatic," he quipped.

Good. He's still lucid, too.

"What do you want with Seth?" Bug's hammer was right back at the ready.

"Kinda excessive, Bug." Moth was at her side, arms akimbo.

Bug shrugged. "He killed dozens of people the other night, and attacked this club with no regard for anyone. I don't exactly feel compelled to be kind."

Moth folded her arms. "Not that I disagree, but you do need to ask him questions, right?"

"Yeah. Looks fine to me, though." Bug spun her hammer, then tapped Leech's left cheek with it. "You're not talking. I'm not very patient right now. Gonna ask one more time, then I crack you open. What do you want with Seth?"

"What . . . do we want with . . . him?" Leech was almost laughing at her, despite trying to regain the full functionality of his brain. "That power, of course . . . belongs . . . to us anyway."

"And who's us?"

Leech chuckled as he tried to stand again, this time with more success. "Who else? The Cloaks, and Hyde himself. That power is . . . ugh . . . ours to begin with."

"Yeah, yeah, yeah." Moth stepped forward, holding a dagger to his neck. "Explain how it belongs to you."

"You don't really think you have any leverage on me, do you?"

"Have you been paying attention? Dagger on your throat, hammer to the head, and, uh, whatever he can do," Moth tilted her head in Seth's direction.

"Gee. Thanks," Seth mumbled.

Moth held the dagger tight to his skin. "So. What do you mean by it's yours?"

For a moment, Leech stood there, glaring at them in turn, then at Moth's dagger at his throat. He looked to her, flashed a demonic smirk, then grabbed her hand and forced her to plunge the dagger right into his own neck.

Moth stumbled away in shock, leaving the dagger lodged within him.

Leech seemed to be just fine with the dagger hanging there, smiling as more of that black ooze spat out of the wound. Slowly, he pulled the dagger out of the crevice, then tossed it to the floor. "You're damn annoying." He may have wanted to stand upright, but the beating he'd taken from Bug's hammer kept him from doing that. "You win this one. Send Aegis our best."

Just as before, his entire body mutated into ooze, and splashed into the nearest crack in the ground.

Bug huffed. "Guess the tentacles are the only part of him that are actually vulnerable?"

Moth nodded. "Seems that way. At least now we know for next time."

"If there is one." Bug pointed towards the opening that they'd rode through earlier. "Swarm of cops waiting for us back there."

"Aegis, too." Moth pointed out the Crown Vic and the SUV awaiting behind the cops.

"Guess they decided to see what we're capable of."

"I don't know how I feel about that." Moth sighed, looking back to Bug. "I can ride through that. The problem now is trying to do so with three passen—"

"I'll deal with the police. I'm a witness anyway." Seth stepped forward. "Go out the back way. We'll talk back home later."

Bug did her best to play confused. "Talk back home?"

Seth turned to her, his eyes narrow, and his voice filled with an anger she hadn't heard before. "Don't play dumb right now. I'm pissed enough as it is."

"Then that makes two of us."

Seth's voice raised. "This is not the time—"

Now it was Bug who cut him off. "Just when were you going to tell me about this then? What, when they managed to capture you and kill you? Oh, of course, that makes perfect sense!"

"Shut it, Pilar." His teeth were clenched as tight as they could be without grinding apart. "You have no—"

"You lie to me, I save you, then you tell me to shut it?" She slammed the hammer into the ground. "No! We're having this talk, right here, right now—"

He grabbed her by her shoulders. "You are my responsibility! You get that? I may not be Dad but you will listen to me, for once in your damn life!"

The ferocity in his stare alarmed her. That alarm turned into anger, and that anger began to twist knots in her stomach she couldn't hope to undo.

"You're right. You're not Dad. Not even close." She yanked herself away from him, shoving him back. "Do whatever the hell you want. Tell them everything. I couldn't care less." Bug made sure to leave venom dripping from each word. "I couldn't care less," she repeated under her breath.

She stormed back to the motorcycle, and slammed onto the seat. "Let's go."

Moth wasn't sure what to do, but erred on the side of caution, leaping onto the motorcycle herself. Without another word, they sped out of the opposite side of the club through the front doorway.

Seth looked up towards the ceiling, chuckling. He ran his hand down his face until he grabbed his chin. "Good job, Seth. Parent of the Year."

15

Pilar sat on the balcony, holding her legs to her chest as tightly as she could. It was the only comfort she had left.

Everyone wanted to interfere in her life, and everyone she knew or even remotely cared about had some ulterior motive. She had become tired of trusting, of letting herself believe in anyone else. She had believed her mother a long time ago, when she'd promised to make up for the time they lost when she was sick.

Her mother had died two days later.

She trusted her father to never abandon her, to always be there for her.

Almost four years had gone by without so much as a word from him.

She trusted her brother to at least be honest.

Even that hadn't lasted long.

The anger in his voice, that look in his eyes . . . it was unreal. It angered her. She'd never been so frustrated with him. She never imagined she'd be so upset.

Her muscles were tensing, her stomach was turning. She didn't wake Bianca. She didn't want to. That was all she needed—yet another person trying to smooth-talk her way into her life.

She just wanted to be alone.

"Shouldn't you be sleeping right now?" The minute she heard his voice, her anger peaked again. She didn't want to see him. Not yet. Not while the thought of him made her ill.

"You're not getting out of class tomorrow, just in case that's what you're thinking."

Pilar wasn't interested in his jokes at the moment. The fact that he was apparently oblivious to her schedule only furthered that. For her, it was just further confirmation of how little he cared.

"I don't have class tomorrow."

He sat next to her, leaning against the wall of the balcony as she did. He didn't bother to ask if he could sit there or not, much to her frustration.

"Pilar, it was a joke. You think I didn't know that?"

"You didn't."

Seth looked to the glass patio door. "Tuesday is History at eight, English at noon. Wednesday is Calc at four. Theory at eight on Thursday. Tech Writing at eight on Thursday."

"Did you study before you came out here?"

His mood dropped when she said those words, but he couldn't let that deter him. "Yeah. Obvious, huh?"

She still refused to look at him. "At least now you're not lying."

"Didn't lie to you. Every night I've said 'I got a gig to do'? I had a gig to do." He lifted his left hand up a bit, observing it. "What I didn't tell you or anyone else about is this stupid ability I have."

"Oh. Is that all?"

He ran that same hand through his locks, bringing most of them out of his face and pulling them back. "Ah. I get it."

"Get what?"

"You're jealous. You think I'm out here being all super-heroic or something. Saving people's lives and fighting off the evil villains or some crap like that."

She had to glare at him for that. *What a stupid assumption!* "Why would I be jealous of—"

"I was about seven when I first used it. I didn't know what it was. Made a cup of cocoa explode before I even put it in the microwave. Told Dad, and he started testing me."

Since he was seven? Pilar couldn't ignore that. *He's had it most of his life.*

"He helped me control it, but I still can't be sure he didn't have something to do with me getting it in the first place."

"And just what makes you think that?"

"He was constantly guilty about it. There was something weighing on his mind about it. I never knew what, but I assumed that was it."

A silent moment passed between them. Pilar couldn't help taking a peek at him, to see if the sight of him still made her angry. But when she saw his face this time, he was somber.

"He told me that someone might want this power someday. They might come after me. But they only have until I reach my thirties, if that. But they won't know that. And once my power starts fading, I might not be able to fend them off."

"How would he know—" The moment she started to say it, she knew what that would mean. "He knew what it was to begin with."

Seth nodded. "So I kept it a secret. No one bugged me about it. Not until almost three years ago, a week after your birthday."

"Around the time that . . ."

"Yeah. When Dad disappeared." He exhaled. "They promised to be back. At the time, I was at peak performance and they couldn't do a thing to stop me. I get the feeling they weren't as powerful either. That Leech clown? He couldn't lay a hand on me back then." He peeked over to her. "But the last time we fought a few days ago?"

Seth raised his T-shirt, revealing the left side of his newly scarred abdomen. "Did a lot more than lay a hand on me."

Pilar flinched at the sight of it. She'd had no idea that Leech had ever encountered her brother before. But hearing what he was saying, things began to quickly add up. "That's why you never told me."

"Now you get it." He leaned back, eyes closed for a moment. "I tried to keep you out of it because I knew if you got involved, I couldn't protect you. A few years ago, sure. But now?"

She didn't want to admit it, not at first. But even she couldn't deny it for long, no matter how stubborn she was. It hurt her ego that she hadn't realized it before.

"So as you can imagine now, when I saw you and Zoe show up—"

"How did you even know it was us?"

"You called me Seth. You almost did it twice."

Her hands quickly covered her face. "Dammit! I'm such a moron!"

"Nah. Just a little preoccupied with the giant man-eating tentacle . . . guy. Probably a little more important."

She couldn't disagree.

"Wasn't the only thing that gave it away, though," he continued. "After all, I was almost your age when the Bug Suit went into development, sis. I'm old, but I'm not old enough to forget stuff like that. Not yet, anyway."

"So you did know about it."

He peeked over to her, his brow raised. "Pilar. Really. You think I never had anything to do with Dad, like, ever? I mean, yeah, I had my issues with him. But you know, he was my dad, too."

It was her turn to get a bit personal. "Do you . . . Do you miss him?"

"Do I miss him? Huh. Wow." He looked to her again, then to the skies. "Yeah. I miss him. I miss them both. And honestly? I don't know what I'm supposed to do with myself now, let alone what to do for you."

"For me?" She looked to her toes, as if they would give her the words to say. "What do you mean, 'what to do for me'? I'm fairly certain that's something I should be concerned with."

"You shouldn't be alone at this age. I grew up with both of them around until I moved out. It's not fair that you get me as a replacement halfway through puberty. I'm a pretty crappy replacement."

Pilar didn't know what to do with that, either. *Crappy replacement? Is that really what he thinks he is?*

Seth scratched his dreads a bit. "Look. I overreacted at the club, and I'm, well, I'm sorry for that. I shouldn't have snapped on you. But, you've gotta understand something."

Pilar tilted her head back towards him a bit, looking at him from the corners of her eyes.

He met her glance with a weary one of his own. "When I took you in and became your legal guardian? I became the very thing I hated when I was a teenager."

She turned her head more to face him hearing that, and her brow naturally raised. "Which would be what, a parent?"

"Yeah."

She hadn't expected that answer to be so blunt. After all, Seth didn't seem to have had a problem with signing the paperwork when it happened. "Then why even do it? I could've gone to Cairo and stayed with our aunt—"

"Please. You'd've run away before moving to Cairo."

She couldn't deny that.

"And even if that were true, I was not about to let that happen. I'll be damned if I just jettison you off to somebody out of the country just because I'm scared I might not do a good job."

That answer perplexed her further. "But then, why?"

"I might be scared I'll do a bad job, but it's my job to do." He propped his left elbow on his left knee, then rested his forehead in his palm. "And whether I'm doing a crappy job or not, you're my responsibility. You're my little sister. I'm overprotective because that's what a big brother does. No one else in our family can say that and mean it."

Don't start making me feel guilty. I'm supposed to be mad at you. Pilar refused to say anything of comfort for as long as she could.

It's true, isn't it? But then, why couldn't she say it? Why was it so hard for her to openly say it, to yell it, to express it? *You're not doing a bad job, Seth. I'm sorry, Seth.* That was all she needed to say. And still, she sat there, silent.

Seth sat up. "Using that battle armor . . . I know that's what you think Dad wanted before he died, but I'm pretty sure he wouldn't want you putting yourself in that kind of danger."

"He's not dead," she shot back.

"Pilar—"

"He's not dead," she said again, far sharper than before. However, she realized how sharp her tone was, and huffed away a bit of that before continuing. "He can't be dead. It doesn't add up, and I need to find out why it doesn't add up. That's the whole reason I even started wearing the suit—to find him."

She could hear Seth starting to object, but as his words started, he seemed to catch himself and just sigh.

He really thinks dad is dead, she thought. *Why? What does he know that I don't? Why won't he tell me?*

Seth had already moved on. "Pilar, I don't know what to say right now. I'm trying to keep you safe. I really am. But at some point, I need you to trust me on that, too."

Pilar glanced at him, then huddled her legs in again.

"We already lost Mom and Dad."

Despite everything in her body wanting to argue back, she held herself in check. *This isn't a battle to pick right now. Just let it be*, she told herself.

"Sis, I love you too much to just send you off like some unwanted package, or sit back and watch you throw yourself right into the hands of these freaky murder-monsters. I want to actually see you grow up and be an old fart right alongside me. You get what I'm saying, right?"

Try as she might, she couldn't keep from at least smiling at that. "I never said I was going to die, Seth. But the suit? It's a part of who I am right now." She looked towards the sky as the dawn began to sneak above the horizon. "It was the last thing Dad left me before he—"

She stopped herself, just as Seth had before. She knew they wouldn't agree on whether he was alive or not. They never had before. *I'll have to prove him wrong.*

"Seth, it's my responsibility to use that suit. And right now, Zoe and I are the only ones capable of stopping monsters like Leech. Aegis can't even seem to handle it. You saw that massacre the other night on the news, right?"

She could tell he didn't want to agree with that. She also knew he didn't have much choice.

"And that was against that one guy. Yet we crippled him yesterday. We made him run. And if not for the circumstances surrounding us? We could've have completely destroyed him." She looked directly at him now as she finished her plea. "Can you really say, with confidence, that anyone else can do that? That they would want to do that?"

Seth silently chewed on her rebuttal for a long moment. "I shoulda just grounded you. Would've been easier even if you didn't listen." He chuckled at his own suggestion as he stood up. "Just . . . sleep on this, okay? At least don't go rushing out again without considering any of this. It really doesn't have to be your job."

"I'll get some sleep. Eventually."

As he slid the patio door behind him, Pilar felt herself trying to hold everything within her again. That pain of losing her mother, then her father disappearing on them, and not knowing why any of it happened . . . it was returning again. Her brother meant what he said, and yet she still doubted.

Why do I feel like I have to do this? Why can't I just trust what Seth says?

She stood from her perch, then walked to the edge of the balcony, resting her forearms upon the steel railing. Looking at the bit of the city she could see from their apartment, her mind jumped to thoughts of her dad again.

Sorry, Seth. I have to find out what happened to Dad. And I have to protect you now, too. If I don't use the suit, then I may lose the only family I have left.

16

Saturday morning.

The duo arrived at Sands's lab at the crack of dawn. The sun brightened the sky, giving them a breathtaking view of the world around the mountainous islet. From there, they could see the glimmering sea on one side of them, and lush greenery surrounding the lab entrance on the opposite side. Zoe looked as though she could bask in this bright, beautiful, straight-out-of-a-painting world for another hour.

Pilar wasted no time trying to get inside of the lab. She could admire nature's millionth picturesque sunrise some other time. Right then, she needed to get on the elevator and descend into her den.

The building itself was unremarkable, and was well rooted into the mountain's side. Its rusted gray outer walls somehow blended in well with the foliage that had sprung up around it. On one side of the building, there were windows higher up that were part of the unused living area. Once they were indoors and in the actual levels of the lab, it would be completely closed off from the outside world.

"Is this place really a lab?" Zoe didn't hide her disappointment in the slightest. For Pilar, that made it all the more entertaining. This would be the first time that she would be showing someone else her inherited lab. It was something of an honor to have the privilege of seeing the root of her genius, and more exciting to show it to someone else.

If anything, Pilar knew it was her own ego being excited to show off just how intelligent she was, and where that intelligence came from.

This was something that she had no one to share with prior. Seth was the closest thing she had to someone that she could talk to about it, and at least until then she had to keep it all a secret anyhow. Despite the brevity of Pilar and Zoe's partnership at that point, she was genuinely excited to share this little bit of her world with someone who at least understood a part of it.

They walked into what looked like a small cave opening. At the back wall of this crevice was a large sliding door, and to its left side sat a small pane of black glass. They stopped at the door, and after a second more, Pilar approached the panel pressed into the wall, laying her open palm against it. It took another five seconds for something of interest to happen.

A bar of bright, blue light slowly glided behind the glass panel. It scanned the handprint and compared it to every other print in its system. After the scan ended, the panel glowed a fierce green, and the thin metal doors before them slid open with a swooshing sound. A bit of a draft left the room within.

Zoe took a natural step back from the cold breeze that Pilar had grown accustomed to. "Izzit really that cold in there?"

Pilar smiled. "We're not even in the lab yet, Zoe. Come on."

"Why are you so, um, happy?"

Pilar's smile didn't fade. She had to admit, seeing Zoe look worried about essentially nothing was oddly enjoyable. It at least made her feel less like Zoe wasn't some stoic being who she just couldn't get to at all.

"Oh, I get it," Zoe concluded after a moment. "You don't get to show off to anyone, do you?"

And just like that, Pilar had the seat of power snatched right out from under her ego. The smile lessened, but she still couldn't completely bury that little smug enjoyment she'd built up.

"Let's just get into the actual lab," she answered with as much ice as she could muster.

The doors slid back shut behind them, and the only light that resonated within was from another panel next to it that glowed blue. Pilar pressed her hand against this one, and her palm was recognized, changing the light to neon green.

The *hum* of a machine gurgled below. A jolt shot through the car. It slowly gained momentum, and the *hum* gained fervor along with it. Glass-covered slits in the walls allowed the amber lights of the elevator shaft to shine through, covering Pilar and Zoe with silver-yellow highlights within the car's darkened confines.

Pilar honestly hated this part of it. She couldn't quite explain it, but the elevator ride always made her uncomfortable, no matter how many times she'd ridden through it.

It was only five seconds before the elevator slowed to a crawl, then stopped. Zoe nearly jumped at the sight of the door that opened behind them.

"Yeah, that one used to scare me all the time." Pilar proceeded through the door, motioning for Zoe to follow. "This way." She found herself smiling again, watching as Zoe walked into the lab. She was clearly awed by the sight of it all.

It was overwhelming. The interior of the underground lab was enormous, almost reminiscent of the auditoriums at RCU. The walls and floors were a bit sterile in color, an almost white shade of grey. It was maintained by a few dozen small robots that scooted about the lab like rodents. They varied in shape and size, and each had a preprogrammed, simple task they were to do each day at each hour: the oval-shaped robot had a trap opening in its top that allowed it to scoop up trash, the robot with two orbs for feet was in charge of buffing the floors and countertops . . . every single one had a task.

Zoe saw another one of the robots that seemed to be stuck running about in a circle, pivoting on its hind wheel. After a few seconds of this, it shot off towards the wall, right at her feet, and careened off of it, only to flip right-side up and start spinning again.

Pilar walked right to it, knelt over, and tapped the top of it with her knuckles. Just like that, it shot off far to the other side of the lab, as if it suddenly remembered that there was a fire to put out. A moment later, they could hear the sound of it running into another wall, and then the sound of it spinning on its heels once again.

Pilar met Zoe's incredulous glance with a sigh. "It gets it right. Eventually," she decreed before moving on as though nothing had occurred at all.

In the center of this large space were two long lab tables, and at each were four stations with a microscope, a light table, and various tools for testing chemicals and repairing wiring. "Chemical research, mechanical development, and repair," Pilar commented as she pointed to each area of interest.

Zoe was beyond amazed. "It's more than I imagined it would be, that's for sure."

Her attention was immediately drawn to the giant monitoring station that sat at the eastern edge of the room. The enormous screen that sat embedded into the wall was eighty inches wide and sixty-seven inches tall. At the foot of the computer console was a small holographic globe. Pilar's hand "touched" the globe; she then manipulated the many buttons upon it as if it were a touch-screen display. After inputting the correct commands, another small computer a few feet away popped open with a slot prepared for a small vial.

She dug into her backpack for the vial she'd recovered from the Aegis massacre, placing it in the slot. The vial descended into the column, which eventually closed. The small monitor connected to it now read "processing . . ."

Pilar sat in the chair by the monitoring station, then smiled as Zoe ogled the lab. "So now you've seen it. Now I have to kill you."

Zoe barely heard the threat, if at all, she was far too busy being fascinated with this new world surrounding her. "This is your lab. Just . . . wow, Pilar. I don't know if I have the words for how awesome this is."

The smile Pilar had gained, soured. "It is now."

Zoe's brow raised a bit hearing that, especially in such a somber tone. "Then who—" It took her a moment to realize what Pilar wasn't saying. "Your dad's lab."

"Yeah."

"Well, um . . . you're putting it to good use, right?"

"Maybe."

"What makes you say that? Pretty sure he'd want you to continue his work and keep the lab going, wouldn't he?"

"Yeah. But it's not like it can keep going forever. Power costs money, money that I don't have."

"How has it been going for this long?"

"That's just it. I don't know. Up until a few months ago it only had minimal power at best. I could access the suit and the basic terminal, but everything else was dead. Including those guys." Pilar pointed to another group of maintenance bots roaming the floors. As if on cue, the rampant loose screw of the bunch shot by again, crashing into another nearby wall before going into its near-infinite tailspin.

"That one could've stayed off, though." Pilar tapped it with her knuckles again, and it sped off into the distance once more.

Zoe giggled. "Yeah well, we can't always pick our family members. Even the eccentric ones."

Pilar's left eyebrow raised high hearing that. "Trying to relate that to something topical?"

Zoe shrugged. "Not important. We should look into who owns this place and who started it back up. It can't be safe just having the lab suddenly up and running, Pilar."

"I know," she answered back. "But until the lab came back online, I literally had little else I could do aside from rudimentary tests on the armor. And even then, that was limited. Seeing the lab back up, I thought maybe Dad . . ."

Pilar seemed to snap out of the small funk she was in when Zoe put a hand on her shoulder. "I get it," she said. "You thought that maybe your dad did it. Like you'd found a clue of his whereabouts."

Pilar wasn't certain how to respond to that. It was exactly that, and she knew how unlikely that was, but she wanted to believe it was him. As though he'd been there, watching over her as she struggled to get the armor in running order, and once she'd reached her final dead end, he gave her the help she needed by restoring the lab to full power.

But that would also mean he was around somewhere, watching her. And knowing her father as well as she hoped she did, there was no way he'd just be there and not confirm to her that he was alive.

Perhaps it was something she knew was true all along, but didn't want to admit. And now that someone else was there, she couldn't just deny it.

Someone else got the lab up and running. Someone that I'm not aware of.

"Are you sure you aren't being watched?" Zoe looked genuinely worried when she asked that. That certainly didn't help Pilar's own fears. Still . . .

"I at least did a thorough security check of the lab after power was restored, and looked over as much of the lab as I could. Every diagnostic, every security check, every scan for outgoing traffic, every camera shot. All came back with nothing." Pilar folded her arms. "I don't know who got the place going, but they don't have their hands on it right now, at least. And I have security programs running sweeps constantly."

"And nothing yet," Zoe concluded. "Honestly? That worries me even more."

"Well, there's nothing I can do about it for now," Pilar acknowledged. "I'd love to build a whole new lab in a whole new location that is completely out of anyone's memory or range, but, you know, money. And needing at least fifty people to move all this stuff efficiently."

Pilar was surprised to see Zoe nod her head so voraciously in agreement. "Well if it's been on for months at this point, I'm assuming the benefactor is on our side. For now. Regardless, this lab would be our best bet at a hideout, don't you think?"

"A hideout?"

"In non-comic terms, that would be a place where we go to rest that no one knows of. Our headquarters, as it were," Zoe clarified.

"It's already that. For me."

"Yeah, but I mean, all this stuff could be used for so much more than what we're doing now, right? What do you plan to do after the Cloaks are dealt with? Or after your father is found?" Zoe seemed to unintentionally wander to one of the monitoring stations, her curiosity leading her to try logging in.

110

"Hey," Pilar quickly swatted her hands away from the console. "I'm not some comic book crime fighter. I have taken over this lab and started my search for my dad's sake and now to tear down the Cloaks. That's all."

"Well, even vigilantes on a singular mission have to have some place they can fix themselves up or figure things out, right?" Zoe looked right into her eyes, just knowing that her point wasn't easy to refute.

Pilar had been so busy trying to get everything to just work properly that she'd never considered the thought of needing to repair it all. She was thinking far too in-the-moment. Her plan was as simple as ever: once everything was done, she would just find the answers she was looking for, find her dad, and be done with it.

But there was always that nagging thought in the back of her mind: *What if it takes longer? What if I don't find the answers?*

No, she had to be honest with herself. It wasn't that she hadn't considered it. She didn't want to consider it.

Her overzealous nature had taken a pause at Zoe's suggestion. Her plan for the lab wasn't absolute, but it was a better use of its power than just tinkering here and there for gathering information. Far be it for her to outright admit that, of course. She didn't need Zoe's head getting any bigger. "Right now, we need to concentrate on our current objective before you turn us into the next superhero television show."

"That's not even what I'm trying to do," Zoe shot back with a laugh. "So what exactly is our current objective, partner?"

"Do you have to say it like that?" Pilar rolled her eyes, then turned her attention to the monitoring station, making sure Zoe hadn't broken anything. "Finding out more about Hyde so we can put him and his group out of commission, of course. I'm almost certain he's the link to—"

Zoe shrieked. Without even looking at the figure behind her, Pilar already knew what had alarmed her: a six-foot-tall robot that looked like a bipedal mud wasp. The robot's metallic skin had been painted to match the color of the Bug Suit, and four metal arms originated from its upper torso. Its feet were large, and the hydraulics that allowed him to make some very impressive leaps were very visible behind them.

"This is Gilgamesh, the supervisor of the robots in the lab. 'Gil' for short. Gil, this is Zoe. Her codename, as it were, is Moth. For now anyway."

Gilgamesh reached out a hand, and although it had no visible mouth, it spoke through a hidden speaker within its cranial area. "It is a pleasure to meet you, Miss Zoe." For something so robotic, its tone was surprisingly friendly and welcoming.

Zoe didn't respond well at first. She reached for him as if she were trying to pet a mountain lion. "Likewise, I'm sure. Certainly. Yeah." Despite her nervousness, she shook Gil's hand, and tried her best not to look petrified.

Gil nodded. "My apologies If I make you uncomfortable, Miss Zoe—"

"No, it'll just, uh, take some getting used to, that's all."

Pilar had to give her credit for lying to make a robot feel better. "Well, in any case, you'll have to get used to seeing him if you plan on being my sideki—"

"*Partner*." Zoe was getting much quicker with the correction.

Knowing that she still needed Zoe's help, Pilar decided not to continue arguing the point for the moment. "Right, of course. *Partner*." She said the word as if it cramped her stomach.

"You really have that much of a problem working with me?"

"It's . . ." Pilar sighed. "It's not you. Or rather, it is not just you. I'm just very used to the idea of working alone. I'm not used to having a . . . ," again she stumbled, ". . . having a partner."

"I'd thought you'd like the idea of having someone to relate to." Zoe leaned against the control console of the monitoring station, arms folded.

Pilar peeked at Gil, then back to Zoe, eyes narrowed. "Kudos for making a good point."

"Wow, kudos? Whatever shall I do with those?" Zoe said with a smirk.

"I give you a compliment and that's what you do with it, huh?"

"Pilar." Zoe said her name with an exasperated little breath. "I'm really going to have to help you appreciate the fine art of appreciating the people around you. Starting with giving compliments that don't sound like you're going to die if you try to be any nicer."

Pilar immediately retaliated with a cheeky, toothy smile that was almost cartoonlike. "Zoe, that was the most brilliant idea that anyone has ever said! Thank you for the wonderful suggestion!" Just as quickly, her expression dropped from over-the-top happy, to flat-out annoyed. "Better?"

Zoe just shook her head, smirking at her partner in crime. "Well, you tried I guess. Kudos for that."

Pilar could feel her own face twitch hearing her repeat that. And yet, now she had to really give her credit.

Well, internally, she had to, anyway.

She cleared her throat. "In any case, once I know what this Leech guy is made of, I'll be ready to tear him a new one. Until then, we can discuss what will happen next and make plans for tomorrow night."

"I thought you were just going to beat him up again. You're coming up with a plan?"

"A plan to draw him out? Yes. A plan to beat him to a pulp? Absolutely. What did you think I meant? That I'd just go out there and wing it? I'm not a fool. Brash, sure. A fool? Not ever."

"You're making progress." Zoe was still nervous to step anywhere near Gilgamesh, but she was making a very credible effort to at least look as though she didn't mind his presence. "Well, we should consider what their next move may be."

When Zoe joined Pilar at the monitoring station, the analyzing terminal that held the material sample form the night before let out a series of tones. The results of the testing were then relayed to the larger monitor—results which were not what they were hoping to hear.

"Inconclusive. Wonderful." Pilar wheeled her office chair over to the terminal and removed the sample vial, eyeing it curiously in the light as she rotated it, shifting the inky material within. "It's lost a lot of its viscosity. Interesting."

"Anything other than turning runny?"

Pilar's glance darted towards her, and a small grin came to her face. "You knew what that meant, huh?"

"Hey, here's a shocker. I'm not dumb."

Pilar hadn't expected Zoe to be so sarcastic. And the more she talked to her, the more her behavior intrigued her. She couldn't nail down just who she was dealing with. Nothing seemed to crack her, even calling her a sidekick. Zoe just kept trying to mentor Pilar at every chance, as though she were a masterful vigilante with years of experience. Even beyond that, she'd assumed the only person she'd ever speak with on such equal footing would be someone with a matching intellect.

Pilar was lost in thought as she stared into the vial, and Zoe was quick to call her out. "I'm getting to you."

She was too psychic for Pilar's comfort. "Let's just focus on our next move."

Zoe nodded. "Sure. So then, what's our next move?"

"Our next move is to get you into that." Pilar flicked her hand towards a wall of tall tubes behind them, pointing directly at another battle suit. "If you're going to be my . . ."

Zoe grinned. "Come on. You can say it."

Pilar huffed. "If you're going to be my partner, I need you to be able to keep up. I'll need to get some more materials from Aegis to finish it, but that won't be a problem for us, considering what just happened. Once that's done—"

"You'll have a way of keeping me in check when I wear that, won't you?" Despite saying something that sounded so insulting, she'd said it with a smile. It was as if she didn't even care about Pilar's ulterior motive.

"What makes you think—"

"Not dumb," Zoe repeated, tapping the side of her head. "I'm not worried, either. I'm pretty sure it has its benefits. But the way you see it, if you can convince me to wear that battle suit, you can probably lock me down or something if I go rogue."

"Well, that makes that part easier." Another huff of frustration escaped Pilar's lungs as she started to realize that Zoe truly was predicting her at every turn. What was more uncomfortable was that she happily went along with donning the new battle suit despite that. "You don't sound insulted," Pilar finally said.

"I'm not. If me trusting you will prove to you that you can actually trust someone other than yourself? That's a good thing. Just, don't get me killed, 'kay?" Zoe winked at her.

Before Pilar answered, Zoe started to make her way across the lab, to the gigantic containment tube holding what would become her suit. "I do have some requests for it, though."

"Requests?" Pilar grumbled. "You don't really expect me to do that."

"It's the least you can do, right?" A bright grin of mischief was her exclamation point.

Pilar's elbow landed on the control console again, as she rested her face in her palm. "No."

"Hey, think of it this way. If we're really going to do this? We should look and feel the part, right?"

"You and this hero talk are starting to irk me."

Zoe shrugged. "I'm good at breaking down people's personal walls. It's what I do."

"Right. Studying criminology and forensics to be a detective. Therefore, you know how people work."

"Like you. You put up a lot of walls, but really? You're lonely. You're not as mean-spirited as you want people to believe."

"And what makes you think—"

"The argument with your brother the other night. Among other things."

Pilar looked back to the monitoring station. "That was different. He's still my brother, and I still live with him. For now."

"You were hurt because you felt he lied. And that's what you want from people, right? To not lie to you."

Pilar wasn't sure if she was irritated, or unnerved. Whichever case it was, she was done talking about her personal feelings, and knew the quickest way to end the conversation.

Unfortunately, the quickest way to end it was to give the girl what she wanted. "Fine, you win. Give me these improvement ideas and I'll see what I can do."

Zoe's smile wasn't nearly as cheerful as Pilar expected. "I'll have the list to you by tonight. A lot of them are things I thought of while we were out the other night. Some of 'em are things I've just, you know, always wanted."

Pilar rubbed her forehead. "Could you, like, not push your luck any further?"

"Hey, to be fair some of this stuff could work for both suits!"

Pilar certainly couldn't help perking up at that. Perhaps having some of Zoe's off-the-wall ideas would help. Try as Pilar might, hers wasn't exactly a creative mind. "Comic book superhero" stuff was clearly Zoe's department. And whatever Pilar didn't like, she could easily explain away, right?

Pilar looked to her own suit, sitting in the containment tube next to Zoe's new gear. "Bring me a list of your ideas, then. I'll see what I can do."

Zoe looked like a spoiled child on Christmas morning.

"Within reason," Pilar added.

"Oh, of course, of course. This is me we're talking about. Perfectly reasonable."

17

The full moon above was plastered by a few stray clouds, making for an eerie scene on the streets below. The city seemed suspiciously empty aside from a few pedestrians and maybe three or four cars riding through the deserted cross streets below.

Logically, this should have been an ideal situation for Bug and Moth. However, the problem was that they were counting on Aegis to be around.

"So. What's our plan again?" Moth sat on the edge of the building, staring down into the streets with a pair of binoculars. As much as she couldn't wait to get her hands on her own Bug Suit, she would have to settle with her homemade costume for at least this one last night.

Bug was a few feet behind her, cracking her knuckles. "Supply shipment comes every Saturday night, through here at about 2:00 a.m. We're going to stop that shipment and take the armor."

"Not very heroic."

"Only way we can get enough Armor Cloth to pad your new suit properly, and make all these changes. Convincing enough?"

Moth didn't bother to look back. *Dad is gonna kill me if he finds out I'm doing this. The plan never involved me actually robbing Aegis!* She stood from her post, putting her small pair of binoculars back into her belt. A sudden, small shuffling noise drew her attention to their immediate left, to a nearby staircase.

Zoe's sudden shift of attention quickly caught Bug's eye. "What?"

"I get this strange feeling that we're being watched." Her hand quickly slid to one of her daggers, but she didn't draw it from its pouch just yet. She held the blade for a moment, waiting.

Bug took a quick look about. "You're imagining things."

"Can't be too safe," Zoe answered back. Her left hand was firmly on the hilt of the dagger. "Pretty sure it's not one of Hyde's creeps, either."

A deep, dark voice boomed from the side of the roof's doorway. "I didn't follow you. I just know your usual route. Or I should say, Bug's usual route."

Both girls whipped around to meet the owner of that voice.

He was a tall, round, black man, dressed in a black suit with a matching black tie and white shirt, wearing shades even in the pitch-black night. If the other Aegis Agents were stereotypical in their choice of suits, then this man must have created the stereotype they used. His very demeanor screamed "Agent Jackson" before he spoke a word.

There wasn't much he needed to do to get on Bug's bad side at that point. Being an Aegis Agent was more than enough. "Who the heck are you?"

"Agent Abel Rose. Head of Aegis Security Division Two."

Bug's heart jumped at least three beats. "Agent Rose?"

He nodded. "You've heard of me—"

Bug drew her hammer, and held it firmly in her hands. The weight of the enormous head caused her to lean in a bit further forward for comfort, but she was starting to get used to the large, blunt weapon.

"I've read of you. Security Detail for Professor Sa—"

"Your dad."

Bug was taken so off guard by his response that she nearly dropped the hammer. "What? How?"

Without answering her question, he tossed a leather sack filled with something heavy in front of them. Bug couldn't hide how tense that made her. "And that is?"

"You need lightweight Titanium Sheet Armor—or rather, Armor Cloth, right? There's about two hundred feet of it in that sack. Should be more than enough to finish her battle suit."

Moth leaned to Bug. "Um, Bug? How could he have known that?"

She made no effort to hide her anger, still holding her hammer before her. "I would like to know that. Unfortunately, I don't have an answer. However he found that out, I'm sure he knows just about everything I've been up to." She looked back to Agent Rose. "Just how long have you had me bugged?"

He nodded. "Sharp, as expected. You're definitely Sands' kid." He took a few paces towards the north edge of the building, looking outward towards the horizon. "I've got a line directly in to your suit's communications. Little hidden trick your dad pulled a long time ago when the suit was still a prototype." He looked over his shoulder, back to them. "He asked me to watch your back should something happen to him and you end up using the Bug Suit. And for some reason, he wanted me to confer with you once things got going."

Bug's eyes scanned the ground for a moment as she mentally searched for a way to understand what Rose had just said. *My dad asked him to track me down and confer with me?* If that were the case, then he had to have some information leading to her father's whereabouts. Still, Bug knew she couldn't just ask for that out of the blue.

She needed to know for certain that he was actually telling the truth.

She retracted her hammer back into its small pole form, then slid it into the strap on her shoulder. "What do you want with me?" Her arms were firmly folded, and her feet calmly planted.

He turned to walk away and descend down the staircase he used to get to the roof. "Meet me tomorrow afternoon at your usual café spot. We'll have a more detailed conversation then. And try not to look too conspicuous." He didn't say anything further, leaving them to make their own decision. He made it clear that he expected them to actually comply.

Bug thought about simply ignoring him just to prove that he didn't have any leverage on them. However, to have the armor she needed thrown right at her feet was something she couldn't easily ignore.

Moth grabbed the bag from the ground, untying it with haste and reaching a hand inside. She fiddled with it for a bit, and shortly after she pulled out a long piece of the thick cloth, as well as a larger piece of the armor plating that would go underneath. "This is what we were looking for, isn't it?"

"Damn." Bug looked back to the stairwell, where Agent Rose had walked to when he made his exit.

"So we can leave it and go about gathering it the hard way, or just meet him and see what he wants, at least. Of course, it might all be an elaborate trap."

Bug nodded. "We don't have much choice."

Moth nodded. "We'll meet with him tomorrow. In the meantime, we should start planning what to do when we do have this sit-down with him." Moth drew a dagger, flashing it to Bug almost playfully. "And we should probably plan for every possible double cross he could pull."

Bug couldn't disagree, giving Moth an affirmative nod.

"So, how did it go?"

Pilar was completely floored when they returned to the lab. The first sight was of Bianca sitting at the monitoring station within. Gilgamesh stood next to the seated nurse, arms behind his back as if nothing was awry. Bianca sat there without a care in the world, prying through files and searching through the database as if it were her database to begin with.

Pilar was ready to throttle her right then and there. "How the hell did you get in here?"

Bianca paused for a second, looked up at both Pilar and Zoe, then grinned as she raised her right hand. She began wiggling her fingers. "Palm recognition."

"You're still in the system?" Now Pilar was completely irritated. *Of course she's in the system. Why wouldn't she be in the system? I mean she was allegedly the sitter right? Why not put her in the system too, Dad? Don't forget the mailman too! Gotta give him access to your super-secret lab filled with weapons and battle suits and God knows what else!*

She looked to Zoe, who just shrugged. Bianca then leaned upon the monitoring station, smiling. "I've been searching through Andromeda—"

Bug raised her hand. "Wait, wait, wait. Andromeda?"

"This old bird's name." Bianca grinned. "At least it was when I first started using it. I don't know if Sands ever changed it again. All this tech gibberish is new to me, though. And this globe thing? Ought to be a hit at parties."

"You could have warned me that you were going to be here." Pilar began taking off her Bug Suit piece by piece, slowly revealing the black bodysuit that she always wore underneath. It looked as though the bodysuit itself was covered in yellow circuitry paths.

"How? What, were you going to stop chasing down bad guys to answer your phone? Which, by the way, love, does you no good here." She slid a smartphone across the surface of the monitoring station's desk area.

It was definitely Pilar's phone, which she'd left behind intentionally. She put her hair back into its usual puffy ponytail, then picked up her goggles from the table and put them on her head. "Well, just so you're aware? There's no reason for me to have this on me when I'm in the armor. Who exactly do I want to talk to while I'm running around trying not to be killed?"

Bianca tapped the side of her glasses. "I'm not terribly great at all the higher functions of this station, but I can at the very least use its basic functions. And I'm sure you could use someone as your eyes and ears when you're out doing all that lovely gallivanting you two seem to enjoy."

"Look. You've already invaded my life in so many ways that right now? I don't think I need another reason to be angry with you. Do you?"

"That's a fair point I guess. Just a thought."

"Also, I already have him—"

Before she could even point to Gilgamesh, Bianca cut her off. "I'm aware, love."

Gilgamesh bowed. "Miss Bianca was a welcome surprise. Her last login to this lab was eleven years ago. I was still in my prototype phase."

"Okay, great. You got in!" Pilar's bright smile switched back to a scowl in the next moment. "Why are you here now? How'd you even know to come here?"

"Seth had to work tonight. And after hearing what you two went through, I knew you'd throw yourself right back into this." She took a heavy breath. "I took it upon myself to make sure you were doing okay."

"I'm fine," Pilar spat.

"That was not convincing."

"Bianca."

"Okay, love, I get it. You're not happy I'm here. But you had to know I'd come here eventually. I had a home here too, for a good while, you know. And I can already guess you're in over your head." She folded her arms. "Am I right?"

"If you are?"

"It's all the more reason I should help here."

"I'll think about it. But in the meantime, I need to work on these suits. So, if you don't mind? Terribly?" She looked to the tube containing the second suit.

"Tell you what, then. I'll leave all the science-suit-things in your capable hands, and focus on any information we can get about what's happening. Is that good enough?"

Pilar huffed as her final retort. "Whatever keeps you out of my way."

19

By sunrise, Pilar had completely passed out at her seat.

Bianca wasn't too far off. If not for the hot coffee that Zoe volunteered to get, she probably would've been out.

Zoe was still trying to grasp all the history she was jumping into, and Bianca wasn't someone she'd heard of yet. If she was going to get some honest answers, she may as well try while Pilar was asleep. In the back of her mind, a very weird, almost paranoid train of thought made her worry that Pilar might be faking.

Pilar's next snoring fit ensured that wasn't the case.

Bianca returned from another room in the lab with a large, blue blanket in hand. She wrapped it around Pilar, then returned to her seat at Andromeda, continuing to tinker about and get familiar with its functions once more. Zoe watched her for two solid minutes, still unsure of how to really start any conversation with her. *I guess I could start with the obvious.*

"So, um, hey."

Bianca finished her current sip, then quickly sat her cup down. "Ah, Zoe, right?"

"Yeah."

"I guess we really didn't get a formal introduction." She extended her right hand as she sat down at Andromeda again. "Bianca Lin."

Zoe shook her hand. "Zoe Shinomori."

"Pleasure."

"So, Bianca. How do you know Pilar?"

Bianca leaned back. "Believe it or not, I used to babysit her when we were kids."

"For real?"

"Quite. She doesn't seem to remember, though." Bianca took a quick glimpse at Pilar, then looked back to Zoe. Her smile was melancholy at best. Whatever she'd dredged up, Zoe could tell, it hurt. "She's been through a hell of a lot. I know that much."

"Yeah. I get the feeling that's why she's put up so many walls." Zoe leaned against the console, arms folded. "Not exactly a healthy response. Wish I could do more to change it."

"Well, why are you so intent on that?"

Zoe's face soured. "I don't really know. I knew some of her background, but I didn't know all of . . ." She looked about the lab again. "Well, all of this."

"Yeah. I can imagine." Bianca finally took another sip of coffee. "God, this coffee is good. Where'd you get it from again?"

"Donut shop a few miles off the coast."

"Oh yeah. I know that place. Never tried the coffee though, oddly enough." She took another long sip, trying her best not to make so many slurping noises. Despite her efforts, she was still fairly loud.

Zoe cleared her throat. "Bianca, do you . . . do you have any idea what happened to her dad?"

"Trust me, if I did? I'd be the first to tell her."

Zoe sighed hearing that. "Yeah. Guess that makes sense."

Bianca turned her chair a bit, to face Zoe. "Why do you ask?"

"Truth?"

They both looked to Pilar again, both wanting to verify she was indeed sleep. When her next snore shook the air, Bianca shook her head at the girl. "Well that hasn't changed. You were saying?"

Zoe continued on. "My dad was working on her father's disappearance. She's literally the only witness. He got forced off the case, but I learned about it through him. Once I met her in school . . ." She looked to Pilar again. "I couldn't just let her suffer like that. If I can help her find an answer, then I really want to."

"Your dad's a cop?"

Zoe nodded. "And I'm studying to be one. Not that being a vigilante is a good start to that, but you know. Gotta get it done somehow."

"And your dad? I imagine he's not okay with any of this."

"He's fine with what I've told him." She gave Bianca a bit of a smirk. "Haven't gotten back to him about all of this yet. He probably won't take it well."

"Can't blame him. If it were my kids, no matter their age, I'd be livid. Honestly, I don't really want Pilar involved in all of this. I thought I might be able to convince her to stop it once I moved in."

"Then you realized she'd just do it anyway."

Bianca turned her attention back to Andromeda's large display. "Something like that. And I realized she's probably the only one who can do this."

Zoe took another look around the lab. The robots that had been roaming about earlier were all hiding now, seemingly resting from the various tasks they had all about the lab. Even the hum of Andromeda seemed to quiet down from before. The lighting in the lab had been dimmed, and even though Zoe knew that sunrise was happening outside, it felt like night had just settled in.

"I'm glad you're there for her. She needs someone close to her age to relate to."

"You think so?"

When Zoe looked to Bianca, she could see the sadness all over her face as she thought of Pilar. She hadn't known Bianca for very long, and yet she could see it, easily. *This hurts her to talk about.*

"When she was little, she didn't have any friends in school. But, she was happy at home. She had her parents. She had her brother. She had me. And over the years, she's been losing that. First me, though that's likely of little consequence to her. But then she lost her mother to an illness. Then her brother became distant. Then a couple years ago, she lost her father. And unlike all the others, she has no idea how. He was just, gone."

Zoe nodded. "Wow. I guess I didn't know. I didn't even know half of that."

"I didn't either. Seth filled me in on much of it. Then I saw her. Aaaaaand she hates me." Bianca rubbed her forehead as she smirked at Zoe. "Probably shouldn't be surprised, considering. But it does hurt."

126

"She doesn't have any friends in school, either. I don't think she really wants any."

"And that's why it's good she has you at least, now."

"I'm not sure she considers me a friend. Probably more a pain in the ass."

"Some would say those are one and the same." Bianca stretched her limbs as far as she physically could, yawned, then stood from her seat. "Okay. Time for me to set out. Need to shower and sleep in my own bed. You should get some rest too. Won't be much help to her if you're half asleep, love."

"I will. Eventually."

With that, Bianca walked to the elevator, disappearing behind the closed doors and leaving Zoe there with far more worries. She'd considered that Pilar was a loner, but she'd had no idea about the rest. At least now, her obsession with finding her father made sense. He was likely the only person she still trusted, and now even he was gone.

Zoe couldn't help thinking about that over and over again. How would she have turned out if her parents had just . . . vanished? If she wasn't sure her sister even loved her? If she had no other friends, and all she knew that kept her sane was her studies? She remembered the argument Pilar had with her brother after the attack at the club. Not that it didn't make sense before, but now . . .

She sat next to Pilar, resting a hand on her shoulder. "Hey."

"Hey. What time is it?" Pilar grumbled.

"Seven."

"Good. Gimme another hour and I'll finish your suit. Don't need to bug me."

Zoe almost laughed at that. She was the one who'd planned to stay up all night, after all. And, of course, she obviously wasn't trying to pester Pilar about the suit. That was the least of her concerns. But that wasn't very important.

"Sorry to wake you up. You sure you don't lie down in your bed? The suits can wait." When her question was answered with a bout of snoring, Zoe knew what the rest of her morning was going to be like.

"Guess I should call home. Tessa probably already started a manhunt for me."

20

Pilar's eyes were drooping as she and Zoe sat idle in the South Café.

"I didn't think you'd actually wake back up and work on the suits again with only two hours of sleep." Zoe took a slurp of raspberry tea through her straw.

"You know, a large part of that was spent working on your suit." Pilar grasped her forehead. "Damn. It even hurts to think right now."

"Well, tell ya what. I'll do all the talking with Agent Rose. You just answer when you can. We'll write it off as you being sick when he gets here. I doubt he'll have an objection to a sixteen-year-old girl not feeling well."

Pilar glared at her from the corners of her eyes. "No way am I letting that happen. I want to see what this Rose guy really knows, firsthand."

"Something else really bothers me about this." She leaned forward so that Pilar could hear her quieted voice. "He's been using the Bug Suit to watch you, but suddenly shows up now? Why not when we were facing down those two demons from the other night? Or the night we ran into Seth?"

"All questions worth asking." Pilar looked just behind Zoe, watching as the man in question walked in the door. He was as tall and brutish as she remembered despite not wearing his normal business suit and tie. Instead, he arrived in a pair of tan slacks, with an earring in his left ear, and having donned a bright pink Hawaiian shirt decorated with a green palm tree print. He looked more like a lost tourist than an agent, but no less strange. Any attempts on his part to blend in were null and void.

Pilar was quick to point that out to him. "How inconspicuous."

"I look normal in this."

Zoe couldn't hold her giggling in. "You look like a salesman from the '80s. The shades don't help, by the way."

"I wear them for a specific reason." He grabbed a chair from a vacant nearby table, and joined them on the opposite side of their current booth. "And they aren't important right now."

"Oh please," Pilar snapped.

He looked to Zoe, then to Pilar, before releasing an enormous breath. He raised his hands to his face, until his index finger of his right hand was touching the brim of his sunglasses. He gently pushed them down, just enough for his eyes to show. His pupils and irises were so very grey that his eyes appeared almost completely white.

"Well that looks . . . different." Pilar tried not to attract too much attention, but even her subdued exclamation drew an ear or two.

Rose responded with an obviously intentional clearing of his throat.

"What?" Pilar said, then followed that with a flippant reply: "Sorry."

Zoe kicked her in the shin ever so slightly under the table. Pilar winced, then promptly reiterated her apology. "No, seriously, I didn't mean anything by it. Sorry, okay?"

Rose gave her a halfhearted wave. "Don't worry about it." He slowly put his shades back into place, having proved his point. "I don't feel like putting contacts on all the time to hide it. I was in an accident years ago that almost robbed me of my eyesight. Would've been legally blind the rest of my life if it wasn't for your dad."

Pilar looked to Zoe, then back to Agent Rose. "Wait, so Dad can suddenly cure the blind now? First I've ever heard of this."

Rose's hands were clasped together before him while his elbows rested on the table. The shift in weight lifted the loose table upward, causing Pilar and Zoe to sit back. It was a rather large table, and yet the hefty Agent Rose was able to tilt it with his elbows.

It was the first time Pilar could remember being intimidated by the sheer size of someone. And yet, she still did her best to ignore his girth. "What role did he actually play, in your eyes?"

He gave her comment a very slight smirk. "Bad pun."

She leaned back a bit, arms folded, and slouching in her seat while grinning. "I know. I'm good at that."

He scratched his right ear a bit. "Your father knew of my situation, and he wanted to attempt to restore my sight back in full. To do that, he had to consult with his colleague, Evandrake Hyde."

"Hyde." Zoe sat back in her seat, cuffing her chin a bit with her right hand while playing with the straw in her iced tea with the other hand "That name again."

Rose tilted his head towards Zoe. "So you're familiar with him."

"Only in name, so far. Coming up a lot."

Pilar peeked at Zoe. "For you too?"

"Yeah. I had nothing to connect it with before, but his name was associated with Aegis. It also seemed to be disassociated with Aegis in the past decade, too."

"I see. Not surprising, to be honest." Rose nodded a bit. "In any case, between the two of them, they did fully restore my eyesight, at the cost of the pigment."

Pilar nodded, thinking back to the photo that Bianca had shared with her. "That shouldn't surprise me considering what I know now, but still, somehow I can't begin to think what they'd even have in common."

"Sands was a highly respected scientist in the field of robotics. Hyde was an expert in combining biological and robotic research," Rose continued on. "They certainly did something I didn't think possible."

"Well. That's an interesting story." Now Pilar leaned forward, arms still folded. She didn't bother to hide the mistrust in her glare. "So, getting back to why you're here?"

"Tough crowd." He leaned forward a bit more, his voice considerably muted. "Aegis has some issues that the public isn't privy to. And a lot of its past problems are reappearing."

Pilar nodded. "Like the monster that killed all those agents."

"Yeah. Let's call that issue number one right now, at least in the eyes of the director." His eyes slowly turned towards the window behind them, observing the somewhat busy street outside. "There's a group of us within the company trying to figure it all out, but we can only do so much without drawing too much suspicion."

"Oh. I get it." Zoe leaned forward again, giving him a snide smirk. "So basically, you want us to do the dirty work."

He grimaced. "I don't want you to do anything yet, aside from lay low. What I'm doing right now is giving you some clue as to why we aren't your enemy."

Pilar and Zoe both looked at him as though he'd insulted their parents.

"Or rather, why your focus, for now, should be only laying low and gathering whatever information on the Cloaks you can." Rose glanced over to Pilar. "Try not to actively engage them again. You know, like the other night."

Pilar folded her arms. "I'm not making any promises, and I have my own questions for them. So if you have any information they might not have, like where my father is?"

For the first time during the conversation, Rose actually looked uncomfortable. He rubbed his bald head for a moment, then looked about the café as if he were waiting for someone to bail him out.

As if perfectly on cue, Pete showed up, smiling that blissfully unaware smile Pilar liked to see. "Y'all doin' alright over here? Need refills?"

Pilar greeted him with the most precious smile she could give him. "Oh, we're fine, really. Thanks, Pete."

"Sure, no problem." She could tell that had actually disturbed him. Pete looked as though he were about to swallow his Adam's apple. "You really sure everything's okay? This guy isn't giving you two trouble, is he?"

Pilar looked to Zoe, then to Rose. "He's a stalker. Please kick him out."

As stoic as Pilar kept her face, Zoe didn't hold in her giggling at her claim. Pete, at least, seemed relieved to not have to follow through on that once they'd all started laughing.

"He's fine," Zoe added. "He's a, uh, a coworker."

Despite Pilar's initial statement, she relented in the face of Zoe's optimism. "Yeah, yeah, coworker. Don't worry. We're fine."

Pete looked to Rose, who just barely looked back. "Well, all right then . . . what's your name brotha?"

The complete change that Rose made right before their eyes put Pilar on edge. Suddenly he was laughing. He shook Pete's hand, shot a few quips with him, shared a sports joke . . . By the time Pete left the table, Pilar was pretty sure they were going to go to a sports bar and compare their favorite teams.

As the laughs died down, he returned his focus to them. "Not a bad guy," Rose said.

"What . . . just . . . happened?" Pilar's eyes were still a bit wide as she glared at Rose.

"What? You thought I couldn't socialize?" He smirked, though it was extremely subtle at best. "I'm pretty good at dealing with different people."

"Well, uh, as cute as that was, we're not done with our questions yet."

"Questions like why I didn't help you when Leech showed up?" Rose said.

Zoe folded her arms, and now scowled at him having heard that. "So you knew about that."

"Hard not to." He took a breath, then continued on, scratching his five o'clock shadow. "Unfortunately, with the RCPD already there and having a perimeter set up, we couldn't do much. Gotta remember, kid, even if we have all kinds of zeal and reasoning backing us up, if the cops say stay out, we stay out of the way. By the time me and my partner arrived, they were blocking the club off entirely."

Pilar sat back in her seat, arms folded as she stared back at her plate filled with crumbs. "Well, that's convenient."

To her surprise, Rose shrugged. "Trust me. If it were up to me, you wouldn't even have the suit to begin with. But your dad, in all his infinite wisdom, thought it'd be best in the hands of his teenage daughter."

"You sound happy about that," Pilar replied. Her face was the definition of smug when she said it.

Agent Rose stood, looking to them both with the same stoic face. "I obviously wasn't exactly ecstatic when he told me to search you out if something happened to him. I'm still not fond of this idea. But he made me promise to do just that. And, seeing as you've already got the Bug Suit up and running, and are working on another one? It sounds like his judgment might be right."

Pilar had to give him credit. At the very least, after all, he didn't completely brush her aside.

He placed a couple of one-dollar bills on the table. "I'll keep tabs on Aegis and help keep you out of trouble. Cover stories, supplies—I can get it to you. You know, without having to try and steal it from us."

"Technically, mine to begin with."

"Not according to the law, vigilante."

Pilar couldn't argue that at all. Even she knew she was operating well outside of any legal protection. "Meh," was all she grunted in reply.

He continued on as if she hadn't said a word. "All I'm looking for is any info you get on Hyde or his cronies in the process. That, and keeping yourselves out of trouble." He gave one of the passing baristas a nod and a smile. "For now, I've got business back at the office that apparently is too urgent to wait another hour. We'll talk again soon, I'm sure."

As the door chime rang through the air, he peeked back inside, and pointed to them. "Remember. Out. Of. Trouble."

"Oh my God, okay already," Pilar answered. "You are really bad at the whole inconspicuous thing, you know that?"

Again, he ignored her critique, and proceeded to leave as casually as he'd entered, Hawaiian shirt and all.

Zoe and Pilar quickly moved their positions at the table, nearly sitting side by side and lowering their voices to a whisper.

Zoe's eyes darted about the café like a bird on a caffeine high. "If he's not lying, then maybe Aegis isn't really our problem after all. And if he's looking for us to gather information on the Cloaks and Hyde himself?"

Pilar smirked. "We could control the flow of information he gets. If we think he's not on our side, feed him some false information and see if he bites."

"Then it sounds like we're accepting his terms. In our own special little way, of course." Zoe shrugged her shoulders, but smiled as she locked eyes with Pilar.

"Of course. In the meantime, we need to get back to finding those Cloaks in the first place."

They stood from their seats, then began to make their way through the café towards the register. "Easier said than done. Thoughts on how?" Zoe was already busy digging through her wallet.

"Nothing so far," Pilar answered, now digging into her own wallet. "We know that they've been after Seth, but they keep throwing out decoy attacks too. It's like they're trying to bait us away from Seth, rather than Aegis or RCPD. There's something they don't want me to get the chance to discover."

"Something like . . . ?"

"Dunno. But probably something they fear about us both."

"Hi!" Zoe greeted the young man at the counter with bright smile. She hurriedly gave him the check, along with the exact change to pay for her meal. She looked to Pilar, realizing that she was trying to scrape together the money to pay for her drink and pie. Before Pilar could protest, Zoe snatched the bill out of her hand, and handed it to the clerk along with her credit card. "I've got this, too."

"I can pay for myself, you know. I was joking earlier about you paying for me."

"Would you stop already?" Zoe couldn't help laughing. "I got ya, okay? Just say thanks and let's go."

Pilar hated the fact she had to do even that much. It wasn't like she needed her to pay. She had the money . . . Realizing that it was a losing battle and a silly thing to begin with, Pilar finally managed a somewhat sincere "thanks."

As they walked out, they instinctively lowered their voices again. "Maybe the Cloaks recognize where the Bug Suit is from? Could explain a lot," Zoe began.

"Which would mean they know something about my father and his work." Pilar followed Zoe's lead, plopping on her motorcycle and holding onto her waist. "We need to stalk every single spot we can."

"You've got an idea?"

"Yes, indeed I do. It is going to require a lot of Burst Bees, however."

"To the lab?" Zoe revved the engine.

"To the lab!" Pilar exclaimed over the roar of the bike.

And a moment after, they were tearing off through traffic, headed back to their comfort zone.

21

Unidentified.

Every sample returned that same result. She'd left multiple vials of the substance in the analyzer at this point, and yet they all returned that same response. After all that time, she fully expected something to change.

And yet, here they were, once again staring at vials that looked like nothing more than old motor oil.

"Maybe there's something about the lab itself that's causing it to be unidentifiable?" Zoe was paying some attention to the sample, but her eyes were mostly on the upgraded armor. She couldn't see it fully within its protective case, but the little bit she could see had her positively excited. "I can't believe you were able to add that, too! How'd you do all this by yourself?"

"Magic," Pilar answered, still staring at the liquid. She wheeled her chair over to one of the long light tables, still carefully holding the closed vial.

"Desk three, on," she exclaimed. And as if she'd flicked a switch, the light table erupted with an off-white glow.

"Okay, that's cool," Zoe said aloud, having witnessed the activation in her peripheral view. She finally made her way to Pilar's side, and was once again fully concentrating on the vial with her. "So how does this stuff even work?"

"From what I can tell? It's some sort of nanotechnology. We're likely talking about millions of self-replicating machines that can mass produce whatever they're told, on the fly. The liquid is probably what keeps them unified as one object."

"Do you have any proof of this?"

Pilar sighed. "That's what I'm trying to find. Aside from visual proof in the way the liquid reforms and what I can almost certainly verify in a microscope, I still can't verify how it manages to repair like that. And the samples we have likely have been away from their source too long."

Zoe folded her arms. "So once they're pulled apart long enough, they can't reform."

"That's the thought. But before I can figure out how they get pulled apart, I need to know what they're made of. Nanomachines aren't an element, and this ooze isn't just motor oil."

Pilar's hand was beyond nervous as she prepared to open the vial. Up until that point, she had been perfectly fine making her observations from the contained sample. But considering where that sample was sourced from, opening the container right there in the lab could prove to be the worst mistake she'd made in her life. Even with a protective shield in front of them, even with her wearing protective gloves as she worked, her fear continued to mount.

There was literally no other way at this point, though. They needed to at least try to understand what they were dealing with from a molecular standpoint.

And there's only one way to do that.

She finally popped the top off the vial, and slowly poured the liquid into a clear dish. "Prepare containment," she commanded. And on that command, an arm lowered from the ceiling, a large glass-like dome within its grasp. That dome interlocked with the glass shielding that Pilar was reaching through, completing the sealed-off container.

They glared at it for at least a minute.

And it proved to be the most boring minute they'd spent in the past few days.

Pilar realized that whatever she was expecting to happen, didn't happen. "Alright. We're clear. Now to see what—"

Before she commanded anything else, the arm above slammed down on the container, trapping it within. All sorts of alarms rang above their heads. Zoe looked to Pilar, panicked as she tried to figure out just what could have happened while they were literally just staring at the liquid.

"Alarm cancel!" Pilar yelled. And on her command, silence erupted around them.

"Holy crap, that was scary," Zoe blurted out. "Is there a reason half the world's fire alarms went off down here?"

Pilar glared back at the liquid again, seeing not even a slight change. They kept staring at it, but nothing happened. *Is something malfunctioning? And if it is, just what is it that . . .*

It took her a moment to realize what had caused the alarm. Once she noticed it, fear spread across her face like chicken pox. "Dammit! Containment units 4B and 7B! Get over here and help contain this!"

"What is it?" Zoe still was utterly unaware . . .

. . . until Pilar pointed her eyes right to it. "Look at the metal under the dish."

At first, Zoe still couldn't see it. The only thing that looked even slightly odd was that the metal plate was slightly bent.

"Wait." Now she started to understand, just as the two robots arrived and covered the sample with two more protective shells. "It's controlling the metal?"

"Yeah, it's trying to nourish itself! All it needed was oxygen and some metal to be in proximity of . . . But something else is making it—"

The sound of a shotgun blast erupted from underneath the containment hold. Pilar and Zoe both fell back from the impact of the sound, as well as the sheer strength of it startling them both. For a moment, they lay on the floor, staring at each other as if waiting for one of them to be brave enough to see what had happened. Pilar realized that if one of them was going to get up, she might as well be first.

It was her lab, after all.

Zoe gave her a nod however, and they both decided to stand, and observe just what had happened.

Pilar breathed a sigh of relief when she could visually confirm that the containment had been a success. The first layer of protective glass had shattered, but the other two service robots had been able to cover it in time.

What did scare her, however, was what had become of the liquid within: It was now a very dark blue color, and whatever parts of it had been on the dish had melted through it.

"Acid," Pilar mumbled. "It's a self-defense mechanism."

"So, if it's weakened enough, or separated long enough, it blows itself up?" Zoe was still standing back a bit, clearly not wanting to be anywhere in the vicinity of that slime.

Pilar nodded. "Yeah. And in this case, the only thing that really threatened it was the exposure to light from the table."

"Let me guess. That won't work on the real thing?"

"Maybe," Pilar answered. "For now, I need to run more tests to see if that's conclusive. If it's true, the last thing I want to do is shine a big light on Leech and have his entire body explode all over downtown and melt everything in a mile-long radius."

Zoe nodded at that. "In the meanwhile, what exactly will you do with this sample?"

"Well according to these robots now, the liquid is no longer sentient. It's just an acidic goo."

"That doesn't sound any safer. You know that, right?"

Pilar scratched her head. "You know what? You're actually right on that. I'll get to work on containing this for now. Think you can handle putting on your battle armor without my guidance?"

Zoe made her way to the armor, grinning all the while. "I can't wait to find out."

"It's battle armor, Zoe. It's not a pair of pajamas. Little more complex than that. Need to be careful."

"Complex, need to be careful. Got it." Zoe was far too fascinated to really adhere to that, and Pilar knew it.

"She's not listening," Pilar mumbled to herself. She began instructing the maintenance and service robots to contain the remains of the experiment, still trying to resolve just what had happened. At the very least, if this fluid was indeed sensitive to light, then it made sense that the Cloaks were only seen during the night. Certainly they were unlikely to just explode from sunlight, but it likely made them far weaker than normal. So at the very least, they now had that one distinct advantage over them. If all else failed, she could try to get to a light source or they could use the light sources already implanted in the battle armor to try to short out this . . . stuff that Leech seemed to be made of. But then again, as she'd clearly just tested, it could make the situation far worse.

The other problem of course, was that she couldn't be sure the other Cloaks were made of that same exact material, or perhaps an even more improved version that did not share that weakness. Her train of thought was interrupted by the sound of Zoe yelling:

"Okay, so, um, how do you actually open this thing?"

Pilar should have been extremely irritated by that, but instead, she almost burst into laughter. She cleared her throat before turning her attention to her confused partner.

Told her so.

22

The beat shook the streets outside. The steady thump made a rhythmic tremor, muffled only by the stone walls that surrounded the club. It was far past midnight, so there weren't any more club hoppers filtering into the club. An hour beforehand, the line to get in was nearly around the block—the bouncers could barely keep the crowd in check.

On the adjacent rooftop, Bug and Moth stood, eyeing the scene below them. Nothing out of the ordinary had occurred yet, but both had a very strong hunch that the Cloaks would show their faces there. After all, they were after Seth, and the melodic bass that echoed out of the club was the work of his hands.

This particular night also gave Bug and Moth the perfect chance to test the modified battle suits. In Moth's case, it was a nearly brand new set of Bug Armor.

Bug had to admit that she was glad she'd taken Moth's suggestions seriously. The suits looked far better aesthetically, and almost all the features Moth had on the list were useful in some way—though, to be fair, there had been some horrid ideas on that list as well.

Moth's body armor and helmet were now deep violet. The suit was form fitting, and underneath its exterior were multiple layers of the Armor Cloth that Bug had received from Agent Rose days before. Underneath that cloth was a flat-circuit suit, used to control the suits functions via the natural reactions of the wearer.

Zoe's suit had a cape that wrapped comfortably around her nape, matching the scarf of Bug's suit. However, when spread wide, the cape appeared to be a pair of symmetrical moth wings, while Bug's scarf appeared like wasp wings. Both served the same function, however, granting them the ability to glide freely so long as they had the space to do so.

The antennae attached to Moth's helmet were also different from Bug's spiraling gold attachments. Instead, Moth's antennae were more akin to that of a luna moth, while Bug's own were more akin to that of a hornet. Though aesthetically they appeared like mere ornaments, they did in fact serve different purposes: Moth's antennae served to neutralize signals or other tracking devices, while Bug's antennae did the opposite, tracking other signatures including Moth's own suit.

The Bug Suit had gone through a few changes as well. Most notably, the entire suit was now black with gold highlights, along with gold lenses in the helmet. The back of the gauntlets were glowing yellow now, as well, instead of pink. While Bug had modified Moth's battle suit with high-heeled boots, her own suit now had flattened shoes that still absorbed impact very well.

Aside from the aesthetic changes, there was also the addition of a unified communication channel. It allowed both Moth and Bug to communicate with each other, as well as the lab, at any time. A camera within the suit's helmet would also display the face of its occupant, and whenever necessary, a Burst Bee could be utilized as a camera as well, and give instant feedback of about a five-hundred-foot radius, cleanly.

"I have to say, Bug, this is extraordinary." Bianca stood at the monitoring station back in the lab, fascinated by what she could see on the screen above. "Being able to patch through to everyone at any time is a significant boost in communication."

"It still needs some tests, but for now it'll do. For something I never planned to implement, I'd say it works fine, though." Bug could see a small digital display of Bianca standing within the lab in her helmet's HUD. "Still no sign of anything yet on our end."

Moth stood next to where Bug kneeled on the rooftop, glaring at the club with a strange wonder. That wonder, of course, came from her trying out every function her helmet gave her access to. "Thermal vision option? Night vision? One-hundred-times zoom?" She was literally giggling, unable to contain her excitement. "Bug, this is too awesome for words. And you had this all this time?"

"Not exactly. Only had thermal before. And quit messing with all that stuff. You're going to cause a malfunction if you keep flipping through modes."

"How can you tell?"

Bug pointed to the lenses of her own helmet. "My suit is the master of all the communication abilities in each suit. It is also the primary controller for the fail-safe in each suit."

Bianca chimed in over the communication line. "Fail-safe?"

"Yes. In case something really bad happens. Like someone gets hold of one of our battle suits and goes on a rampage in it." Bug returned her gaze to the club. "Don't worry, your suit is the backup fail-safe to my own. So if I somehow lose my mind or my suit gets stolen, you have the authority to activate its fail-safe remotely."

"What . . . exactly are these fail-safe things you have?"

"Completely not important right now." Bug's helmet loosed a ringing beep in her right ear; she whipped around to her right, but saw no one there aside from Moth. "Please tell me you heard that too."

Thankfully, Moth nodded. "Yeah. Kinda hard not to hear. Is that some sort of warning?"

Bug nodded, then began looking all around the roof they stood on. "Someone is stalking this area. But so far I have no sign of who or even what it is."

Moth quickly realized as she looked at Bug that the eyes of her helmet seemed to be reacting to her speech. "Am I imagining things? Or are your helmet's eyes—"

"Yeah. You wondered if I could add that. Figured I'd try."

"And you did all this in a day?"

"Lab assistants, robots and stuff, but other than that? Yeah." Bug continued to swap the viewing abilities of her helmet, but nothing out of the ordinary appeared. "Hey Bianca, are you seeing anything out of the ordinary on Andromeda?"

"Nothing yet. No news reports, not one oddity."

"Crud. I know something's up. If it were just me then maybe it'd be a malfunction. But both HUDs?"

"What happened?" Bianca asked, her voice shaking.

144

Bug could see the concern starting to spread all over Bianca's face, even in that tiny electronic display. "The helmets are built with a limited energy detection protocol. If any large amounts of electricity or other types of power get within a certain range, we're immediately alerted."

"And that alert just went off for both of us, but we don't see or hear anything," Moth added. "Kinda freakin' me out right now."

"Believe me, you're not the only one." Bug drew her hammer's hilt from its holster, and quickly expanded it. "Something's here, and it's about to sneak-attack the club."

For a moment, there was nothing but the sounds of the club music, a car here or there, and the wind current above the city.

They could hear the sound of Bianca slamming her hands on to the control console even over their com-link. "Behind you!"

Almost immediately, Bug and Moth's displays lit up with warnings aimed directly behind them on a rooftop across the way. There were at least eleven different targets standing there, glaring at them as if they were nothing more than prey that had been cornered.

"So! Eleven of them huh? Not sure how I feel about those odds." Moth drew a dagger in each hand. "They were able to mask themselves from us, weren't they?"

"You want the honest truth?" Bug took a pensive step backward. "Either way, it really doesn't matter much now. They're not getting Seth. I won't let them."

Neither of them had realized the decrease in numbers in front of them. By the time they did notice that their targets had reduced to just ten, he was already standing behind them, smiling. The smile on his face seemed bright and pleasant like a sunny spring morning. And yet, Bug was completely unnerved by it. Whatever lay behind that smile frightened her to the core.

He pushed a few strands of his long, silky black hair from his perfect face. "We meet again. I can't say I'm surprised."

Bug could feel herself trembling slightly. She couldn't recall a time in her life where the mere smile of a man made her so nervous.

No, not nervous. Petrified.

It was the same as that night.

Mantis.

Regardless of that, she knew that he was after her brother. She couldn't let him proceed.

Mantis was quick to notice that. "Oh. You're protecting him, aren't you?"

"Uh, yeah?" Moth was able to speak up after a moment, but even Bug could tell Moth was at least just as frightened as she was by the vibrato in her voice. "Why else would we be here?"

"Well, I just felt that you should probably be more concerned with yourselves. Since actually, we're here for you two." He tilted his head. His eyes narrowed to near slivers as he stared them down. "Not really my idea, but you know how it goes. Orders are orders."

When Bianca overheard that, she had to fight her emotions to keep calm. "Bug? Moth? I'm fairly certain that this brouhaha won't end well. You need to flee as soon as possible."

Bug heard her request over the communication link. "One problem with that, Bianca. We're not exactly in a fleeing position."

"I might be able to help get us out of here. But there's another problem." Moth looked back towards the club. "If we do run away, there'd be nothing to stop them from assaulting Seth again."

Bug quickly understood the folly of their plan: they'd known that Seth would be attacked again and figured that, at most, two of those monsters would show up. Two of them, they could handle. This was supposed to be their trap. Instead, this monster used their trap against them.

Bug still held her hammer before her, but she was much less steady with it. "I really don't have a plan for this, guys." She made sure to keep her voice as quiet as possible, since the three of them could hear each other regardless.

"Then we're doing things on the fly."

Bug nodded. "Yes. But first things first. Battling up here is a distinct disadvantage to us right now. We need to get them to the ground level."

Moth nodded. "Maneuverability. I can agree with that." She quickly placed her daggers back in their respective pockets on her utility belt, and reached in the far right pouch of her belt. Seeing that none of the cloaked monsters bothered to move, she whipped three of her toxic smoke bombs from the pouch, scattering them upon the roof. The massive, violet swarm of gas clouds that erupted from the silver globes made it nearly impossible for Bug and Moth to see. Of course, their helmets protected them from the smoke and gave them other means to see where they were headed.

Thanks to the improvements that Bug had made to the "feet" on their respective armor, they were able to bound down the sides of the buildings. Within seconds they'd safely landed in the alley between their perch and the neighboring RCU Bank building. As soon as they fled the alley, however, eight of the eleven goons began to land in front of them, each hitting the ground with a tremor-inducing thud.

"Um, Bug? There's literally nothing for them to bound off of on this side of the bank," Moth whispered. "I didn't track them, but if they really met us down here, the only way I can think of is—"

"They literally jumped off from thirty stories up." Bug found herself losing her fear and becoming more agitated with the cretins. "Because, of course they can."

Moth looked to Bug, but only for a quick moment. "Whatever these guys are, they're durable as hell."

"Pointing out the obvious really is a talent of yours, you know that?"

Mantis seemed to be thoroughly amused by their apparent attempt to flee. He stood a ways back, behind his eight minions. "We need you to be the control for our tests on them."

The cloaks draped around those eight beasts ripped apart. Thousands of pieces of torn, black cloth floated through the air. And in the midst of this shedding, there stood eight shadowed figures, each one with a gas mask covering its face. Their torsos looked like nothing more than thin pipes, and their thighs and forearms were just as thin; however, enormous, rounded shells that looked similar to the Bug Suit's oversized gauntlets covered their shins and their lower arms. They stepped into the light a bit more, and it became clear what Bug and Moth were up against: robotic, bipedal cockroaches. Their long antennae dangled from their heads, and as they scurried about, the metal in their feet clicked constantly.

Bug could literally taste the leafy salad from her dinner resurfacing in her throat.

"Why cockroaches? Of all the things in the world they could have been, why cockroaches?" Moth wasn't too thrilled to see their actual form either.

Despite how repulsed she was by the sight of them, Bug could not continue to hold back and play defensive. They'd stalled for long enough. It was time to attack them instead. Within seconds, her fully functional hammer was tight in her grasp again. Held by both hands, she wound back and then pummeled the nearest of the cockroach robots directly in its chest. She fully expected it to crack in two once the hammer collided with its thin frame.

Instead, her hammer bounced off of it as if it were nothing more than rubber, and its body didn't even get scratched!

"These are the advanced models. Roach-Bot Type 0A." Mantis stood there, arms folded under his cloak, as he smiled at the vigorous display. "Sorry, they can't be damaged so easily. Of course, now that you know that, you can see where this will go soon."

"That doesn't sound good." Bianca cupped her chin. "Not too many things that can kill a cockroach to begin with."

The Roach-Bots began their own frenzied attack; Bug hoped that they would perhaps be clumsy oafs. Instead, Bug and Moth were barely dodging the rising onslaught of attacks, and all of their efforts were being repelled.

When one of the robots did manage to strike a clean blow, the pain was also much more intense than Bug imagined it would be. They hit hard. She realized that if she hadn't improved the suits at all, her spine might have freely flown from her body from the impact of even one fist. She couldn't deny that there was a dark part of her ego relieved to see that Moth was struggling just as much as she was. The more logical side of her knew that she'd be invaluable in getting out of the situation alive. Somehow, despite their pain and the sheer number of robots assaulting them, they made their way back to each other, and stood back to back as the machines remounted their assault.

Moth barely repelled an enormous wing from one of the robots with her daggers. The force of the blow caused her to lean backward, pushing against Bug's back. "Too many, too strong!"

Bug barely blocked a swing from another of the robots, forcing both her and Moth in the opposite direction. "I'm aware of that!"

The two of them spun to each other's opposite side, now leaning against each other's backs but both looking to their right. "Options?"

Moth put away one of her daggers and pulled three obsidian globes from a pouch on the right of her utility belt. "I can make 'em go boom if need be."

Bug looked about, realizing just how much of downtown they'd probably damage in the process. "Not yet. Not a good spot."

They had a moment to breathe, and it was likely the only chance to get a clean scan of the robot's bodies with her helmet's analyzing options. With the press of a discreet touch-button on the side of the helmet, the program was activated. Bug affixed her gaze to one of the robots and let the lens run a visual print of its system through its own. Before the analysis could be completed, one of the robots leapt forward, forcing her to guard against it with the giant electric hammer that had been so ineffective thus far.

She avoided its leap, and jabbed her hammer into the gas-mask-like protrusion that was likely its face. Moth and Bug both watched in awe as it stumbled backwards, into a pair of its "brethren" as it tumbled to the ground in a spray of jolts and sparks.

Bug looked to the completed diagnostic that her HUD displayed, and as if to confirm it for her, the green image of the robot was highlighted red directly in its cranial area.

"Bug, love? Your helmet just sent some fascinating data back to Andromeda." Bug had turned off the visual display form the lab, but she could still hear Bianca's voice. "What exactly is this?"

"A snapshot of our current problem," Bug answered back over the com-link.

"Snapshot?" Bianca didn't sound any less confused when she repeated it.

"I'll explain it when we get back!" Bug's aim shifted to the next Roach-Bot in line. Her hammer quickly found its way to the robot's face. The shower of blue, sparkling electricity that hailed from its body was mesmerizing.

Without a word, Moth quickly went to work. Her daggers began to find their way into the face of every robot within reach. Her leaps were still a bit awkward as she continued to get used to the battle suit, but she still made it look all too easy, as if she were simply dancing about. It was the first time that Bug actually saw this much of a display from her, and she found it hard to concentrate on her own melee without feeling a tinge of jealousy.

She had seriously underestimated just how skilled Moth was.

Within moments, the numbers began to swing in their favor. They'd gone from eight, to three, to one, to none. There was a long area of roach parts strewn about, some which were still wriggling around as if trying to survive without the rest of the body.

"That was more painful than I expected." Moth pulled out another set of daggers, holding three in each hand. "Still, this suit is phenomenal, Bug! It made it so easy to look so awesome! I swear we were part of the Gorgon Zola Nine just now!"

"Part of . . . who?"

"That girl spends too much of her time watching cartoons, hon." Bianca sighed. "Besides all that, there's still at least three targets surrounding you according to the Burst Bees nearby."

"Good thing you can see them, because we can't." Bug looked about again, just to confirm visually that the others had completely vanished. "I can't even find a hint of them, even with the helmet."

150

"Maybe they ran off?" Moth was at Bug's side once more, holding a pair of daggers as if they were short swords. "Not that I actually believe we'd be that lucky."

A gleeful clap came from a few yards behind them. Mantis and the others had returned, standing upon a small donut shop and bearing down on them. It was Mantis who had given them the strangely disturbing round of applause, his hood hiding his face in its shadow.

"Well, it looks like they have a fatal flaw after all. It just took someone with a bit more skill to find it. Too bad for those Aegis agents it took you so long to get here, I guess. But they knew the risks of taking that job, right?" Mantis pulled his hood back off again. "You like Aegis as much as we do, right? Which is pretty much not at all. They are an evil little company. They're the reason we exist the way we do right now."

"You're saying Aegis created you," Bug nearly growled as she spoke. "And that somehow gives you the right to kill them by the dozens?"

Mantis's disappointment was palpable, to say the least. "It doesn't matter anyhow. It would seem you have caught the attention of Hyde. You must be something special for him to make the trip here."

The shadow that loomed behind them could only be described as "literally freezing." Even under her armor, the back of Bug's neck felt cold and naked against the darkness that had arisen, blocking out the moonlight as it emerged from the cracks in the cement. She and Moth turned to face it, and without even seeing what the shadow would form into, they took five steps backward.

The blob of black material then formed itself into a figure that resembled a man wearing a long, flailing cloak. On its head sprouted two large horns at either side. The sense of panic and fear within Bug started to take over. She held it in—

Then she saw those eyes . . .

It's him . . . It can't be him . . . It can't be him!

"That suit. Interesting that you are wearing it."

The voice was the same as the nightmare that had haunted Bug for the past two years. That voice was what she thought about destroying every day, and yet also feared hearing every time she put on that Bug Suit. Her entire body felt as though it had turned to stone. Her mouth, her eyes, her legs, her arms . . . Nothing worked. She couldn't even blink.

"Sands. So you are an agent of his, are you?" The deep, hissing vocals were seeping into Bug's subconscious. Before she knew it, she was back in that lab again, watching her father become wrapped in that shadow, in that black fog that consumed everything around it.

Moth's screams brought Bug back to the world for at least a moment. She looked to Moth's feet, already partially trapped in his shadow, sinking into the ground where he had managed to extend it beneath her. "Bug! Snap out of it!"

There was no scientific reasoning behind this monster. How could she destroy it? How could she free Moth? It would consume them, then everything surrounding it!

Before she knew it, Bug had taken two steps away from them all. Two steps away from her ally, and away from that demon.

"You're going to run, aren't you?" The demonic shadow cackled at her. It taunted her with Zoe's life. "You won't get far. I'll consume you too, you know. I'll consume that suit, and then everything that you know? I'll know."

Bianca's voice rang in her ear now. "Bug! You have to get Moth out of there and escape!"

I can't . . . I can't . . .

Something within Bug snapped. It was as if every muscle in her body exploded at once. Her mind entered some sort of violent euphoria. Before any of it registered with her brain, she'd leapt high into the air, and pulled back her right fist. When her fist slammed into his shadow, she yelled from the darkest parts of her heart. The only thought on her mind was to kill him. Destroy him. Erase him!

An enormous spout of indigo light erupted like a column, surrounding her entire left arm as her fist obliterated the shadow-covered cement below. The part of her mind that wasn't completely locked into another world could hear his agony as the light shot multiple slices through his shadow, then through his inky, black "body." Moth had broken free of his grasp, and the residual power that escaped Bug forced the other Cloaks to retreat as well.

Bug's body had emptied everything. She had nothing left.

Moth fell to her knees, panting. She could see Bug lying in the street, completely still. She forced her legs to bend, to push her upward. The concrete beneath her was unforgiving. Even through her armored boots. it felt as though she were walking on spikes.

"—oth . . . hea—? Wha—? Agent Ro—" She could barely make out Bianca's scattered voice in her own helmet. Whatever that energy was that Bug had unleashed, it had done the suits' functions no favors either.

Moth fell to the ground again, grasping Bug's limp body into her arms and trying to wake her. Most of Bug's helmet had been destroyed—Moth could see Pilar's vacant eyes as she lay there, barely breathing. Her entire body was cold to the touch, despite the display of destruction she'd accomplished moments before.

Police sirens slowly echoed through the city streets, growing louder as they zoomed towards the scene of destruction. Moth had no idea what to do, how to help her friend. For the second time in her life, she could feel the hurt of knowing that she could do nothing for someone close to her.

She would have to explain it all to the police later. She definitely had to prepare a story for her father and her sister. More important than that however, was thinking of what to tell the hospital to even get Pilar the care she needed!

A black SUV shot out of the southern end of the street. Before Moth could try to react, to see just who or what was coming, the SUV whipped around right in front of them, tires screeching as it came to a halt a few feet away.

Agent Rose nearly jumped out of the rear doors of the truck. "We've got to go, now!"

Moth didn't question it. She didn't have time. She was so frightened by Pilar's condition that nothing mattered. "Please . . . help her . . ."

Agent Rose slowly took Pilar's limp body from Moth's hands, and rested her across the back seat of the truck. The two of them jumped into their own seats. The driver was another agent, a brunette woman in a similar suit to Rose's own. She shifted the truck into drive, whipped it hard to the right, then peeled out, shooting the truck through the debris scattered upon the road.

"Pilar'll be okay." Agent Rose tried to give Moth some sort of comfort. "She'll be okay."

Moth barely responded for a moment. "Where are you taking her?"

"The hospital. Don't worry, Bianca's working on a cover story for the both of you as we speak. She'll meet us there."

Moth's eyes darted in his direction, narrowed. "Do you think I give a damn about a cover story right now?"

Rose turned his sight towards the road ahead. "Yeah. I think you do. They're going to want to know why a sixteen-year-old girl and her nineteen-year-old friend look like hell, and why they should be treated immediately."

The ferocity in Moth's glare left the moment she heard that. She looked back to Pilar, watching her breathe as she lay there with that vacant look in her eyes. "I'm sorry. I know. I know." She could feel her eyes welling up. "She'll be okay. I know she'll be okay."

He could do nothing but watch as the police swarmed the grounds.

He couldn't understand how a simple experiment could have gone so badly! All they'd needed to do was test those robots against someone a bit more formidable than the RCPD—which wasn't difficult— and Aegis's Security Agents. Leech had dispatched dozens of them with ease on his own, and he was by far the least powerful of their group, so those two girls running around in power suits should have been a decent challenge for those roach-based robots. However, he never would have dreamed that those stupid metal abominations would have such a stupid flaw!

And then, on top of that, she'd tapped into something that had nearly killed them all in one fell swoop.

Widow was holding up what remained of his body—minus the large chunk missing from his left abdomen—and helping him stand. She had been fortunate. The "blades of light" had just barely missed her. Had she not recognized that something was wrong and moved accordingly, she wouldn't be there holding Mantis upright.

Leech had lost his right leg. His right arm-tentacle stretched to the ground to keep him steady. He was still trying to figure out his own error. The robots he'd built had been nothing more than cannon fodder to them. He'd followed his predecessor's designs perfectly. There was nothing that he could have missed.

Unless . . .

"That bastard." Leech slammed his free left arm into the brick wall nearby. "He knew! He designed the mass-produced line with a fatal flaw, just in case someone tried to use his work against—"

His words were quickly halted by the long, black shadow clenching at his throat. The claw that grasped him extended from far behind him. The shadowed arm was attached to a large, black crystal, partially shattered. Through the gaping hole in that crystal, part of an elderly man was visible. He mimicked the claw's action, with his own weathered hand reaching out, clenched.

"You didn't account for that. Not a very smart move on your part, good doctor."

Leech's eyes were filling with that same black ink-like substance that his arms were born of. He could barely speak, or breathe, as the hand clenched further.

"I don't have the patience for such stupidity. And quite frankly, you have failed me multiple times. Is there a reason aside from compassion that you should be left alive?"

Leech managed to chuckle despite the lack of air. ". . . Come on . . . kill me . . ." He was barely breathing. His eyes had gone black.

"That could be arranged." The shadow gave a slight grin before letting go of Leech. "You will not get off so easily. You are bound to my cause. Your life ends when I say it ends."

"Hyde, we still have a significant problem." Mantis was still smiling despite the horrific damage done to his body. "Just what was that power she utilized? She nearly killed us all with it, but she didn't seem to know what it was herself."

"Sands was a very meticulous man, dear protégé" He smiled. "His paranoia of his own work is peculiar, and yet it might be quite successful in stopping our evolution." Hyde nodded. "Indeed, it could be the end of us entirely."

"You sound eerily pleased with that."

"Not so much pleased as I am curious! Still, that child could become quite a pest if she is not taken care of immediately." Hyde's crystal prison shattered, crashing to the ground before him like pieces of frail glass, until only a pile of fine, black sand remained. He shoved a bit of the sand away with his left boot. Without the cocoon that once protected and obscured him, Evandrake Hyde appeared to be nothing more than an old scientist with an odd hairline and a vicious smile. "Of course, we are in no condition to do that, thanks largely to her."

"It would be in our best interest to recover. Chances are, if she survived, she will be in no condition to defend herself. And Seth is already vulnerable." Mantis raised his claw to the skies, eyeing it for damage. "Still, it's a crushing blow to my ego to be defeated by that girl so easily."

Hyde chuckled at that. "Your ego? I'm hardly concerned with your ego. Now hurry back to Ninety-Nine. We need to prepare for our next move."

24

Her eyes didn't open for almost two days.

When they did, they were greeted by the early morning sunlight. A few blinks were all she could do to try and ease the transition, but even then, Pilar found herself having to shield her eyes from the light. She was in a hospital bed, a place she truly did not want to be. In truth, even seeing the hospital gown made her deathly afraid. To Pilar, there was never a good reason to be in a hospital. It pretty much meant that something had to be wrong. She wanted to write it off as some sort of bad dream, but she knew that certainly wasn't the case.

Pilar barely sat upright before realizing just how weak she was. She could recall some of what had happened. One moment that continued to sting her was when Zoe called out to her for help, and she'd hesitated. She couldn't fathom it.

She . . . had actually thought about abandoning her.

To complete the irony, Zoe opened the door to the room as she finished the thought. She was carrying a bag filled with plastic cups and a gigantic jug of orange juice.

"Good, you're awake! I didn't want to have to drink this all by myself!" She was far more excited than Pilar had expected. *How could she be so happy to see me after what I did to her?*

Zoe sat on the opposite side of the bed, grinning ever so happily. "Are you feeling better?"

Pilar gave a meek answer, unable to look her in the eyes. "I'm better, I guess." She was surprised by how weak her own voice sounded.

"That's good to hear. You had me worried when you went unconscious." She took a long swig of juice, before belching. "Excuse me."

"Shouldn't you be ready to kill me for almost leaving you there?"

Zoe began to fill up a cup of orange juice, then handed it to Pilar. "Kill you for being scared? Hardly. I mean, I was too, you know." She handed her the cup, which Pilar swiftly drank.

"Zoe, I know . . ." Pilar took an extended breath, trying to gather the bit of strength she could. "I can be a real jerk sometimes. I don't like working with other people, I don't like having to constantly watch my back. I don't even like talking to any of you unless I absolutely have to."

"Well, this sounds positive so far." Zoe sat back a bit, folding her arms.

"Look, what I'm trying to get at is that I'd never do something like that. I never even thought I'd think something like that." A heavy breath went in, and again a heavy breath left her lungs. "Abandoning you should have never crossed my mind."

Zoe leaned back in her seat next to the hospital bed, smiling with her arms folded. "That's good to know, Pilar. But you didn't have to tell me that."

"I'm learning to appreciate the fact that you're my teammate in all of this."

Zoe's mouth was agape for a solid three seconds. "Okay. So I should prepare for a tornado to touchdown any minute now, shouldn't I?"

"I say something semi-nice and you tease me for it?"

Zoe's laughter was infectious. Pilar tried to resist it, but found herself giggling, then chuckling . . . then laughing at it all.

Slowly the laughter died, as they realized that they weren't laughing at a rather average joke, but instead laughing because they were just lucky to be alive.

Pilar cleared her throat. "I should explain why I reacted the way I did, shouldn't I?"

"There's a particular reason aside from fear?"

Pilar nodded. No one had been privy to the whole story except Seth, but Pilar felt that Zoe, at the very least, deserved an explanation.

"I've had nightmares since my father disappeared. Every time, I see myself entering my dad's lab one night. And I always see that . . . thing, that same monster. He's engulfing everything, until I'm all that's left. I try to run, but I can't move. Soon the same shadow begins to consume me. The nightmare usually ends while I'm suffocating."

Pilar looked to the blinds, peering at the bright blue sky of mid-morning sunlight. "That face. I could never forget that face."

Zoe leaned back. "So could you have seen him before and just blocked it from your memory?"

"I don't know. What happened on the day of Dad's disappearance has eluded me since it happened." A slight smile followed her breath. "Anyway, I guess I just . . . I never expected to actually see that monster outside of my nightmares, you know?"

"I can imagine." Zoe rubbed her forehead with her left hand. She then poured another cup of orange juice for herself, gulped about half the cup down, then exhaled in delight. "This really is good." She smiled at Pilar, whose askance glare quickly brought Zoe back to the serious discussion. "Do you think you'll be able to face him again?" Her demeanor was a bit drier now, and her smile was filled with worry.

Pilar's eyes were lost in the sight of the hospital gown on her body. The mere thought of that monster brought a chill over her entire body again. She clenched her own bare arms. "I can't really answer that right now. I wish that I could, but, I can't."

"Hey. No rush. Seriously. Can't really say I'm ready to face that thing either." Her eyes glided to the floor as she stared at her own ankles.

Pilar knew why she'd looked down.

"What exactly happened when you were grabbed by that shadow, uh, thing?" She still wasn't sure what to even call it! It was hard to admit that the old man was literally commanding his shadow like some sort of extra limb. Even worse, it had actually tried to eat Zoe alive. But no matter what she wanted to believe or whatever logic she wanted to apply to disprove the illusion, she could not deny that she actually saw it. Leech and the rest of those monsters' mere existence was an anomaly, but she couldn't figure out how they had come to be. The answer had to lie in that sample she'd collected,

160

but she hadn't had a chance to try and analyze it again. With all their stalking of Aegis, retooling their armor, picking fights with the Cloaks and trying to study, where could she even find the time?

Zoe's smile slowly became a saddened grin. "Hard to describe. Only my feet up to my ankles even got submerged in it, but it felt like . . . something was reaching into my skin. It was something cold. Then there was this pain that shot through me, like my feet were being ripped from my body."

Pilar could feel herself cringe just hearing that. "And I wasn't seeing things, right? That was definitely his shadow?"

Zoe's gaze tilted down slightly. "No doubt about it. I don't wanna sound crazy, but, you know, is what it is, right? His shadow attacked me."

Pilar nodded. "I think it's more than that. Maybe it's not his actual shadow. In fact, it may be very similar to the sample that I got from Leech a while back."

"Wasn't it inconclusive or something the last time you scanned it?" Zoe barely remembered the sample herself.

Pilar sat up. "Yeah. But I also didn't have this experience to go on, either."

"Do you think Rose may know something about it?"

"I'd love to ask him, but he's not exactly easy to get in contact with."

"You . . . do know he's here, right?"

Pilar's eyes opened fairly wide hearing that. "He's what?"

"How did you think you got here? I mean I'm awesome and all but I'd have a hard time trying to get us both here, considering."

Pilar had to smirk at that one. "Fair point."

Zoe stood, and made her way to the door. Just as she got within a few steps of the doorknob, it started to swing open. When she saw Agent Rose standing in the open doorway, she turned to Pilar, laughing. "Well, that was easy."

"What was easy?" Agent Rose walked in to the room, his sunglasses firmly planted on his face and wearing a white lab coat over his green Hawaiian shirt and tan Dockers. Pilar almost burst into laughter just seeing it, but managed to somehow hold it in.

"Nothing, nothing. You've just got really good timing, that's all." Zoe closed the door, and returned to her seat as well. "At least that saves me a walk."

Rose sighed. "Guess you're both doing better?"

Pilar gave a lethargic nod. "I'm alive, so I guess that counts as better. But I couldn't tell you anything else. I feel completely weak, though."

"You're right. Your injuries and fatigue are not anything life threatening. So, the good news? You're not dead."

"Then why am I—"

He knew that question was coming and quickly cut her off. "Because I had to explain why you were unconscious, somehow. Bianca came in handy for that."

"Bianca is here?" With everything that had happened, Pilar realized only at that moment that Bianca of all people had likely heard and seen everything that had happened to them, and had been helpless to stop it in any way. She deserved a big, heartfelt "thank you," at the very least.

Rose nodded. "She'll be here in a little bit. She's grabbing your brother. Both of 'em have been here for the past two days just waiting on you to wake up."

"They didn't have to do that. I'm fine, really."

"No, you're not. Really."

"Didn't you just—"

"Again, the good news is, you're not dead." Rose raised his shades upwards, resting them on his forehead. Despite the strange color of his eyes, Pilar managed to look into them this time without being awestruck by them. And yet, by the look in his eyes, she could tell that something was wrong as well.

"Pilar, what you dealt with two nights ago was a part of a much larger experiment. The monster Zoe described to us—big shadow, horns on its head, glowing eyes and mouth—what was its name?"

That name was hard enough to think of, let alone repeat. It just wasn't something that Pilar felt needed to be brought up again.

"It was Hyde." She nearly spit his name from her mouth.

162

"Pretty much who I thought it was." Agent Rose sat in the small rolling chair, and the moment he did, it creaked loudly. He slightly altered his position in the chair as it continued to buckle under his weight. "I know I'm not that heavy."

"For that chair?" Zoe scratched her head. "Rose, have you, uh, looked at it? Not much of a chair to begin with."

After clearing his throat, Rose stood from the chair. He paced the room, thinking of what next to say.

"You're stalling for some reason," Pilar finally blurted out after a full minute of his marching.

"Trying to put a few things together mentally. Gimme a sec, kid."

"Not 'kid,' by the way. 'Pilar' works fine."

"The fact you're saying that proves my point." He made his way to the nearby counter, leaning his back against it for support. That was definitely a better option than the heavyset agent trying to fit into the petite little chair.

"Indigo."

Zoe and Pilar both looked at him as though he'd grown a third eye. Zoe actually spoke their suspicions of his insanity aloud. "Indigo? Okay. And that means what?"

"I should say it properly. Project Indigo. It'll make more sense with 'Project' in front of it, right?"

Again, they exchanged awkward looks, and Zoe responded. "Uh, no. Not right."

He cleared his throat again. "Indigo was supposed to be a sort of 'living material' that could replicate itself. Its general application was to be for self-repairing armor. As you can imagine, this was something Aegis would've loved."

Pilar nodded. "Sounds like it. Living material? I assume it was supposed to be some sort of gel-like metal?"

"That was a later modification by Hyde, I assure you."

Pilar folded her arms. "I'm not surprised. What else do we need to know about Indigo?"

Rose shrugged. "Not sure what info you already know. What have you seen of it so far?"

"It self-destructs if enough light is applied to it," Pilar answered. "Or at least, that's what happened with my sample."

Rose nodded. "Well a small enough sample, probably. But a larger quantity requires far more than that. It's sensitive to light, but you're not going to shine a flashlight at it and vaporize it."

"Well yeah, there's that and the fact that when we put a little light to my sample, it blew up real good and turned into acid. Wasn't exactly a great moment in the lab."

Rose rubbed his chin as he thought. "If you've run into Hyde and Leech, then you've already seen two examples of Indigo in action. As for Aegis, the higher-ups know he's responsible for the slaughter over in District 10."

"District 10?"

"The place we first saw him," Zoe answered in place of Rose.

"Of course." The window behind and to the right of Pilar's bed was open, and the breeze that had started through it was actually relaxing her.

"At the time, we weren't fully aware of what our agents were walking into. By the time the teams we sent there understood what was happening, it was too late. Couldn't get 'em the backup or the weapons they needed."

"You have weapons just for these guys?" Pilar asked.

"Well, we did. How effective they are? Not sure. That suit you've been wearing's got a whole lot of different functions. I'm sure you know most of 'em."

"Don't insult my intelligence, please. I know every one of them—"

Rose was quick to stop Pilar's argumentative reply. "Every function except the one that you used last night."

There was absolutely nothing Pilar could say to counter that. He was right. She had absolutely no idea what she'd done, or how she'd done it. "I remember a lot of light, but other than that? Nothing."

"After we got you two to safety, we had some other agents take the opportunity to survey the area, and they found samples of what was left of the assailant. We weren't sure until we analyzed it, along with Zoe's description." From the lower right pocket on his lab coat, Rose gingerly pulled out a small, glass tube containing a thick, black liquid. It was immediately recognizable to them. It was the exact same as Pilar's previous samples.

Rose handed Pilar the vial and she held it to the light, trying to see if there was anything beyond its viscous surface. "It's what they're all made of, isn't it?"

Rose focused his eyes on the vial as well as he continued. "As far as we can tell, each of those 'Cloaks' is a scientist that worked on Hyde and Sands's research team. They were all involved with the prototype of Indigo, but when they proved that Indigo was too volatile and couldn't be kept in check, the project was immediately halted, with Sands at the forefront of the stop."

Zoe looked at Pilar. Her glare then slid to Rose. "Hyde didn't halt it, huh?" Inwardly, Zoe hoped he wouldn't confirm that, but it was inevitable.

Rose nodded. "And we think he infected himself first. He knew its potential, but not its side effects. Then he started infecting others. Some failed—for now, we assume that the three remaining are the only survivors. Not including Hyde himself."

"If you've got their info—"

"We don't. There were dozens of scientists on their team, and their records were deleted the moment Project Indigo was canceled."

There was a moment where the only sounds that could be heard were the hum of the power flowing through the building, and the whisper of the air flowing through the vents.

Zoe gave the answer they all dreaded: "Aegis sanctioned the project under the radar."

"Can't prove anything, but we believe that a certain portion of Aegis's higher-ups did in fact sanction it after the initial accident that got it stopped. The Cloaks themselves were barely on anyone's radar, until that massacre a few days back."

Pilar's eyes widened. "The results."

"And now you get it."

She'd gotten more than that. "Agent Rose, with all due respect? There's no way my father was involved. You know that, right?"

He raised his left hand. "Yeah, I know that much. But, Project Indigo may have something to do with his death."

"Disappearance," Pilar corrected him. "No idea if he's dead yet, and I doubt he really is."

Agent Rose rubbed the back of his neck. "Right, yeah. Disappearance. My bad."

Zoe had no hint of a smile on her face. Instead, her eyes narrowed, and her arms were folded. "You still haven't told us what exactly happened to Pilar."

"Professor Sands informed a few of us during Project Indigo that the Bug Suit's strongest function was the ability to render Indigo useless by sending an enormous surge of power through it. Anyone under its influence would need to get the hell away to have any chance of survival."

Pilar's brow raised hearing that. "Even if what you're saying is true, that still doesn't explain how—"

"It partially destroyed the suit? In your panic to help Zoe, you overdid it. Sands also made it clear that the function was a last resort, as it wasn't fully tested yet. There was no telling what the results would be."

"But he knew I'd figure it out or need it, right? Then why wouldn't he . . ."

A bit of silence fell over the room. They all knew the question that Pilar was about to ask, but they also knew just what that question would implicate.

Zoe eventually got around her own fear, asking the hard question. "If he knew his daughter was going to be using that suit, then why not warn her? Why not tell her what it was and how to use it?"

Agent Rose looked to Pilar before beginning his answer. "If I could answer that, I would. Sands left a lot of this stuff half-assed." As if on cue, the moment he finished that sentence a small chirp rang out, followed by a familiar melody. "Get some rest, Pilar. Can't have you running around just yet." He reached into his right pocket, pulling out a small black smartphone. With a slide of his finger across the screen, another voice became audible. He continued out of the room, leaving them alone once again, now with his information to swim through their heads.

"So the suit has some powerful weapon hidden in it that's the only thing that can stop them." Pilar looked to Zoe.

"Probably only in your suit, too."

Pilar clicked her teeth. "From what I know of the suits? Probably. I'll have to verify it once I'm home. Which should be soon, right?"

Zoe looked into her eyes with a smile that was as innocent as a toddler's. Her hand found its way to Pilar's left shin, and without even the slightest warning, she slapped it.

Pilar nearly screamed from the pain, managing to turn it into a fierce yelp before it got any further than that. Covering her mouth helped somewhat, but the tears welling up her my eyes were all the sign of pain that needed to be seen.

Zoe's grin was startling. Pilar couldn't tell if she was happy that she finally understood how badly injured she was, or if Zoe found her pain humorous somehow. "Yeah," Zoe continued, "he said that the good news was you're alive, which you really seem intent on ignoring. You're still bruised all over the place, and that shin's in pretty bad shape."

"Great. How did that happen?"

"Probably during the fight with those . . . roaches."

A shudder involuntarily escaped Pilar. "Those things. And I'm sure there's more of them."

"You probably weren't hurt that badly, just bruised. But whatever that suit's secret weapon was, it probably made things worse."

"Sounds about right."

"If you were actually trained to take hits and taught how to properly fight back, your body wouldn't be so bruised." Zoe's matter-of-fact grin immediately irritated Pilar.

"And of course, you can train me, right?"

"Of course."

Though Pilar still wasn't anxious to be taught, she couldn't rule it out now. After all, not knowing how to fight properly may have been a larger part of the reason she was in a hospital bed. The bare basics of combat that she'd been taught by her dad were clearly not going to cut it.

"Well anyway . . ." Zoe placed the jug of orange juice on the table by the hospital bed, along with another cup. "Rest up, okay? Don't try to rush your recovery right now. We'll get down to the specifics later, and if anything happens, I can handle it in the meantime."

Pilar sank back under her covers a bit. "Yeah. I don't have much of a choice, huh?"

"Nope."

As she headed for the door, Pilar stopped her. "Hey."

"What?"

"Well, um, it's just . . ." Pilar took a quick breath. "Thank you, Zoe."

Zoe left with a tender gaze.

25

Somewhere between morning and evening, she'd fallen asleep again, and apparently that sleep was even heavier than before. When her eyes fluttered awake again, Seth and Bianca were both in the room, likely unaware that they'd fallen asleep together. Bianca's head rested firmly against Seth's shoulder.

Pilar couldn't help herself —she gave a loud cough. Bianca was the first to wake up, and she looked at Pilar as if she had five eyes on her face.

"That's cute," Pilar answered to Bianca's glare, pointing a finger at Seth. Apparently she'd guessed correctly. Bianca had no idea she'd fallen asleep that way and jumped from him as if he were an virus-infected beast. That woke him up, and he was as slow as ever to respond.

"You awake this time?"

Pilar's brow raised. "This time?"

"Yeah. Last few times you were awake? You mumbled some stuff, rolled your eyes, and fell back to sleep." Seth's eyes caught Bianca's rose-red cheeks. "You okay?"

"Yes, of course. You should be asking her that, shouldn't you?"

"Pilar's not blushing."

Bianca's change of subject was swift. "So, Pilar! How exactly did this happen?" She couldn't be any more obvious.

Pilar just chuckled at the unnerved woman. "To be honest? I'm not fully sure myself. You heard what was going on over the com-link, didn't you?"

Bianca's blush was slowly going away as her nervous smile gave away her worrying thoughts. "Honestly, love? I couldn't see anything, only hear. And even then, there was a lot of yelling and screaming that . . ."

It became clear that she didn't want to relive what she'd heard. Honestly, Pilar couldn't blame her—she'd been there, after all, and she certainly didn't want to think about it.

"But I heard," Bianca managed to continue, "that you ran into their leader."

"Yeah," Pilar huffed, looking to Bianca. "I made a miscalculation last time. I thought they'd go after Seth again for his power. But the Cloaks used that against us."

Bianca nodded. "So I gathered. The whole lot of them were there as well. It was a trap from the beginning."

Pilar sat up a bit and reached for the orange juice that Zoe had left her. "So our next task is to—"

"Rest," Seth interrupted. "Stop even thinking about this stuff, Pilar. You need to rest."

"Seth, this hospital bed is the closest thing to 'rest' I'm getting until I figure out more of this."

"Yeah, you're gonna make me seriously ground you this time, aren't you?"

"That's just heartless. Grounding me while I'm in the hospital?"

His smile didn't last long. He stood up from his seat, hands gripping his waist, eyes glaring at Pilar as though she really were an undisciplined child. "You do understand what just happened, right? The whole 'almost dead' thing? That both of you were almost killed."

"You don't have to remind me. I was kinda . . . there."

He rubbed his hand through his dreads, scratching his scalp. "Then you get why everyone has been on pins and needles the last two days, right?"

A nod was Pilar's only correct answer.

"Good. Then do us all a favor and do what I ask. Just this once? Rest. Sleep. You're not going to be in here the rest of your life. A couple of days won't hurt." He didn't bother to say much else. He really didn't need to. He took a slow walk out of the room, trying his best to keep from slamming the door but failing.

Bianca waited for a moment before she started in. "He was moments away from hunting down the Cloaks himself, you know. It took everything I had to calm him down."

"Everything you had?"

Bianca's eyes widened. "What in the world are you even thinking?"

"Nothing, nothing. It just doesn't surprise me." Pilar smiled. "I'm starting to understand, I guess."

Pilar was a bit surprised by Bianca sitting on the hospital bed next to her. "Should you be sitting next to me right now?"

Bianca gave her an askance look. "You don't have a communicable disease do you?"

Pilar felt obliged to answer. "I have the flu."

Bianca just shook her head, smiling. "Being cheeky as always, I see. Who do you think saw you first, before you got here?"

Pilar's eyes creaked to their left corners, eyeing her. "Zoe."

Bianca huffed. "After that, smart aleck."

"EMS?"

Bianca gave up trying to goad the answer she wanted out of her—probably because she knew Pilar was well aware of what she'd done to protect them. "They think it was a motorcycle accident right now. By the time you got here, your suit was off thanks to Zoe's help."

"It's back at the lab, right?"

"Yes, but that's hardly the point! You were nearly comatose when you came in! That simply cannot become a common occurrence!" She was much more stern with that. "I do not want to come to work one day and have someone from the RCPD telling me you've died!"

"Bianca, wow . . . okay, calm down. I'm not going to die. I didn't die this time, right?"

"No, but you're acting like it can't happen, and that's the problem!"

Pilar was staring at her bedsheets. "Believe me. I know it can happen. I'm more aware of that now than I ever was." Her hands found their way to her shoulders, and she hugged herself, as if to verify she was still alive. "That wasn't pleasant."

A strange silence lingered between them. Neither seemed to know what to say, where to go from that thought. It was Bianca who pierced the silence with a question that was no lighter than their previous topic:

"Pilar . . . are you certain this is really your fight?"

This was the moment that Pilar had known was coming, but she was had never been sure how she'd get there, or who'd ask her that question. What worried her the most was that when Bianca asked it, it took her much longer to answer than she'd once thought it would. That night she'd almost died. If not for whatever had compelled her to use that armor's power, they would have both been consumed—eaten alive by that monstrous shadow.

Or worse.

And yet she needed to pursue them. They were the only clue she had to her father's whereabouts. *If he's still . . .* She stopped the thought from even entering her mind.

But there was another thought now. This wasn't just about her finding her father anymore. Her brother was at risk, Aegis agents were at risk . . . everyone she knew and even people she'd never met were in danger of being consumed. She couldn't just watch, with all that power, and honestly tell herself it "wasn't her fight."

For starters, Zoe certainly wouldn't allow her to.

"Bianca, I'm not going to let myself get killed. But, I need to stop them. I'm probably the only one who can."

Bianca reached her right hand around Pilar's shoulders, lightly hugging her. "I know. It's just not something I'm comfortable accepting yet."

"I'll take it easy for a little while. A few days at most. But after that? I'm not promising anything."

Bianca sighed. She then forced herself off of the bed and to the chair she'd recently occupied, to remove a leather bag from behind it. She quickly brought it back to the bed, and now it became familiar.

My laptop bag?

Bianca's little smirk was more devious than Pilar would have expected. "Seth would kill me if he knew I'd brought you this," she commented as she placed it next to Pilar on the bed.

"Not going to be hard for him to find out at this point."

"I know. And I also know what it's like to feel helpless, to want to do something even if you know that for the moment, you can't." She wasn't looking at Pilar when as she said it. Instead, her eyes were flatly staring at the laptop itself, as if whatever she was remembering was trapped there, staring back at her.

"Not something you're going to talk about, is it?"

Bianca jolted a bit, but quickly shook it off, looking back to Pilar with a smile. "No. It'd bore you to death."

"Because this place is sooooooo fun."

"Just . . . do your research, Pilar, okay?" She thumped Pilar's forehead slightly. "Make sure no other nurses or doctors know what really happened, alright? I went through a lot of trouble to get that whole accident story to work. Even had Agent Rose wreck a motorcycle."

Pilar wasn't sure she wanted to know how that had gone. "Yeah. I'll keep it quiet . . ."

As Bianca left the room, Pilar pulled out the purple-tinted laptop, and flipped it open. A yellow sticky note was attached to the screen, and the only reaction she could have once she saw the note was to shake her head and laugh at it.

RESSSSSSSST! - Love, Seth.

Seth was already ahead of us, she thought, realizing just how aware he really was. *He's more clever than we give him credit for.*

26

Pilar was getting used to hobbling around her own hospital room, if nothing else. Having to sit and stare at the same four walls so often made her start to question how she tolerated it at home. She wanted to blame the lack of things to do in the hospital room aside from doing random research on her laptop and talking with every visitor that entered.

Of course, it was the same small group of visitors every day, too. But she didn't really mind.

It was a very, very odd feeling. Pilar spent so much of her life feeling like extra weight, like something that everyone just put up with out of obligation. Seeing people show up there, even if only to ask "how are you doing" gave her a feeling she couldn't really explain. For as long as she could remember, she'd been a burden to everyone but her father.

After all, her brother hated her. At least, that's what she'd told herself for the past few years.

And yet there he was, still in her room, half asleep, not bothering to go home after work. He practically lived there with her, despite everyone, including Pilar herself, telling him to rest in his own bed for once.

She'd spent the past few years making it her mission to ignore him. A part of her had never forgiven him for how he'd left. That moment when he'd hit their father and blamed him for their mother's death never left her mind. And she couldn't resolve it. She couldn't begin to understand why he'd dropped contact with her, either. His problem was with their dad.

At least, before she couldn't understand it. And she had dragged that along with her for three more years.

The truth was, she was the one that hadn't wanted to talk. She was the one who hadn't wanted to reach out. So many times, he'd tried to include her and she'd shunned him.

Pilar just wanted to find a rock to crawl under. There he was. After all the crap she'd given him, trying to put distance between them, there he was.

As she hobbled to the open window, her eyes snuck a peek at him as he slept in the rolling chair Agent Rose had almost busted days before. "Who knew?" Pilar mumbled, then found herself mumbling a promise eerily similar to the one her had mother made before she'd passed. "I'm going to change things when I get out of here. And I'll try to be your kid sister again. Promise." She worried that it was a bad omen that when her mother had made that promise, she'd died two nights later.

That won't happen this time. I won't let it. And there's too much left to do.

The woman who suddenly opened the door and peeked her head in was strangely familiar to her, though Pilar was sure she didn't know her at all. "May I enter, madam?"

Pilar and Seth both glared at the golden-haired woman as though she had eight eyes. "You know what knocking is woman?" Seth leapt out of his seat and started charging towards the door in a huff.

"Hey, whoa, calm down there champ, Agent Rose's boss sent me!" She quickly entered the room, and closed the door swiftly behind her. Seth had made his way right in front of her, staring down into her eyes with a scowl that could scare a serial killer.

The woman flashed her badge right alongside her huge grin. "Agent Madriella Mars! See? Grin matches the ID and everything!" She forced her grin even harder when Seth met her gleeful claim with harsh, unforgiving silence.

"Agent Rose's boss sent you? For what? I've already got Agent Rose's help." Pilar leaned against the windowsill. "Aegis is suddenly warming up to me a lot lately, considering."

"Well, that's because you weren't really the big concern. Actually, that's probably not right to say." She tapped Seth's shoulder. "Come on, at least let me explain, cutie!"

"Not a chance. Been a long week." Seth didn't budge a step.

"Let's hear her out at least," Pilar added.

"For what?"

"I'm not even sure, but if she really was a threat, she could have killed me already," Pilar motioned to her bandaged leg and arm, "considering."

Seth shrugged, then made his way back to the chair. "You've got exactly one solitary minute to convince us, Madriella."

"Oh, you can just call me Madri! No need to be that formal!"

When her welcoming statement was met with dead silence and Seth started the stopwatch function on his smartphone, Madri cleared her throat. "So, to be honest? I'm here because I wanted to meet the legend for myself: the genius daughter of Professor Sands."

Pilar folded her arms. "I'm flattered."

"No, seriously! You're so dope! I've heard all about how fast you passed all those tests and stuff!"

"So you've been stalking me." Pilar looked to her brother, then back to Madri. "Yeah you can go now—"

"Wait wait wait! Okay I know that came off a little creepy! But hear me out, okay?" Madri cleared her throat then straightened her black skirt. "So here's the deal. I'm here to make sure all the paperwork goes through, and that your stories hold up—and also as extra security detail in case they try to finish you here."

"No offense? But I'm not feeling safer." Pilar peeked at Seth. "Convinced yet?"

"Got, like, twenty seconds left," he answered as he looked up from his phone.

"You really hate Aegis, don't you?" Madri sat on the end of Pilar's bed, legs crossed as she grinned right at her.

"Something give it away?"

"Nah, nothing at all, just taking a wild guess." Her smirk weakened. "But you know, we're on the same side. Well, at least the little group the director put together."

"What group?" Pilar folded her arms. "And what is the deal with this director? If he's taken that much of an interest in me and what I'm doing then why isn't he here now, and why the hell isn't he out there clearing my dad's name?"

"She," Madri pointed out. "And that's an easy one: Because she can't."

She looked to Seth, who just raised his phone up to show the stopwatch. It was clearly at zero.

"We know what happened. We're trying to figure out why, same as you are." Madri's smile softened. "The director seems to have based her life on succeeding, though. That much I know for sure, babe."

"Did you just call me 'babe'?" Pilar's brow nearly folded in on itself as she said that.

"Sorry! Got a little carried away there!" And just like that, the bright, cheery smile returned. "In any case, your help would get her one step closer to the truth about Sands' disappearance, something she can't do on her own."

"Oh? And what's stopping her, or any of you, from getting that info?"

"Public opinion? Inner turmoil? Stock market? The board of directors?" She huffed out a huge breath, falling back onto Pilar's bed and staring up at the ceiling as she carried on. "We're trying to get answers and stop those other monsters, just like you. But we don't have the freedom you do. And we aren't completely prepared for what they can do."

"So what you want—"

"Is your help!" Madri sat up like a giddy little child, only to collapse into a depressed funk and lay right back on the bed. "But we can't really do that outright just yet. So, we've got to wait around before we can get a concrete plan going, and watch your back in the meantime."

Pilar looked to Seth, then back to Madri again, but this time the sarcastic eye rolls and smarmy voice weren't present. "The director wants my help?"

Madri peered over to her, and smiled. "In a more direct way than you think! But I can't talk about that just yet. She just wanted me to give you notice, and help out the other agents. Seems you've really got those demon-hoody guys' attention."

Pilar sat on her bed. "Lucky me, I guess."

It was a strange thing to ponder. The director of the very company she'd been chasing after; the very people she thought might be responsible for her dad's disappearance but were definitely responsible for his disgraceful termination from the company . . .

Wait a damn second.

"How does she not know what happened to him? She's the director! She had to sign off on his firing!"

"Unless the board was all like, 'nope, nope, we got it from here, he's gone-zo'! Then it kinda doesn't matter." Madri sat up, then folded her arms. "You don't know how things work at Aegis, do you?"

"Of course not."

"I got it," Madri exclaimed, clapping her hands together and wearing a proud smile. "You need a tour of the place! That's perfect! It'll put everything into perspective!"

Pilar looked to Seth, who just grabbed the bridge of his nose. "The girl's nuts."

Pilar looked over Madri again, and chuckled. "I knew I remembered you. You're the girl with the batons."

She waived a flippant hand. "Nice to meet you! You know, um . . . again!"

"Pleasure's yours, I'm sure."

"What a nice thing to say!" Madri looked to Seth, grinning. "You should try being nice like her, you know? She even gave me the chance to explain myself!"

"I can still kick you out of here," Seth answered.

"I wouldn't exactly stop him," Pilar added.

"Geez, you two are mean as hell."

"We try," Seth added.

After giving him a bit of a scowl, Madri turned her attention right back to Pilar. "So hey! Having that battle suit must be cool, huh?"

Neither Pilar nor Seth uttered even a word back. They just pointed to the door. Madri didn't put up much of a defense aside from an audible whine and a roll of her eyes. "All right, all right, fine! But I'll be back to quiz you about stuff! I don't know what stuff, but it'll be . . . stuff!"

Pilar remembered the snarky little smile Madri had given her earlier and returned one of her own. "I'm totally looking forward to it!"

Sticking out her tongue at her like a defeated five year old was Madri's last line of defense before she left, leaving the siblings in the room.

"Well," Seth started, "I'm not even sure where to go from there."

"Seth, I don't understand something."

"Considering who was just in here? Not surprised."

"Seth."

He sat on the opposite side of her bed, arms folded as he glared at the doorway awaiting any more surprise visitors. "I don't understand anything about them, either. The only one of them to even give a damn until a few days ago was Agent Rose, so this sudden burst of concern is off-putting."

"You knew Agent Rose already?"

"Yeah. Not by choice, but yeah." Seth rubbed his neck. "He was the one that contacted me when Dad, uh, vanished. He knew where you were." He leaned against the counter near the window, standing at Pilar's bedside. "I kept off and on contact with him after that, especially the first year you started living with me."

"Needed advice, I take it?"

"Yeah. I think I was calling everybody I knew for parenting advice by that point. Agent Rose, though . . ."

Noticing that her brother was glaring at the door ahead of them as though a monster lay in wait on the other side, Pilar looked to the doorway as well. "Waiting for the next interruption?"

"Nah," he whispered back. "That Madri chick is probably standing on the other side of the door, listening in. Probably with some sort of really expensive mic."

Pilar's lips said "great minds" perfectly as she tapped the side of her head. They were on the exact same page.

Seth stood up, and quietly made his way to the door. Once he was firmly pressed against it, he inhaled a bit before yelling right at the metal frame: "How you holdin' up out there, girl?"

They could hear Madri fall over herself from the shock, literally screaming obscenities as she tried to right herself. Seth quickly made his way back to his seat, and sat nonchalant while Pilar again found herself trying to hold in laughter. This was absolutely a side of him she'd never expected to see, but she had to admit . . .she'd never really tried to, either.

When Madri burst back into the room completely unkempt, the laughter escaped from Pilar's body before she could contain it.

"You are so mature," Madri snapped at Seth before slamming the door behind her, opting to stay in the room. She was still straightening herself.

"Eavesdropping is bad for you," he retorted. "But if you're going to do it? Probably maybe kinda try not to be so obvious, yeah?"

Pilar finally calmed her laughter completely and cleared her throat. "In any case, maybe it's good we talk directly to you. I've . . . no, we've got questions that need some answering. You might actually prove qualified to answer them, after all."

"Oh, how flattering of you two!" Madriella Mars huffed before plopping back onto the foot of the bed. "Fine. Let's try this again, then. From the top. But could you speak up please? Think ya annihilated my eardrums."

27

He needed a plan to escape.

Confronting Hyde directly wouldn't get him any reprieve, that was certain. No, all that seemed to do was further push Hyde to torture him. Hyde and his comrades were in a fantastically poor position, after all. They were tied to Hyde's power, and to his bidding, but they weren't allowed to die until Hyde deemed it so. He himself had already tried more times than he cared to admit to push Hyde into killing him, but each time . . .

"No, no. Not yet. You do not leave that easily."

He had already been defeated by that vigilante once, and he could tell that Hyde knew something about her, but wouldn't share it with any of them. Why? Why would he hold a trump card like that so closely to his chest?

There was only one logical conclusion to draw from that.

Hyde knew that the girl had the potential to kill them all. Her accidental release of that power during their assault was proof. The only reason he could even have this one moment of clarity was because that girl had injured Hyde so badly. Normally, any of his thoughts were easily readable due to their connection to him.

It wasn't as though it was something they'd volunteered for. They, at one point, were captives—experiments. Leech seemed to be the only one who still remembered that now. There had been six of them at the start. One had been killed by Hyde outright, as an example. Then his control had tightened. The others had stayed loyal out of fear, and slowly . . . their humanity had gone.

Leech wouldn't dare act as though he cared about other humans at this point—they were nothing but food to him now—but becoming some lifeless pawn, some pitiful zombie that followed only his cravings and the words of his foolish master?

He refused.

But, he needed a plan. That part . . . that was the difficult part. Due to their attachment through the Indigo, anything he could think up would be snuffed before he could enact it. This was the first opportunity in years to be independent of that old fool. It wouldn't last long, though. He needed to figure out his goal, and figure it out fast.

Of course. If I gain her suit and her power . . .

He had to keep some way of remembering his goal close at hand, something that would not be traceable once the Indigo reactivated completely— something it would not grasp; could not understand.

He scoured his lab space, stumbling about in the dark like a dog mad with hunger, looking for the bloody meat its nose could smell all about. He lumbered to a table far in the back of the darkened room and latched on to a knife in his excitement. On his right arm, he rested the blade, grinning madly.

"It's you that shamed me, and you that freed me." His eyes looked to the blade he held as he plunged it into his skin. And slowly, within his arm's flesh, he carved his note.

KILL BUG

It wouldn't be long before the network was fully repaired and his body and mind were trapped in Hyde's influence again. But that scar, that would be his reminder, his flashback. That was the weakness he'd found in Indigo long ago, after all. And, to his knowledge, only he knew of it.

He needed to absorb her all on his own. She and that suit of hers needed to be his. If he could meld that power into himself using Indigo, he could very well turn himself into an insanely powerful specimen—the ability to not only control Indigo, but to erase it, all wrapped in one body.

There would be no question. He would be perfect. And he could wipe them all out, those so-called allies of his.

He salivated at the thought as he stared at the dripping wound. "Kill Bug, kill Bug, kill Bug, kill Bug . . . ," he continued to utter the phrase under his breath.

He could feel the network restarting. He could sense the Indigo in his body beginning to stir, as his master had healed enough to establish the link once more. The moment he did, anything Leech spoke or thought would become a live spark transmitted straight to Hyde. His thoughts would no longer be his own.

But Leech had been preparing for that for years. The others were far more loyal pets, especially that spider. Leech's loyalty had never existed, and Hyde knew that. But, despite the likelihood that Leech would kill Hyde with his own bare hands if given the chance and the power, he was also the best at ensuring he was never caught. After all, this wasn't the first time Hyde had been severed from the Indigo.

Leech fell to one knee, grasping his head as the surges of electricity ricocheted through him. The nanomachines that made up the bulk of the Indigo were fantastic creatures, able to jack themselves directly into the nerves of their hosts without hesitation and transmit perfectly to and from their lobes. Widow's scream reverberated from halfway across the compound. Leech couldn't help smiling when it reached his ears, despite the pain ripping his mind asunder.

And then . . . as if it were nothing but a dream, an immense calm swelled. His entire body relaxed. And with that calm, his every thought became nearly unified with the others.

He stood. "Lord Hyde awaits our arrival," he muttered as he marched out of the door.

Within each footprint was a single spatter of blood.

28

It's good to be back home in this apartment.

When they walked in the hall, their neighbors across the way—a young couple who had been there for about a year—happily greeted them on their way out. Of course, they were probably more than a bit curious to see four of them headed into the three-bedroom apartment, when for the longest time only Seth and Pilar had ever been there.

Seth chuckled a bit at their inquiry. "She overdid it at a school event and hurt her leg. This is our new roommate, Bianca," he gestured to Bianca. "And this is her friend from school, Zoe."

Pilar was a bit startled by how naturally he told the cover story. *Way to sell a lie, Seth. Just when I was starting to really trust you too.* She tried to keep her smirk internal, but she was sure the little cocky grin had leaked to her face, at least a bit.

They laughed at Pilar's apparent misfortune, but the guy seemed pretty genuine with his well-wishes. "You'll be done hobbling around here in no time," he added. "If you guys need anything, just let us know."

"We'll, um, do just that," Bianca added, after finally fiddling with the lock for five minutes and getting it open. "Wrong key," she mumbled, handing the keys back to Seth.

"Oh yeah. Silly me."

"Reminds me, I need to get that key duplicated."

As they closed the door behind them, Seth handed the house key back to her. "Have fun."

"You don't need it tonight?"

"To go where? I'm chillin' here until she's good, at the very least."

For a brief moment, Pilar was slightly disappointed hearing that, thinking it meant she couldn't sneak out and go hunting around like she usually would. Her brain took a moment to recall the fact she couldn't if she wanted to, and even if she could, well, he already knew everything.

She still hadn't gotten used to all that. And she realized too, what he'd done. He'd taken time off, just to be around while she recuperated.

She was far less used to that idea.

The apartment itself felt like a utopia to Pilar when they walked in. The windows were open, and two fans were on in the living room. After dealing with the sticky air that had built up outside, the cooled apartment was invigorating and inviting.

"So, what exactly am I cooking again?"

They argued for a few moments amongst themselves, but eventually Bianca gave the deciding vote to Pilar, "since she's the injured party here and she probably could use it, I'll make steak this go-round."

"She gets to use her injury as an excuse to get what she wants. Great moral lesson there," Seth laughed.

"Battle scars," Pilar answered back, very satisfied with herself.

"I've got more of those, if you remember."

Pilar rolled her eyes. "Yeah, yeah."

"Don't take that so seriously, sis." He'd quickly made his way in front of her, moving things out of the way and opening the door to her bedroom. "Take it easy, okay? No practicing acrobatics in your room or anything like that."

"Oh my God, you are such a goof." Though she'd said that while shaking her head, again she smirked at him.

"I'll bring dinner to you once it's done," Zoe added before hastily leaving the room. Pilar assumed it was to grab her laptop and bring it to her.

Seth sat her down on her bed, then made his way towards the door. "Everything alright?"

She nodded. "Yeah. Thanks."

"If you need anything, let me know."

Pilar almost didn't say anything, but eventually found the bit of courage she needed.

"Seth?"

"Yeah?"

She couldn't understand why she was so nervous, but she stuttered for a second. "T-Thank you for taking me in. And taking care of me."

"What . . . ?" He laughed a bit. "I swear we had this discussion already."

"I know. But it wasn't until the other day that I understood why we had that discussion. I just . . .wanted to thank you honestly this time."

"Don't need to thank me. But can I ask you an honest question?"

"What would be a dishonest question?" The look he gave her made her clear her throat and try again, without the snark. "Yeah, sure."

"What made you hate me for so long? We've been living together for years. I don't remember giving you any reason to think I didn't care."

She looked to the bed, trying to find a comfortable sight while she gathered her thoughts. After all, he'd asked her something she still wasn't fully certain of herself. But rather than run away from it, she decided to tell him just that.

"I don't really have a concrete answer. For the first few months I was just trying to figure out what happened when Dad vanished. Why I ended up in the basement of the lab by myself. And why I couldn't remember anything about the few days up to that point. I didn't want to talk. I just wanted to be left alone."

She peeked at him for a moment, but found herself looking back to the bedsheets again when she realized what she was about to admit.

"After that? It was . . . spite. I never let go of the day you and Dad fought. I still don't know if I really have."

"That wasn't a fight." Seth sighed. "That was me lashing out. And I shouldn't have. Especially not with you right there."

"Then do you still think . . . Dad had something to do with mom's death?"

"Not anymore. I haven't for a long time. And I wish I had the chance to talk to him about it before, well," he hesitated. "Yeah. And it didn't help that I just left without coming back to talk to you. You didn't deserve that. Not after what we all had just gone through."

Now it was Seth who couldn't seem to look her in the eye. "I was an ass. Acted like a brat. And, without even thinking about it I took it out on you in the worst way possible."

"By not saying anything." Pilar folded her arms.

"Yeah."

"That's why I thought I was just a burden to you. That you took me in because you felt you had to, not because you wanted to. And I hated that. And I hated you for that. I decided I'd deal with you as little as possible. I couldn't just avoid you once I lived here, and I couldn't just act like I didn't care at all. You're still my brother."

"But you could just keep me out emotionally." He nodded, confirming his own thought. "And me being me, I just . . . tried to bury myself in my work. 'It'll turn around eventually. She doesn't hate me.'" He smirked. "I never was the best at lying, not even to myself. I just didn't know how to really talk to you. How to say anything."

"I guess," she added. "Like you said, you became a parent."

"Yup. Not something I expected."

She exhaled, finally expelling some of the guilt and doubt she had, and looking her brother in the eyes. "I guess we both needed to grow up a little."

"A lot. We still have to. But, we came a long way in the past couple weeks."

Pilar rubbed her neck. If the past few days of events had done anything, it had given her the evidence she often sought in regards to her brother's intentions. Her mind went back to the photograph Bianca had showed her, and she unconsciously grinned as she thought about it. *Maybe things can be closer to how they were way back then.*

She looked to Seth, looking right in his eyes, unwavering. "I'm going to put the suit on again once I'm better. You understand that, right?"

"Heh. That." He nodded. "Understand it? Nah. More like, I'm just going to deal with it. It's your decision." His eyes wandered for a moment. "I don't like it, not even slightly. But hey, Dad—in all his infinite wisdom—thought you needed to do this. I'm not going to waste our time arguing about it. And really, what can I say?" He leaned against the door's frame. "You're doing what I tried to do."

"Which was?"

"Fight back."

She was surprised to hear him say that. If anything, she'd figured he'd be even more adamant about her putting the suit away for good once they got out of the hospital. To hear him admit that even he wanted to fight back . . .

"I'm gonna do some homework, for once."

Seth left her with a sincere, worried grin. "Not sure how many times I'm going to have to repeat this but, get some rest. Seriously, sis. Just rest for now."

"I'll try. Honestly."

29

Dinner had long since come and gone. Zoe and Pilar were in the bedroom with their laptops, unable to shake off the itch to search for whatever they could on Aegis and the history behind them, as well as the Cloaks.

Unfortunately, they weren't getting very far by conventional means. Information on the Cloaks was nonexistent. Barely any news coverage was aimed at them. Whenever there was a news story that could have involved them, it was blamed on "other parties" that wouldn't strike as much fear into the city.

Meanwhile, Aegis had plenty of information out there, readily available. The problem for Pilar and Zoe was that the information was usually wrong. It was exactly what they didn't need: information that gave them no clue to anything connected to the Cloaks or even a hint about their employees. There was barely a passing mention of Evandrake Hyde or Emmanuel Sands.

They still continued their research, hoping that something somewhere would spark a memory, a thought, an idea, a sneeze . . . something more than what they were getting. All they'd earned was agitation from running into so many dead ends.

"Not finding anything on your dad at all." Zoe looked up from her laptop, staring at the full moon outside. "Any ideas of what might have happened to him? Are there any news reports that caught your attention? Anything special?"

"Not really, Miss Twenty Questions, no."

Zoe had to laugh a little at that answer. "Sorry. It's what I do."

Pilar shook her head, then turned her attention to the small laptop in front of her. The sound of the laptop snapping shut alerted her friend. "Zoe? There's something I've been meaning to ask you."

Zoe looked up for a moment, then back to her own laptop screen, smiling. "Ask away."

"What's your real reason for doing this?"

She nearly choked on her own breath. "Why wouldn't I be doing this?"

"Because even I wouldn't be doing this if I really didn't feel I had to." Pilar's eyes didn't waver as she stared at Zoe.

Zoe's glance lowered a bit as she looked to her own laptop. She wasn't sure she wanted to tell Pilar. *No, she deserves at least some sort of explanation by now. I can't just keep everything from her. I need to tell her.* She inhaled heavily, her chest inflating visibly before she exhaled.

"My dad has been trying to resolve a case involving Aegis for years. It's been haunting him. Problem is, Aegis is in real tight with the RCPD."

"That's not surprising. It's why they don't interfere with each other, right?"

Zoe brushed some of her loose hair from her face. "Yeah. It's also what makes it hard to get the RCPD to really do anything to check Aegis. They know Aegis can usually handle the threats they can't."

"Go on."

"The case he was working on was against your dad. But, eventually he became my dad's best source of information on Aegis. Professor Sands knew everything that was wrong there and he needed it to be stopped."

"So you picked up your dad's old case?"

Zoe nodded. "When your dad disappeared, my dad's job was put in turmoil. And I took it upon myself to find out what happened." Her gaze shifted to the window as she tapped her fingers on her lower lip. "I found out, through my own research, that Aegis was into some seriously grimy stuff."

"Uh, 'grimy stuff'?"

"Yeah. Grimy. Dirty. Bad."

"I know what grimy is."

Zoe wasn't going to argue the finer points of that. "So anyway, there was a lot of hush-hush experimental-type stuff. I hadn't heard about Indigo, but I'm also still going over everything my dad went over."

"How long ago did you start?"

Zoe looked to her laptop, then to Pilar, a bit of a grin on her face as she thought it over. "It wasn't until the start of this year that I picked it up. As for the costume? Maybe two weeks ago."

"Why the wait?"

"Not being able to find anything on the case, all the frustration . . . my dad finally retired this year. But we all knew he wasn't ready to. He thought he could walk away from it, but he was still sneaking in whatever time he could reviewing his case notes. It was driving him insane." She looked to Pilar again. "You're really the last lead either of us had."

"And I don't remember anything surrounding my dad's disappearance, so I'm not exactly much help."

Zoe reached out and gently shook Pilar's uninjured leg. "Hey, that's not true, you know. You've been helpful in a lot of other ways. And even if you weren't, this is about much more than the case now."

Pilar bowed her head a bit. "So, what was your plan from there?"

"Donning a costume was the first step, but I really had no idea where the hell to go from there." She looked back to Pilar. "Then you showed up. Or rather, the Bug Girl showed up."

"You know I hate that name."

Zoe laughed at that, knowing it would get under Pilar's skin a bit. Still, she continued on without bothering to correct herself. "I knew who you were from studying the case for so long, but the Bug? That was new." She leaned forward a bit, resting her right elbow on the desk and then resting her chin on her palm. Her eyes looked squarely into Pilar's own. "Essentially, you're a part of the case. I'm helping to protect my only possible witness. Having that witness also be my best ally is a bonus."

Pilar fell back onto her bed, staring at the ceiling. "I see."

"You're getting the wrong idea." Zoe leaned back in her seat as well, looking at the ceiling just as Pilar did. "You're thinking I'm using you and that's the only reason we're friends."

Pilar's gaze darted back to Zoe. "Is that true?"

Zoe smiled as bright as she could. "Yup. It's absolutely the only reason we're friends. If it weren't for that, I wouldn't even bother talking to you."

Pilar couldn't keep from smiling back at that. "I'm rubbing off on you."

"Friends do that."

"Okay, okay. Enough with the friend stuff. Getting too mushy." Pilar sat back upright, propping her laptop back open.

"So, any useful information?"

"From everything I've searched? Nothing." Pilar rubbed her brow as she thought. "Our best bet is probably going to be returning to the lab. The Andromeda system might be able to hack more clues than anything else."

"Well, you can't really go there in your present condition."

"That's where you come in. I need you to be at the lab tomorrow, okay?"

Pilar's mischievous glare was startling. Zoe wasn't certain what to expect, but at the very least, at that point she'd learned to trust the girl more often than not. After all, the last time she had, she'd wound up in some of the most advanced armor created in the world. All crafted by one sixteen-year-old genius inheriting her father's work.

Zoe looked to her partner, a nervous smile on her face. "Uh, sure, yeah. I'll be there."

30

"Pilar . . . what on Earth are you, um, wearing?"

Pilar knew full well that Seth was referring to her baggy pink pajama pants and shirt. It didn't help that she had her goggles on while indoors. "Good morning to you too, dear brother."

"I suppose that translates to 'I like my weird-scientist-stuck-in-a-bad-'80s-movie look,' right?"

"How did you get all that from 'good morning'?" Pilar answered his insult with a scowl.

He shrugged in reply. "It's a gift."

"Well, hate to interrupt our lovely morning conversation, but I've got important things to do."

She tapped a button on the right side of her goggles, activating a "screen" in the upper-right corner of her vision. She could see everything that Gilgamesh could see in the lab on this miniature display in her goggles, similar to the way the HUD in the Bug Suit's helmet worked.

Zoe was at the lab as requested, though she seemed hesitant about being there. "So, I'm not sure this is a good idea, you know? I mean, the Cloaks could come back at any time and attack, right?"

"We don't have that to worry about," Pilar added. "The lab is the most secure place to be right now. And there's a lot of work to do at the lab. Particularly, I need to figure out how to counter this Indigo stuff, and get back to work on repairing the Bug Suits."

"Uh, Bug? It's secure how?"

"Would you just relax already? It's secure. The only way anyone not authorized is getting in is through a defense system grid that even I couldn't get past with my suit. No one else will bother."

"Ah, I get it." Zoe looked into Gilgamesh's eyes as if to see Pilar. That was impossible however, as the control goggles only worked one way. When she did look through Gilgamesh's eyes, the bent lenses made her look warped in Pilar's view.

Pilar held back as much of her laughter as she could.

"Hey! Why are you laughing?" Zoe didn't hide the fact she was insulted.

Pilar tried to wave it away like a dying campfire. "Nothing, nothing! Let's just get to work on that liquid, okay?"

Zoe huffed a bit, folding her arms while giving Pilar a snarky little grin. "You've changed."

"Huh? I have? Since when?"

"Hard to pinpoint exactly." Zoe gave Gilgamesh a very cautious pat on his head. "Well Gilgamesh, are you ready to get to work?"

"This will be strange indeed," Gilgamesh replied, his electronic voice sounding as though it had raised half an octave. "But I welcome the chance to assist you and Miss Sands in any way I can, Miss Shinomori."

Pilar smiled, hearing the conversation through her goggles. "Well. I didn't think flattering me was in your programming."

"What is this 'flattering' you are speaking of, Miss Pilar?"

Pilar sighed, grabbing the bridge of her nose a bit. "I'll explain it someday. Maybe. Anyhow, we should honestly get to—" Yet another interruption came, this time a knock on the front door of their apartment.

Pilar wanted to punch a hole in the nearest wall.

"Could you get that, sis?" Seth yelled from upstairs.

"Why should I get that? I'm in my pajamas!"

"Well hey, I'm in the bathroom! Sounds like my situation is way more awkward!"

"You didn't have to share that!" Pilar yelled back.

"What the hell, Pilar? You asked! It's not like I said I'm in the bathroom taking a whiz or something!"

Pilar tried her best to ignore that, quickly heading for the front door to get the intrusion out of the way as soon as possible. She'd pulled her goggles off of her face, to keep herself from looking too strange at that time in the morning.

The woman that greeted her was a familiar, annoying sight.

Pilar's eyes rolled as far back as they could. "Oh great. You." She cleared her throat, then forced a smile to appear on her face. "Hello, Agent Mars."

"Hey, there's no need to be so formal! Madri or Mars, either of them works fine!" She quickly stepped inside. "Mind if I do?"

Pilar rubbed her forehead as she eyed the girl. "Because there was definitely a point in asking."

Mars at least looked more like an agent that day, wearing a black business suit with a white blouse, though her tie was nearly undone and she generally looked unkempt. The peach girl was oddly bubbly as ever as she peeked around their apartment. "For some reason I expected this place to be a lot more, uh . . ."

"Messy?" Pilar already knew what she was thinking, because Pilar thought the same herself.

Madri plopped onto the tan sofa. "Guess I don't need to beat around the bush with you, right? Yeah. Messy. Considering the two of you are always so busy and all. When do you have time to clean?"

"That's not how it stays this way."

"Then how?"

Pilar folded her arms. "We're barely here."

Pilar gestured for Madri to take a seat at the kitchen table rather than the sofa, and she seemed to happily oblige. "Sorry. It just looked so comfy, you know?"

"Sure." Pilar joined Mars at the table, keeping her arms folded and her scowl ever present. "So, why are you here, exactly?"

"Well, it's probably better if I wait until Rose gets here." Just as she finished that sentence, as if on cue, another rap echoed off the front door.

Madri herself jumped up, heading for the door as casually as possible. "Oh, don't worry, I got it!"

Pilar could only stare at her. She wasn't sure if she was amazed by how comfortable and free-spirited Mars was, or outraged by her having the audacity to answer her front door.

Either way, Madri let Rose in.

Pilar had at least something she could reliably make fun of as Madri closed the door behind Agent Rose. "My parents told me never to let in strange secret agents who frequently wear bad Hawaiian shirts. Sorry, but you've gotta go." She pointed at the garish pink shirt Rose wore so proudly.

"You wouldn't know I frequently wore these shirts if I were a stranger."

Pilar's eyes went wide hearing that from him, of all people. *Did he just jokingly catch my mistake?*

"Someone's in a good mood," Madri shot back at him, that cheeky grin of hers still permeating her face. "You got a raise, didn't you? After all these years, I knew you'd get it!"

Pilar almost burst into laughter when Rose glanced at her. His eyes seemed to say, *I am holding everything back so I don't snap at this girl.*

Pilar again pointed them to the kitchen table, just as Seth finally returned from the bathroom.

"Abel Rose. Not sure I should be worried or panicked to see you." Seth's glance fell to Madri, and he let out a bit of a laugh. "And you again. Kinda surprised to see you here."

"Well, I mean, I do work with Rose and he's technically my partner right now. Kinda necessary I tag along with him."

Pilar immediately got to business. "So let's get to the meaningful part of this."

Rose leaned back in his seat, arms folded. "We need to start getting you two moved out of here."

Pilar looked to Seth. "So much for recovery time."

Madri shrugged at that one. "Well, you two can't really be surprised by that, right? I mean, from what Zoe said about the Cloaks after you did the whole, you know, beam-thing? They were pretty much wrecked. They probably just went to lick their wounds for a little bit and they'll be ready to go at it again."

Rose gave a nod. "They'll probably send everything they can at you both. And we have no idea of how many people they'll kill to get at Seth's power again."

Seth sat at the table opposite Madri. "I'm assuming the reason you're here is because something happened that moved up the timetable."

Pilar hoped against all hope they'd answer with a firm "no, we're just being cautious." But she knew full well that was unlikely. When she saw Rose look to her, then back to Seth, then nod in silence, she could feel the stress in her own mind start building.

Pilar tried not to give away her worry as she watched Seth grab a fistful of his locks, whining a bit under his breath. "Well this is perfect timing, isn't it? I'm steadily getting weaker, and Pilar is still recovering."

Madri peeked over at Pilar. "Those robot roaches you guys fought? They're what we've been dealing with this whole time."

Pilar nearly choked hearing that. "Then the times I've been following you guys to see what the big deal was about, was those things?"

Madri looked to Rose, as if to gain permission. He again nodded, not saying a word. Madri continued, "The RCPD isn't equipped to handle 'em. We are. So, they've been letting us patrol and work with them to stop those things. Back before we ran into you, they were just kinda showing up here and there in the city, destroying property that seemed to be random."

"Seemed to be?" Pilar asked.

"We realized right around the night me and you fought that there was a pattern to their attacks. They were hitting near the homes of high-ranking Aegis employees. The area around my parents' house was their target that night."

Pilar noticed immediately that, for the first time since they'd met, Madri wasn't leaping out of her seat with excitement. She looked defeated. Perhaps even more so, she looked angry.

"Gathering intel." Pilar had almost forgot about Zoe on the communicator in her headset until she'd said that. "They're gathering intel on Aegis employees to try to narrow something down. Attacking certain areas means questioning. Questioning means—"

"Luring people out," Pilar concluded. She realized the others weren't privy to her conversation with Zoe as she said that, but they seemed to get the point regardless.

"That's our guess. The last time there was a high concentration of those robots in an area, we fought 'em." Madri sat back, then exhaled. "The last time a bunch of them gathered, that Leech dude showed up. Don't think I need to tell you how that went."

Pilar quickly put it all together.

"They've been spotted near here."

Rose looked to Pilar. Even with those sunglasses on, she could just feel his eyes glaring at her.

"More than we've ever seen in one place."

"Wait," Pilar heard Zoe preparing to object over their communication link. "They made it sound like they were debuting those things when we fought them. Now we're saying they've been around?"

"They debuted that version," Pilar added. "The versions we fought that night were probably made stronger on purpose. New models made to deal with Aegis agents more efficiently, and to deal with our suits."

The silence that struck was maddening to Pilar. It gave her time to think, to realize the truth. They knew who she was now. She would likely never be safe again.

It was always something she had to consider when she put on that suit, that searching for her father, trailing Aegis, it may all lead to endangering anyone around her. But she'd never expected it to happen so suddenly.

There really was a stark difference between what she planned, the results she imagined, and what would actually come to fruition.

"You need to make sure you stay off the radar. Period," Agent Rose reiterated to Pilar. "We have got to move all of you sooner than expected, but we can't have any of you doing something out of the ordinary that might clue these robots of his into where you're at."

Pilar looked to Rose, smirking a bit at that. "I don't have much of a choice. The Bug Suit isn't even repaired yet, though Zoe's about to help me with that right now." She tapped on her goggles.

"She and Gilgamesh are at the lab right now helping me work on the suits."

"Gilgamesh?" Madri rubbed her brow.

Pilar raised her hand in a flippant manner. "Robotic lab assistant. Long story. Not important right now. So, just how much time do we have and where are we going to go?"

Rose tilted his sunglasses downward slightly. "Not sure on a time frame, but we've likely got a couple days at best. As for where? Not sure yet. The best place we've got available is an Aegis site near the north end of the city."

"No offense, but I'm not sure I want to stay anywhere that has the name Aegis in it right now." Pilar leaned forward. "Cloaks aren't exactly happy with you guys, either. And even if what you're saying is true? I don't know what the rest of Aegis is up to. I've kinda got outstanding issues with them. You're about the only one I kinda trust right now."

She peeked over at Madri. "I guess you too, maybe. Still a work in progress there."

Rose smiled back at her. "I'm flattered." He looked to Madri, then back to Pilar, his eyes unwavering behind the shades. "Suppose it's about time you realized that, too."

"Realized what?"

Rose folded his arms. "How did you think your dad's old lab was suddenly operational again?"

As soon as he'd said those words, Pilar realized just how ridiculous her efforts had been from the start. "Aegis has been keeping it going all this time?"

Rose looked to Madri, and she answered in his stead. "Nah, Aegis doesn't even know that lab exists. Once the suit was seen as operational, a certain someone within the company decided to give you the bit of a boost you needed, to see what you would do once everything was active again."

"A certain someone within the company?" Pilar looked to her brother, eyes wide and bright at hearing those words. *Could it be my dad? Has he been hiding in plain sight all this time?*

"It's not Sands," Rose added, "if that's what you're thinking."

"Then who?"

Agent Rose was firm with his answer. "The director."

"What?"

"Our boss. The director of Aegis."

Madri raised a wagging finger. "Ah, well, now, to be more correct, she's the director of our division of Aegis: Security and Sciences."

Pilar's eyes widened at hearing that. *Security and Sciences? Dad's Division?*

"Why would your director even . . ." Pilar was at a loss for words. All that time she'd thought she was tailing Aegis, that she'd been on the right trail, following the leads they had to find the truth she needed, only to find out now that she'd only been able to do it because they'd allowed her to? Because the director made it possible?

If the director had never given that lab power . . . Pilar didn't want to admit it, but it made perfect sense when she looked back at it all. The lab itself just suddenly returning to full power had always seemed off. Still, until that point it had been one of those things she wished she could solve. *But I overlooked it, I ignored it because I wanted to believe it was Dad's doing.*

Never in her mind did she think that Aegis's director would be her benefactor.

Still, it stung to know that the director of the very company she'd suspected were hiding something was also helping to keep her battle suit operational.

She needed to focus for now. There would be time to solve all the logistics of that mess once the Cloaks were no longer a threat to the people around them.

There was really only one place she knew would be safe from their onslaught, if they appeared again.

"The loft in the lab would still be a better place," Pilar concluded. "At least there, I can guarantee that the lab's built-in defenses will be able to repel the Cloaks and those Roach-bots if they return."

"There's that, and the fact it's pretty far from the city limits," Seth added. "I mean I'd rather stay here too, but we've got to go somewhere, I can't think of any place better than that."

Pilar was certain that her bewilderment was obvious on her face. "Did you just say you don't mind going to the lab to live?"

"Temporarily, no, I don't have a problem with it," Seth answered back. "As soon as this all blows over, I want to get back to my nice, normal life, but at this point staying here much longer is probably asking for hell."

"All right, then. It's settled, right? That's where we're going to stay at," Pliar answered.

"Yup." Seth stood. "We should start getting ready to move as soon as possible. I'm talking tomorrow morning, before sunrise."

Pilar nodded. "That sounds feasible, even for me right now." She looked to Rose, her crooked little smile making its way onto her face. "So, think you can give us a hand?"

Rose stood from his seat. "Me and a few other agents. I'll make all the necessary prep on my side."

"Prep?"

"I'm not letting this thing get out of hand. Getting agents ready to escort you there, getting protection for this place ready just in case there is another attack? It's going to take some doing." He grabbed his phone from his left pants pocket. "Gotta call the boss. Sure she'll be thrilled with the change of plans."

"Just who is she, anyway?"

"Director Delacruz." Madri looked back to Rose, and her smile widened. "The two of them go way back. I'm talking like, way back."

"So your boss is your wife," Pilar said, eyeing Rose as she did so.

He laughed outright at that. "Nah. We've known each other since grade school, though."

Seth heaved heavily, stood from his seat, then slowly marched towards his room.

Pilar could tell that despite his answer being so logical, he really wasn't fond of their plan to move to the lab. She found herself wishing she could do something more to help him. She knew just how hard he'd worked to keep everything afloat, and after everything they'd talked about, she appreciated it that much more.

And yet, here he was, being forced to leave what he'd maintained for years, all on the whims of a fanatical group of science-gone-wrong criminals and their obsession with his power.

She found it more amazing that he'd managed to keep it hidden for that long.

And he did so because he was trying to protect me. Guess that means it's my turn.

Pilar stood up and slid the goggles back on her eyes. She stretched, and cracked her knuckles before reactivating the audio connection again. "Zoe? Gil? You two there?"

Zoe ran back into the camera's view. "We're still here. You ready?"

"Yeah. We've got a lot of work to do today."

31

Zoe's help was far more fruitful than Pilar ever expected. If there was one thing she could give Zoe, despite not being as technologically sound as Pilar herself was, it was that she wasn't hard to teach at all. Pilar was worried that teaching Zoe—or anyone really—would be nearly impossible for her low level of patience. It wasn't as though she had plenty of experience teaching others. After all, who would she have taught?

By nightfall, the enhancements were nearly complete, something Pilar hadn't expected. Another thing she'd had to admit was that Zoe was much better at coming up with the aesthetic side of the designs than Pilar ever would have been. Pilar also hadn't expected to be so worn out before the sun set, either.

Zoe decided to head back to Seth and Pilar's apartment, Bianca picking her up on the way home from her own work at the hospital. They were quickly informed of the situation by Agent Rose, and without hesitation agreed to help make the move to the loft above the lab.

Zoe had to be told numerous times not to worry about Gilgamesh though, to which she made it abundantly clear that they weren't being mindful of how he "felt." While it seemed necessary to remind Zoe that he was a robot and didn't "feel" anything, Pilar knew she had a point. It wasn't his feelings that Pilar was worried about, though. After all, without them there, he was practically sitting in the lab either powered down, doing much of nothing, cleaning up, or doing maintenance on any number of things in the lab—menial tasks at best. Pilar had never really gotten around to checking his programming in case of emergency.

Still, she figured that he'd be much more helpful in the lab than in the apartment. And if the Cloaks did attack, Gilgamesh actually did have some combat functions available, even if they were a bit underwhelming.

Pilar lay in bed, restless. With everything that was going on, she couldn't settle herself. Her thoughts began to drift to her missing father. *Where was he? What really happened?*

From what she'd been told, Seth had found her in the lowest level of the lab, crying. The strange thing was, she didn't remember anything of that day, or even the day before.

What was even more strange was that despite whatever had occurred there, she had no fear of re-entering the rest of the lab. Even with as little as she knew of the human psyche, one thing that was certain in her mind was that most people had an innate fear of returning to the same place where something traumatic had happened. Perhaps whatever happened, whatever had caused her father's disappearance, didn't happen in the lab at all.

He'd disappeared on her fourteenth birthday, that much she did recall perfectly. It had made birthdays a special bit of hell for her for the past few years.

Her next thought was that perhaps he was trying to hide. But, why hide from her? He had to know that his help would be beyond necessary considering the situation they were in, and yet he still hadn't shown up.

Unless, of course, he was counting on Pilar to continue his work while he investigated further in secret. Perhaps he'd been captured trying to find out the ultimate weakness in the Cloaks' plan. Or, perhaps he feared being captured.

What the hell is their plan? What is their end goal?

Her stomach wouldn't stop bothering her, and after a while of lying in bed in agony, she realized why: the burritos Seth had bought everyone for dinner. She knew they should have waited for Bianca to cook, but of course, that would require patience.

Guess that wouldn't have worked out anyway, though. After all, half the stuff here is already packed. We're moving in the morning. Cooking was out of the question.

She forced herself out of bed, making her way towards the restroom. She eventually dragged her body back to her room.

Don't remember it being this cold in here. Even in her baggy pink pajama pants and pink camisole, she was shivering in her own arms; she searched the room for the source of the frigid air. She fixed her gaze on the open window on the right side of the bed. She looked to the floor next to her, where Zoe lay, and realized that it was likely she who had opened it while Pilar had made the trip to the bathroom.

Pilar slammed the window shut, intentionally trying to wake Zoe, if she could. Her plan was a success. Zoe darted awake, glaring at the window, then at Pilar.

"Pilar?" Zoe sounded miserable in her drowsy stupor.

"It's cold." Pilar slipped back under her comforter, and rolled over to face away from Zoe.

"Geez." Zoe's laugh was obviously not one of humor this go-round. No, it was disdainful in every way. *I guess even she would be cranky after being awakened in such a way at 2:00 a.m.*

Zoe couldn't hide her foul mood. "You could have just closed it like any sane person would."

Pilar didn't care much, either. "What was that? Couldn't hear you over the harsh wind that started shooting through my room a few minutes ago."

"You're really going to be an ass about this?"

Pilar turned to face Zoe and was so pleased with herself that she smiled right at her. "Maybe."

"You know what? You do that." Zoe wrapped herself in her own white comforter, turning away from Pilar with a roll of her eyes.

Pilar realized then that she might have pushed her a bit too far. "What? You're seriously mad?"

Zoe looked back to her just enough to let Pilar see her agitated grin. "No. Not at all. Not the least bit angry."

"Oh come on. This isn't like you. And even you couldn't have been asleep that long if you opened the window."

Zoe turned her head just enough to peer at Pilar over the covers. "Of course it's nothing like me! You just woke me up at two o'clock in the—" She stopped herself. Her eyes widened. "You thought I opened the window."

"Right. That's what we're discu—"

"Pilar, I haven't been up from this spot since midnight."

Their eyes met, and paranoia quickly kicked in. They grabbed the little bit of weaponry they had available to them. The suits were nearby, but they weren't sure they'd need them yet. After all, it could simply be a normal, human burglar who picked a very bad place to sneak into.

No need to blow their identity on a random thief.

For the time being, they'd be able to do something to the possible intruders. Zoe had her smoke bombs and her utility belt holding her daggers, among other things. Pilar had her electric hammer. Without the Bug Suit on, the hammer was far more unwieldy, but she could certainly manage for the moment. Had it been a few days earlier, she'd probably still be in bed trying to figure out how to defend herself.

Slowly they crept towards the bedroom door, trying to hear the sounds outside the room above their own. Pilar's breathing hastened. Her heart was racing.

Zoe's hand was only a few inches away from the doorknob. She reached for it, barely placing her hand upon the cold metal.

A light knock on the door from the other side made them leap about ten feet back, tripping over themselves and ending up on the floor in a complete mess.

"Are you two okay in there?"

Great. That was who was on the other side of the door? Pilar couldn't help feeling like a moron.

"Yeah. Just peachy." Zoe groaned.

Bianca opened the door to the sight of Zoe clumsily trying to put her blue t-shirt back on properly, and Pilar, bum-over-head, looking at her upside down. Pilar was just thankful that she wore actual pajama pants to sleep—otherwise, it likely would have been a much more embarrassing moment. Zoe quickly straightened herself, nearly knocking Pilar over in the process as she stood. Once she was upright, she reached a hand to Pilar, helping her stand as well.

"Uh, do I even want to ask?" Bianca looked at them about how Pilar expected her to look at them: befuddled. "What in the bloody hell were you two doing?"

"Sorry. You sorta startled us." Zoe quickly made her way to the chair by Pilar's desk, where her jeans were, and hastily put them on. "We had this feeling that an intruder of some sort made their way in here."

"Really? That's what you're going with?"

Pilar nodded. "Yeah. We have a hunch." She pointed to the window with a scowl on her face. "This window wasn't open until a few moments ago."

"Uh, Pilar? That window's been open since two hours ago."

"I'm pretty sure it hasn't."

Bianca folded her arms. "I came in here to check on you and see how you were feeling, and you said you were sweating. So I opened the window."

"I did?"

"You did."

Zoe looked to Pilar and let loose a happy little grin that was just as condescending as ever.

"Oh, shut up," was Pilar's only retort.

Zoe put away her dagger. "Well, I'm awake, no use going back to sleep now. Wanna grab something to drink?"

Pilar shrugged. "Fine. I'll—"

If there was any question something had been wrong before, there certainly wasn't when the explosion erupted. They were all shaken off balance, and crashed to the floor as the building's foundation rocked from the impact. All sorts of fire alarms went off, and they could see the orange glow from outside the window.

"What in the hell was that?" Bianca's voice was abnormally shrill.

Pilar got to her feet as well as she could, although she was still fumbling around with her bruised body. The two falls she'd taken in a row hadn't helped ease her pain.

Pilar knew what this likely was. It wasn't some strange accident. This was an attack.

They're back early!

They immediately went to Emergency Plan A: pack up shop. Pilar packed her and Zoe's laptops into an empty backpack and tossed it to Bianca, then Pilar and Zoe grabbed their collapsed armor, which was still in its "backpack" forms. Pilar, for a moment, considered putting on the armor.

A second explosion hit much closer to home. "No time," Pilar yelled, scrambling back to her feet and following the others out.

Seth ran through the hallway right by them and headed for the front door. "I've already contacted Agent Rose, he and Madri and whoever else they can spare from Aegis are on their way!"

"Well I'm glad you had them on speed dial!" Pilar didn't stop moving for long. "I'm not complaining!"

He flung the front door open, and the couple from across the hall greeted him with panic. "We were just going to get you guys! You hear that explosion?"

Seth wasn't nearly as confused about the blast and didn't hide his emotional panic. "You've gotta get out of here, right now!"

"What? And just leave all our—"

"Yes! Leave it! Go!" Seth yelled at them. They didn't dare second-guess that. The two of them ducked outside the main hallway and made their way into the parking lot.

They could hear fire trucks pulling in from nearly every single side of the complex, police sirens ringing through the air.

"Good," said Seth. "They shouldn't be able to do much more than this for now. At least, I hope that's the case."

"We need to take a back way out," Zoe said to her friends in a low tone. "I'm carrying a sword and she's carrying a hammer. And I'm pretty sure there's enough incriminating crap on both these laptops to put us in jail for a few years. Oh yeah, and the suits. Let's not forget those."

"Whatever! Let's just start getting these people out of this building!" Seth started knocking on every door he could. Zoe followed suit, knocking on as many doors as she could on the opposite side. Their neighbors weren't exactly idiots, of course; most of them left their homes without much of a fight.

Pilar didn't know what to think. She danced between panic and anger with every second that passed. *Some part of me still hopes this was a freak accident.*

The sounds of three more fire trucks whipping around the building reached her ears. *Please let it be a freak accident!*

32

It was obvious that the man he held in his grasp had no clue what was happening. But that didn't matter. After all, he was simply an example.

Amidst the blaze, Mantis stood there, holding the man by his forehead, hoisting him a foot off the ground. Mantis's smile was still as innocent as ever, as though he had no idea the man he held there was in so much pain. The screams of pain did nothing to change his demeanor.

He was enjoying this.

"So, you really have never seen this man named Seth?" Mantis looked over to his two companions, who wore black-hooded cloaks similar to his own. "That's unfortunate, huh?"

Mantis's grip on the man's head strengthened. His cries rang throughout the burning building. The thick black smoke and dancing flames were suffocating his vision, not to mention his lungs. And to top it off, his head was being crushed.

"You're hungry, right? Go ahead, Leech." Mantis tossed the man to him like a slab of raw steak.

Leech looked to Mantis, then to the fearful, feeble man who lay before him like some sort of tribal offering. He was insulted by the very thought of it. "Please. You give me this cowering piece of meat? My worms wouldn't dare lay a finger on such an unworthy meal."

The "meal" before him scurried to his feet. If there was any chance for him to escape, he was going to take it right then.

He stood no chance of dodging the sharp talon as it dove through his chest. It went straight through, and Mantis hoisted him into the air with little effort, holding him by the obsidian blade that emanated from the man's own back like an extra limb.

"Sorry, but we can't have you escaping. The more of you who die, the more likely it is that Seth will find us." Mantis tilted his head slightly, still eyeing his prey. "Still, this wasn't exactly the way I'd planned it."

"Be thankful I sped things up," Widow added, walking by him with a smile on her face. "Not that I don't trust your judgment, but sometimes you can be a bit too patient."

Mantis turned to face her, still hoisting his victim aloft. "I know, I know. Don't worry, I'm not upset. Besides, this is likely a more entertaining plan, anyway."

Widow returned his smile with a wistful one of her own. "I'm glad we agree."

"We usually do."

Leech wasn't enjoying what he was seeing. If there was one thing he hated about working with the two of them, it was that they acted like newlyweds, even on such a grim occasion. It honestly sickened him. He cleared his throat.

"You two can handle this yourselves, am I right?"

"Yes, your assistance isn't really necessary."

He smirked at Mantis's reply. The bright grin Mantis gave him was the last bit of sarcasm Leech could stand without attacking the little mite himself.

Stupid kid. You and this little puppy of yours are in my way. But you'll be out soon enough. His physical form began to morph, until his body became a thick, black liquid. The liquid then drained into the nearest floor vent, quickly disappearing in the darkness.

Widow rolled her eyes as she returned her glance to Mantis. "He really thinks he's better than us."

Mantis shrugged at Widow's statement. Further behind him, the body of his tortured victim slid off his bladed arm, plopping to the ground like a sack of potatoes. "He thinks he's better than us. But the truth is, of course, that he's not even close to what we are."

"How far do you think he'll make it?"

Mantis grinned. "Not very. At the very least, once it kicks in, he'll make a fantastic distraction."

Widow smiled, then turned her eyes to the next row of buildings in the apartment complex. "While we wait, shall we continue our search?"

Mantis walked beside her. "Huh. Search. What a strange sense of humor you have."

Widow glared at the tall building before her. Her red-black eyes glowed such a deep, full crimson that it looked as though she had miniature suns in her eyes.

Panic barely described the whirlpool of emotions inside Pilar as she ran through the complex, hoping against all hope that more explosions would not follow. She eventually ran into Zoe, but Seth wasn't in sight.

"Where'd that idiot go?" She yelled above the crowd of evacuees and various alarms.

"He said he was going to make sure people were getting out of the other buildings! I tried to stop him but he's even more bullheaded than you are!"

"Seth! You moron!" Pilar turned to go after him, but instead she was met by something else entirely.

It's one of them! Dammit, it's one of them!

"And where do you think you're going, Pilar Sands?" It was the woman from before, the cloaked girl with the glowing red eyes.

Pilar had already drawn her hammer, fully extended its handle, and held the massive weapon before her. "Move!"

Despite the sheer weight of it and her lack of recovery, she swung the hammer with all her might. It wasn't until after she'd swung and missed that she realized just how heavy it was without the suit.

Widow's lithe body simply swayed out of the way of her swing. She didn't even bother to capitalize at all.

"They want me to bring you back with me—alive, as it were. Personally, I'd rather you all died here." She removed her hood, and now they could see her face: she was a red-haired woman in a black body suit adorned with red, curved markings. The only true abnormalities she had were her positively enormous fangs, and her six glowing red eyes, instead of two. She grinned. "We don't always get what we want though, do we?"

Zoe pulled out a pair of her daggers, holding them like short swords. "Good point. Now move."

"Oh, I don't think that will be happening. Hyde wouldn't like that." Widow cranked her neck to the left, and it looked as though her head would go fully sideways like an owl. "See this part? This is what I warned you about. You should have stopped interfering that first night. After what you did, Hyde is now very interested in you both. And I'm in no position to argue."

Zoe and Pilar both took a step back as Widow stepped forward. "Although, I could just . . . devour you myself. The rest of the food here is a little overcooked for my taste."

"Hey!" They could hear Bianca calling from the doorway behind them. "What are you doing! Get out of there!"

"Kinda busy!" Pilar yelled back.

In the time it took for Pilar to respond, the humanoid-arachnid had leapt to the left stairwell, then scuttled her way to the ceiling on all fours, clinging to it like the spider she was. Her voice was deep and raspy. Her eyes narrowed as her smile stretched further. "I should definitely feast on those little mutts out there right now. Especially her."

Zoe didn't waste another second listening to her threats. She tossed a silver globe right into Widow's face. The eruption of black smoke that spiraled out as it flew through the air was terrifying for a homemade weapon. Pilar couldn't stop her eyes from tearing up, and covered her mouth to try to stop the gagging and coughing.

Realizing her partner's distress, Zoe grabbed Pilar's hand through the smoke, her other arm covering her own face. They fled through the hallway, out through the back door, and towards the back parking lot, hurrying to meet Bianca.

They were panting and wheezing as oxygen swarmed back into their lungs. For a moment they continued to wheeze, trying to regain their breath after inhaling so many vile fumes. Once she could inhale properly again and her eyesight began to clear, Pilar saw no sign of her brother outside.

Another explosion took them off their feet. The smell of fire and something akin to burning trash began to fill the air. Dancing red-orange flames erupted on every possible side of the building. The three of them—Bianca, Zoe, and Pilar—stood at the eastern side of the complex, where the fire trucks and authorities had not arrived. They were still dealing with the few residents who'd escaped, and trying to control the fire from the first explosion.

Over the distant roars of sirens and the sound of the crackling blaze, Pilar screamed from the very the center of her body, yelling her brother's name, praying for an answer. It was Zoe who held her back. Pilar would have gladly run back into that fiery coffin, even if she knew there was no chance he would be alive. Her heart sank further and further, and the more anguish she released, the louder her cries became. Until then, she hadn't understood the depths of what those monsters were capable of. They were willing to kill hundreds, just to capture one.

"Look! Up there!" someone shouted. A small crowd of residents had gathered, and they all drew the attention of the people around them to the barely stable roof. There was someone standing there, shadowed by the gold light of the fire below. In his right hand, he held another man in his grasp as he struggled.

The skies themselves seemed to flash, forcing the onlookers all to wince, masking their eyes. A vicious popping sound cracked the air. When they could once again look to the man, he'd already tossed his victim to the earth below. They could only see the body as it sailed through the air, a trail of smoke leaving his body.

Pilar knew. Before she could even get a glimpse of the man soaring through the air, she knew.

34

Seth slid to the ground a few feet away from them. Pilar couldn't understand how, but he looked as though he'd barely been burned. He breathed, but it was minimal at best. He coughed, then gasped for air. His eyes were barely able to open. He couldn't form a word. Despite the weakness Pilar felt in her lungs, she ran to him and held him, barely able to stand the heat emanating from his body.

Zoe and Bianca were at their side. Zoe was quick to try and ask the inevitable question, but she couldn't even stand to finish it. "Is he . . ."

Bianca checked his pulse, then visually scanned him for any sign of injury. "There doesn't seem to be anything external, but heaven knows what the hell is going on inside his body." Bianca ran a hand across his cheek. "Just hang in there, okay, love? Please just stay with us." She turned her eyes to Pilar. The cracking in her voice and the water welling in her eyes couldn't be stopped. "We need to get him somewhere I can care for him. Somewhere far the hell away from these demons."

"Pi . . . lar . . ." Seth had found his voice, but it was faint at best.

Pilar had never heard him sound so pitiful. She wanted to cry just hearing him force her name from his lips. "Don't waste your strength, okay?"

"Protected myself . . . with power . . ."

Pilar hugged him close to her chest. Her eyes started to overflow. "I'll stop them," she uttered. "I swear, I'll stop them!"

They'd been so focused on Seth that they hadn't notice Mantis bearing down on them— that childish, innocent smile his greeting. At his side stood Widow.

Mantis looked directly into Pilar's eyes and his devil-be-damned smile enraged her. And the more enraged she grew, the more he seemed to smile. After a moment of glaring at his handiwork, his gaze fell to Seth.

"He managed to protect himself, even in that state? I have to say, I'm impressed by that." Mantis continued to walk towards them, undeterred. "I was sure I'd discarded him with barely any breath left in his body. Widow?"

Widow nodded. "He looked dead to me."

Pilar was beside herself. She gently laid Seth down to let Bianca do what she could for him. She extended the her hammer, holding it before her with both hands. The usual weight that she felt from it was nothing now. She didn't care. That blunt, metal weapon was her only means of vengeance, and she wanted it. She stood between them and her brother. Not a word left her lips.

"You're not serious are you?" Mantis grinned. "Come on, Pilar. You're a genius right? The odds here clearly aren't in your favor if your brother—with his power, no less—could not stop me."

Zoe stood next to Pilar, two daggers in her hands.

"You too?" Mantis sighed. "I can't say I'm surprised. But at least put those Bug Suits on. You both seem so naked without them."

Before her mind could catch up to her instincts, Pilar sprinted at Mantis. She couldn't stop the pain coursing through her, and despite knowing that her only weapon against him was her electrified hammer, she couldn't stop herself from attacking. She didn't have any armor protecting her. All it would have taken was one single attack, just one slight wound.

She could die right there.

But she didn't care. She couldn't plan every attack, she couldn't sit and cower in fear. No one else was going to die, unless it was Mantis and Widow.

She trusted herself to endure it, and ran at him not with fear, but instead with reckless abandon. There was a sense of freedom she hadn't envisioned before. And she recognized that freedom. It was the same as when she had attacked Hyde. It was a part of herself returning to her.

The sound of Mantis's claw rushing through the air towards her was like a jet roaring overhead. Pilar could feel the wind. She could feel the sheer force building up against her right side. She flailed the hammer to her right, knocking away the claw without losing even a slight bit of momentum. Mantis tried again from the left, and Pilar quickly held the hammer to her left, deflecting the attack. This time she was forced to slow down to intercept another attempt before getting closer to him.

Mantis seemed pretty happy with his ability to repel her. "That was anticlimactic." But his eyes widened as Zoe leapt over Pilar, her daggers in hand and aimed directly for his head. She did not waver from her path, and because of Pilar's unintentional diversion, Mantis was forced to try to evade her rather than retaliate.

Zoe was too swift. Mantis's body was caught by her daggers digging into his right shoulder, his blood spraying out from the wound and causing him to stumble back. With his right hand, he held the wound, though he smiled all the while, like a child discovering mud for the first time. "This is good. Really good. You're a lot more resourceful than I expected."

"I'm not afraid of you anymore!" Pilar charged at him again, and before he could react, her hammer connected with the left side of his jaw, sending him in a spiraling heap to the ground.

Meanwhile, the spider woman stood back, arms folded, watching.

A knot started to furl in Pilar's stomach. Something isn't right.

Mantis stood, looking slightly woozy. "That was quite a show of strength." He cracked his neck to the left, then to the right. "If you've got some more of that to get off your chest, go ahead."

"Shut up!" Pilar held her hammer upright again.

"So what will you do, Pilar? We know who you are, where you are, and where you will be. What do you plan to do from here?"

There wasn't anything within her that was ready to submit. All Pilar could continually see was this strange anger that had boiled inside her for so long.

"I'll fight you. That's what I'll do."

Mantis was annoyed to hear that answer. "I suppose that's the optimal choice, right? Not fighting us wouldn't help you much. And we can't do anything to you without drawing eyes to our organization, right?"

"What are you saying?"

"I needed to drain your brother's power. Though what he had left was far below what we expected, I accomplished that. Our leader will now be focused on Aegis, and likewise, so will we."

Zoe stepped forward, still holding the daggers dripping with Mantis's black blood. "You slaughtered them that night. You intend to keep doing that. We aren't going to sit back and just let you kill innocent people."

"Innocent people?" Mantis sounded almost dejeected. "Well. It's unfortunate that you feel that way. But you're missing a valuable point."

"Which is?"

"Hyde has plans that will destroy this entire city in order to test his theory. We intend to stop him—for our own reasons, of course."

"And we're supposed to accept that after what you just did?"

"I didn't destroy the entire city, just these few dozen lives! Though considering the look in your eyes, I guess I should add yours to that total, huh?"

No one could see his claw as it whipped through the air, but the long, thin blade that reached out of his back missed Zoe by only a few inches. Had she not flinched, he would have impaled her with that mantis-like serrated blade.

A second blade shot towards Pilar, and she barely tumbled out of its way. A third blade erupted from his back, then a fourth, then a fifth, then a sixth. Zoe and Pilar were constantly crossing each other's path as they tried to evade each blade. And as they began to tire, Mantis became even more gleeful with his spree of spawning blades. "You know, I can do this all day. I can summon millions of these."

Not good! Pilar continued to leap to and fro, but her adrenaline was starting to die down. The pain from her previous bruises started to catch up with her.

In the midst of her next leap, Pilar stopped. A blue flash of light covered the area around them. She and Zoe stared at Mantis as he erupted in pain, electricity surging through his body.

Pilar's eyes darted to Bianca. She stood only a few feet away from Seth's body. In her right hand she held a Taser, which she'd plunged deep into one of Mantis's extended, bladed arms.

The arms Mantis had already extended quickly crumbled apart. And as his body emitted smoke, he looked to Bianca with a fiendish grin. "So, the devil's daughter remembers how to be a devil."

Bianca spit at him. "Hyde didn't give me this. Sands did. Never put my name with the likes of you swine again."

"Well, now we have a whole slew of targets." Mantis dusted himself off, and his evil grin had returned to that of the jovial trickster. "Did you get all of that out of your system?"

Pilar held her hammer before her. "So, we didn't really do anything to you?"

"Apart from a small bit of wasted time? I'm perfectly fine." He looked to Widow. "I guess I am a little bit agitated though."

A new wave of fear settled into them all when Widow stepped forward. "You? Agitated?"

Mantis shrugged. "Sounds like we may need to retreat anyway. We'll have company soon and I don't feel like dragging this out any further."

Before anyone could make another move, a swarm of black SUVs ripped into the parking lot, aiming all sorts of spotlights at Mantis and Widow. Mantis chuckled a bit at all the Aegis agents who poured out and trained their weapons on the duo.

"These humans are ready to die, apparently." Widow's scowl was malicious.

Mantis shrugged. "I'm kind of bored, actually. And, aside from that, we got what we came for. No need to waste more energy than that, right?" He looked back to Widow. "Let's take a break for a while. We've got so much other stuff to do and I could use a rest."

Widow now took a more feral stance, on all fours. "You're kidding, right?"

That still didn't make Mantis budge. "We need to retreat. Don't forget, we can't make him too suspicious. And we've still got another weapon out there." He was still talking to her like he was pampering a child.

Widow moaned away her frustration. "When are you actually going to show an interest in killing these unevolved beasts?"

"They're kinda fun to toy with. Still, we should be more patient, shouldn't we? There's no need to start a war yet."

Widow's six eyes all rolled. "Of course. Patience. Your favorite word." Despite her obvious annoyance with his order, she smiled.

As the Aegis operatives all opened fire on them with a variety of ammunition that littered the skies, Mantis and Widow nonchalantly leapt into the air. They vanished as if they were nothing more than pieces of obsidian paper, dispersing against the dark night skies.

Agent Rose quickly grabbed Pilar by her shoulder. "We need to get you out of here before people start asking questions."

When Pilar looked back, she noticed that Bianca was already carrying Seth into Rose's SUV. She took another look at the blaze before her, what used to be her home. This is what they were capable of. *Unevolved beasts. They think that little of human life.*

Zoe was still standing there, her fists clenched, eyes draining. Pilar noticed that her daggers were trembling in her grasp. She realized as well that she could barely hold her hammer steady.

"Zoe."

"Yeah?"

"How . . . how serious were you about training me . . . to really . . . to really be able to fight?"

"I was serious before. Now?" Her eyes glanced here, there, then back, looking at the remnants of the building for an answer.

Pilar nodded, and her eyes returned to the blaze as well. "Is that . . . still an offer?"

Zoe's eyes deviated towards Pilar, slightly. "Yeah."

"I don't want anything like that night . . . or like this . . ."

Zoe put her daggers back in her pouch. She walked to Pilar, placing her hand on her shoulder. "I know. I know."

"We should get going." Agent Rose gestured towards the SUV.

They slipped into the SUV amid the panic and confusion, and sat in the back. As they prepared to pull out, another agent stepped up to the driver side window. He looked about the inside of the vehicle, eyeing each of the passengers.

"They all right?"

Rose nodded. "Yeah. A little banged-up, but all right."

"Seth doesn't look a little banged up." When the agent said that, Pilar's attention was driven right to him.

"Yeah. Keeping an eye on him."

"I'm okay . . . Swords, right?" Seth gave it his best effort, but Seth didn't sound convincing. He'd winced even as he'd said those two words. "Really . . ."

Swords peeked at Pilar. "I think he's the only one that believes that," he said to her.

Pilar managed to at least return a small smile. "He'll be okay. He's just stubborn. Like me."

Swords nodded, then looked to his colleague. "Get going, Rose."

Rose responded with a nod of his own. "I'll get in touch with the director when I can confirm they're safe. We'll talk later."

Agent Swords tapped the side of the door twice, then ran off to the other agents behind him, quickly barking orders in the loud tone that Pilar was familiar with.

Not once did she think that of all the people she'd run into, these would be her allies.

35

She hadn't expected Rose to whip the SUV around with so much force. At just about every corner it felt like they were riding on one wheel, pivoting the truck around the curves as if it were being launched from a sling. In the back seat, Bianca did her best to patch up Seth and Zoe's wounds. Pilar looked at the seat beside her, staring at her backpack.

My armor.

During the rush to save her brother, she'd forgotten she even had it! Fighting off Mantis the way they had . . .it started to sink in just what kind of insane risk they'd taken. Despite the soreness in her arms, she hoisted it up.

"And we did it without the suits," Zoe said to her, grinning nearly ear to ear.

"That wasn't the smart thing to do."

"No, but it was what your heart made you do." Zoe tapped her chin with her right index finger. "Actually, it was probably adrenaline that made you ignore it."

Pilar continued to examine the armor. "We just didn't have a good chance to put it on. That and . . .I was . . ."

"We all were," Bianca added. "We all wanted to fight them."

"Zoe's bike was recovered and transported to Aegis HQ as well," Agent Rose added. "Don't worry. We aren't ripping it apart to examine your work. Yet."

When Zoe saw Rose, of all people, look back at her and give her a sly little smirk, she had to question everything. *Did . . . did Agent Rose just make a snarky joke? And smile about it? Did I pass out after that fight and wake up in some alternate dream world?*

The feeling of pain shooting through her leg confirmed the truth. *Nope. Definitely still alive.*

Zoe smiled ever so slightly, despite the pain that still ran through her body.

After a moment to collect her thoughts, Pilar detached the right arm from the backpack, and slid it over her arm. The warm fibers and circuitry within latched onto her arm, and she was quick to put the other arm on afterwards.

"Pilar?" Zoe looked at her while trying not to flinch. That was hard to do as Bianca continued to put alcohol on her open shoulder wounds.

"I'm curious about something."

"About what exactly?"

"My body shouldn't have felt that rejuvenated. Even given the human ability to heal, my leg was in bad shape. Yet earlier I was able to jump about and run as if it were just bruised."

"Adrenaline can do that, especially when concerned about a loved one," Bianca replied as she wrapped a bandage around Zoe's bare, injured shoulder.

"This didn't feel like adrenalin." Pilar put her helmet on, and looked about. As the helmet came online, she could see her vital information. "Well, this is functioning properly," she mumbled. As she looked about the car, the helmet's HUD began identifying everyone's body signature. The girl in the front passenger seat surprised her.

"That thing doesn't have X-ray vision or anything, right?" Madri's smile was as goofy as ever.

"It does. And that is an absolutely weird question to ask me, Madri." Pilar tapped the side of the helmet, just below the jaw, and the view changed once again. "According to the suit's readings, I'm at sixty percent, at best."

"How exactly does that work, love?" Bianca had moved on to Seth's wounds now, though he seemed reluctant to let her even touch him.

"You're done with her already?" Seth tried to sound as jovial as he could, but he only further highlighted just how pained he was.

"Oh, stop your whining and lay your head on my lap, you."

"It's not . . . that bad . . . really."

"Seth, you have a head wound, lacerations on your arms, your jaw looks like you're holding bags of jelly beans in there and

I'm guessing by the way you're struggling to move your arm away from your ribs, there's probably a couple of those damaged too."

"So . . . not that bad?"

Despite his verbal rejections, Seth did as asked, and Bianca began treating his wounds as well. He didn't give her another word. When their eyes met, he just smiled before closing them again.

"Hey, Pilar, you wouldn't happen to have an extra one of those suits around, would ya?" Madri was nearly in the backseat as she turned to ask. Her eyes were lighting up from the sight of Pilar even having only parts of the suit on.

"No," Pilar flatly said.

"No, you don't have any?"

"No, as in this isn't even a conversation we're about to have."

Madri's smile turned into a disgruntled, childish frown just like that, and she snapped back into her seat. She slumped a bit, folding her arms. "So selfish," she grumbled.

Pilar started to reply, but just as she opened her mouth to form the words, the HUD fed back a reading that put her in shock immediately.

It stood directly in front of them, lumbering forward like some mindless robot. It refused to escape their path. Once her helmet's secondary scan finished, it fed back the name of the target before them.

"Agent Rose! Stop the ca—"

Before she could finish, Rose was already slamming the breaks, nearly spinning the SUV off the side of the road and into an office building. "Everyone all right?" he managed to ask, as he himself tried to catch his breath.

"I think so," Bianca replied. "Seth? Zoe?"

Seth nodded. "Can't get much worse."

Zoe nodded as well. "I'm good. Pilar?"

Just as she asked, the side door slammed. Pilar, her armor and her hammer were all missing. Zoe repeated her name as though it would make a difference, but she knew where her friend had obviously gone.

Madri was quickly unfastening her seat belt. "You know she went out there to stop that guy, right?"

Seth started to chide Madri, until he looked over to her and realized that she was actually serious. She quickly scoured the back seat for a weapon. "Hey Rose! What did you do with my—"

"And you'll do what?" Agent Rose shot back. "Hell, she shouldn't even be out there in her condition!"

This was the first time Zoe had seen the agent truly angry. And yet, there was no way she could leave her friend out there alone, either. Her own injuries were superficial at best, after all.

Just as Zoe started to stand, the truck was rocked off its wheels, leaving them all grasping at whatever seemed stable. When it landed upright again, amidst a bursting cloud of dust and smoke, they all tried to gather themselves and peer out at whatever sent them hurtling.

Bianca was quick to get Seth lying back down, realizing that his injuries were worse than she already feared, and tumbling around the truck's innards wasn't doing do him any favors. "Seth's barely conscious," she yelled to Rose.

Relatively unscathed, Rose gave her a nod while getting himself back in the driver's seat. "We need to grab Pilar and get Seth to a hospital. Whatever's attacking us now—"

"He isn't attacking you!"

Rose, Zoe, and Madri could see her now, as she stood upright a few meters from the truck, her armor completely covering her. She was Bug once again, despite the injuries.

Bug had no choice but to ignore those little aches.

"It's Leech," Zoe barely spoke.

They could all see him in the distance ahead now, those leech-like appendages leaking from every part of his body. They were far more out of control than before—it even appeared that one was erupting from his mouth.

Pilar knew that this was close to suicide. When facing Mantis they'd had no choice but to go without their suits. Whatever happened to put Leech on this destructive path, they would not live without the armor here. And Pilar could not fight this monster alone.

Zoe quickly snatched her backpack and leapt out of the rear passenger side door. "Get Bianca and Seth somewhere safe!"

"And leave you two here?" Agent Rose didn't even bother to start the engine. "Get your asses in this car. I've got to get you safe—"

"There is no safe right now!" Bug yelled back. "Leech has gone berserk! If we leave him be, or try to outrun him, he'll kill us and everyone he can get his hands on! He wants me and Moth, so he'll get me and Moth!"

Zoe had already ducked off to the side, getting her armor on as swiftly as she could before Leech made another move. Seeing that, Bug kept her focus on the beast ahead of them. She wasn't far from the eruption point of the first leech that tried to rip her asunder . . . it was that tendril that had toppled the SUV. If there was anything she could already note compared to their previous encounters, Leech's strength had grown tenfold.

When Moth stood at her side again, daggers drawn, she couldn't help but feel relief. That wasn't something she could recall feeling so strongly before. Considering the night they'd had until now however, she couldn't think of it as an oddity. They'd stared down death just minutes before—without their suits—and fought it off.

I trust her.

What threw her off was Madri standing on the other side of her, with that casually blithe smile.

36

"Alright, so what's your plan for this?"

"The hell, Madri? Why are you here?" Bug's attention was quickly split between keeping her eyes on Leech, and trying to get Madri to return with Rose and the others. But just as she said it, the SUV pulled away in reverse, before whipping about and shooting off around a darkened alleyway.

"He's taking a shortcut," Madri answered Bug's curious glare. "Trust me. I'm probably more combat ready than you are right now." She whipped her batons forward, smiling as she showed off the glowing weapons.

"That's what you used on the roof that night," Bug mumbled.

"They were set low then. Little bit of zap. Now? Whole lotta zap." She gave her a wink, then stepped forward. And, without warning or even provocation, she yelled to Leech:

"Hey, psycho-worm guy . . . uh, thingy! The hell's your problem?"

Bug whipped Madri to her far right, tossing the larger girl off her feet and out of the way of the impending attack. Another of the gigantic leeches erupted from the ground, only a foot away from where Bug now stood. Moth was quick to slice the head of the leech off, and it fell to the ground, exploding in a magnificent splash of black gunk on impact.

"He's unstable," Bug uttered. "Somehow he's been made unstable. Just like the sample."

Moth was once again at Bug's side. "This is a good thing, right? Means we can actually, really, harm him this time?"

Bug shook her head. "Harming him is one thing. But, being unstable is something entirely different. When Indigo goes unstable . . ." the remnants of the evidence batch she'd kept at the lab as it exploded and turned into acid was the first thing that came to mind.

Moth was barely audible as she remembered what Pilar said before. "If he goes acidic, This entire city block could be . . ."

"He's a time bomb now," Pilar confirmed. "And if my helmet isn't lying, he's completely unstable and his powers are extremely unpre—"

He was right there, right in her face. He was staring down at her, his eyes wild, his body nothing more than a black shadow bubbling from every side. He looked like a living puddle of tar, with gigantic leeches dragging behind him like heavy chains, imprisoning him. His arms stretched to the ground, dragging at his sides and leaving traces of the Indigo along the ground as they crept.

Crap! How? How did he . . .

Leech leaned closer, his rancid breath fogging the lenses of Bug's helmet. He crept closer as she stepped back, the three of them so taken by surprise that they couldn't react properly.

Leech leaned ever closer, all the while whispering, "Kill Bug, kill Bug, kill Bug, kill Bug, kill Bug . . ." His voice continued to rise. He was getting anxious. He was getting frantic. He was absolutely manic.

Pilar batted his head clean off his body with her hammer, and yet it simply rolled onto its side, screaming.

"KILL BUG KILL BUG KILL BUG KILL BUG KILL BUG!"

She could see the slashes on his arm, carved right into what was left of his skin.

"So, my guess is, he wants to kill me," Bug said aloud as she wound up her hammer. She quickly swung it around again, this time aiming directly for the slash-filled arm. Much like his head before it, the arm detached easily, rolling on the ground and leaving traces of itself as it did. Eventually the naked limb lay still, with his declaration still scarred into it.

"He's already dead," Bug mumbled. "His body is nothing but a husk. The Indigo—"

Bug hadn't realized just how stunned she was by it all. She came to her senses when Madri tackled her to the ground as one of the leech mouths leapt through the air, driving through the cement where Bug had been standing.

"Well, I evened out that debt quick, huh?" Madri helped Bug to her feet. "Might want to have your inner monologue later, kiddo!"

"Kiddo?"

Madri quickly turned about and whipped at a smaller leech as it tried to take them from the side. It quickly dissolved upon contact with her charged batons. "No time to argue it now! See? I'm clever, I did that right when—"

"Whatever! Regroup!" Bug quickly yelled the command to her ragtag team, signaling for the three of them to duck behind a nearby garbage truck. Once Moth slid around the corner and joined them, Bug knew she had to warn them as quickly as possible and try to come up with a plan.

"He's far worse than I thought, Moth. Whatever was left of that scientist before is gone now. The Indigo is not only unstable, it's in complete control and possession of his knowledge." Bug stood on one knee behind the garbage truck's side, as did her other allies. "He was already insane before. I don't know how it happened, but he is positively unhinged now—whatever's left of him that's alive."

Madrid nodded. "Good to know! So, how do we stop him?"

Bug looked to Madri, then to her batons. "Please tell me you have something else aside from those that's effective against these things."

Madri shrugged. "I'd love to, but I'd be lying. And you don't want me to lie, right?"

A sigh was Bug's only answer. "Of course." She stood up and began inching her way out of cover. "This could go very, very badly. But, it's the only way to find out, isn't it?"

Bug gave one last look back to Moth and to Madri, and though they could not see it under her helmet, she smiled at them. "I'm counting on you two to distract him, okay?"

"Distract him?" Moth peeked at Madri, who looked just as puzzled. "What's your plan?"

"If I told you . . ." She didn't bother to finish. She didn't need to.

Bug leapt out of their cover, and with her hammer in tow, she ran right for Leech's still-headless body. Another giant black leech launched out of the ground, and she leapt at it, hammer first, crashing the flat edge of it against the leech's jaw. As it cracked apart and fell to the cement, Bug used the force to carry her, sailing through the air, ever closer to the monster at the root of their problem.

Two more leeches spawned, and two more fell. Another rose, nearly clipping Bug's leg. This one was stopped short of snatching her within its maw by Moth and Madri, as Moth's blade ripped through its lower body and Madri's baton knocked its top half clean off.

Bug was within reach now. She just needed to destroy that body! It was the only thing giving off insane readings that wasn't replicating. This had to be the core of Leech's Indigo instability.

Her solution was to ensure that he was completely destroyed.

I have to summon that power again. I don't even know what it is, but . . . I have to figure it out, now!

She felt the world shift from underneath her. Before she could catch her footing, the entire slab of concrete street tilted nearly vertical, threatening to slide her downward and into the void that waited below. At the bottom of the concrete slide lay an enormous, street-wide mouth that fell into nothing but a bottomless void. Its teeth mashed at all manner of things that were sucked into it. Try as she might, her grip on the street did not hold. Her body quickly began sliding downward, headed towards death. She could feel her adrenaline rushing throughout her body. And yet, nothing came to her.

Three of the tendrils wrapped themselves around her left leg, and began to cling to the suit, almost as if bonding with it at a molecular level.

"IKR Active" flashed across the display before her, with a schematic depicting how to set up the weapon that could save her life.

"Level Four Failsafe, off!" Bug yelled, commanding her suit.

The eyes of her helmet emitted an indigo light. The globe on the back of her right gauntlet sunk inwards, emitting a similar glow to the suit's eyes. As more of the leech's tendrils encased her like a massive silk cocoon, she rested her hammer on the back of her gauntlet.

She could hear her allies yelling to her. She peeked to either side of her, and saw them rushing through as many of the Leech death traps as they could to aid her. Even without a suit, Madri fought onward through the monsters, without hesitation. Even with her injuries, Zoe's daggers cleaved the beasts in front of her for the sake of her ally.

Pilar kicked a large tooth loose of the Leech's maw, then aimed her hammer directly into its throat.

"IKR . . . fire!" She yelled the command with such fervor and desperation that she didn't even recognize her own voice.

The immense beam of black light that fired from the head of her hammer was so full of power that it pushed her up the cement wall she'd been held against. And as it sailed through the air, anything made from the Indigo formula literally unraveled just from being in proximity of it! Bug was quickly freed from the tendrils that held her in place. She found her footing, then leapt off the left side of the concrete wall, stumbling as her leg injury reminded her she wasn't recovered yet. Both Zoe and Madri were at her side, helping her stand and then helping her run as they each hoisted her by a shoulder.

It felt like the entire planet was crumbling around them. She feared looking behind them in that she might witness the vacuum of space sucking the world into oblivion and massive explosions they could never hope to outrun. So much smoke and dust permeated the air and obstructed their vision. Indigo leeches fell all around them, splattering into a harmless black goo as they collided with the ground.

The trio collapsed, having gotten as far from ground zero as their legs could take them. Madri was the first to stand, quickly whipping out her smartphone and dialing as if nothing occurred.

"Juneeey! Hiyyee! You mind driving through a miniature war zone and picking up me and two of the packages? Sounds like fun, right? Oh, Rose already sent you this way? 'Kay! Oh and hey . . . there's . . . um, some construction to be done here, too."

Bug removed her helmet, and immediately gasped for air. She could barely breathe. Sweat covered her face and matted her hair to her forehead. Her eyes were soaked with water, so much so that she was amazed she could see anything at all, even if at the moment most of it was fantastic blurs of paint.

"Pilar? What . . . what was that?" Zoe was sitting at her side, giving her a place to rest her head.

Pilar gladly accepted. "I'm not completely sure. When the suit detected that a source of Indigo was trying to break through its defenses, it just activated."

She looked at her hammer, then raised her gauntlet into the air. "IKR."

"IKR? And that stands for?"

"'I Know, Right?' Duh. Right?" Madri looked pretty happy with herself for that.

Pilar wanted to berate her, but she could tell by the goofy grin that Madri knew better.

"Indigo Kill Ray." Pilar finally stood up, with Zoe's help.

"Well, the name's definitely accurate," Zoe replied.

Pilar looked about, still unnerved and completely spent. "It destroyed whatever was in the fluids that commanded the chemical change. It literally killed the nanomachines before they could enact their suicide switch."

Zoe looked about the destruction left in Leech's wake. "Hey. I think I see someone over there."

The two of them began a slow march towards the figure they could see kneeling where the giant leech used to be. Once they were closer, it became obvious that the figure wasn't kneeling. Its legs were completely meshed into the pools of useless gunk that had threatened their lives moments before.

"Leech?" Pilar recognized him now. His head was reattached to his body, but the scarred arm was no more.

"He knew . . . He knew it was you . . . Fears . . . you . . ."

Pilar still held her hammer ready.

What was left of his body erupted into that familiar black sludge and dispersed into the ground, becoming a corrosive acid which Pilar and her friends jumped away from. All about the ruined streets, the remains of Leech began to harden. Whatever hadn't corroded was quickly melding into the gunk that was once his armor, the beast that was once his very skin.

"Well, those were some oddly uplifting last words," Zoe said as she approached Pilar's left side.

"You guys should probably put your helmets back on, you know. Once the dust starts to settle, people are gonna notice." Madri continually shot looks about the area, and Pilar had no idea what for. Still, her advice was surprisingly sound.

Madri cleared her throat as she helped Pilar walk on her injured leg. "Sooooo, you have any more of those battle su—"

"Not. Happening." Pilar shot her potential request down with cold precision. "Moth was lucky. A combination of timing and fortune, and her own persistence. That and I had a near-finished second suit to work with."

"Well, what I meant—"

"Not only that, but I don't exactly know if I want to put a powerful superweapon in your hands. You're more insane than we are." Pilar said this without worry, despite Madri now being the person holding her up to walk. Even then, she couldn't help letting a bit of a smile leak.

"That, and I work for Aegis, right?" Madri looked to her, smiling an unbelievably bright smile. Pilar thought she could rattle the girl a bit, but instead she seemed to be even more emboldened. "I am the person responsible for getting you a ride out of here, you know."

"We could get back on our own. Eventually." Zoe tried her best to say this with confidence. It was obvious none of them believed it, including Zoe herself.

Another black SUV whipped around the corner. Pilar could see a pair of agents inside as their truck barreled towards them. Eventually it spun to a halt a few feet away.

"But could you get out of here in style like this?" Madri pointed at her coworkers' vehicle.

A female agent swung the door open and hurried them in. "My partner filled us in on everything," she said, pointing to the older man with the silver ponytail in the passenger seat.

Pilar nodded. "Swords, right?"

He gave them a once-over, then pointed to the back. "We need to get you all someplace safe and out of the eyes of the Cloaks."

"My lab," Pilar answered. "We'll be safe there."

As they piled in, Swords peeked at his small phone, swiping at the screen quickly and then putting it back in his pocket. "Sound like Bianca had the same idea. They're in the loft back at Sands's old lab. Your brother just woke back up."

Pilar nearly leapt out of her armor hearing those words. Of all the things to be worried about after seeing what Mantis did to her brother, seeing him near death . . . She wanted nothing more than to get back to her lab. The longest night of her life seemed to finally be ending.

37

Who would have thought . . . I'd be so happy to see a sunrise?

There wasn't much in the way of furniture in the loft aside from a rather cheap cream sofa and love seat, and a humble twenty-four-inch television. Even the kitchen was fairly bare, lacking in any useful food entirely. There were four bedrooms, with only three of each having a very basic cot within.

Pilar was aware of why the rooms were set up in that manner. It was her father hoping to bring his family together again someday. Before he could, their mother passed, and their family splintered further.

It was ironic then, that the company she'd suspected was responsible for his disappearance, and that she blamed for so much of her turmoil, was now responsible for bringing her and her brother there, together.

Well, partially.

Knowing that only this small shadow group within Aegis was aware of everything was oddly comforting. For the first time in a very long time, Pilar didn't feel like she was completely alone. She had people around her who genuinely cared about her, who had a similar goal or were at least on the same path. It wasn't something she was used to, by any stretch.

After they made certain that Seth was stable in one of the bedrooms, and that no one else was seriously injured aside from herself, Pilar was at least able to relax for a moment. She let things sink in as she stared out of the large, glass balcony doors. As unsure of Madri's sanity as Pilar was, she had to admit that the girl was surprisingly thoughtful. She'd volunteered to gather supplies, including tea, coffee, a kettle, and food in general.

Considering the night they'd had, Pilar couldn't deny how good it had felt to take a shower, and now to be able to drink a cup of coffee this morning. She wasn't even much of a coffee drinker to begin with, but she found it extremely soothing now.

To say she had a new appreciation of things would be an understatement.

Zoe left the kitchen with a cup of coffee of her own, and plopped down on the sofa. "So you've had access to this place the whole time, huh?"

Pilar nodded. "Yeah. I didn't need it and couldn't really stay here, since I was living with Seth. Would've been suspicious. But now?"

Zoe took a sip in the silence, then continued Pilar's thought. "It's probably going to be our home for a good while."

Pilar's eyes turned back to the sunrise that greeted them. "Looks like. Are you okay with that?"

"It's not like I can really say no," Zoe answered, laughing a bit at the question. "I can't risk putting my family in danger, either. And honestly, I wouldn't want to leave you here to deal with all of this by yourself."

Pilar happily accepted that answer, and yet still didn't feel right. "Can we really be sure anyone else we know isn't in danger at this point?"

Zoe stared into her cup for a moment. "I can't, really. The only safety we have now is knowing that they rarely seem to operate during the day."

Pilar nodded, then returned her gaze to the glass doors. "Yeah. I didn't even consider things turning out like this. All those people . . ."

"Don't blame yourself."

"It's hard not to. If we would've left that day, and not gone back there—"

"Then they would have attacked while we weren't there," Zoe concluded. "They had no idea we were moving here. They found Seth's address, and went right to him. If we hadn't been home, there might not have been even one survivor. The only blame for last night rests on those monsters." She made sure to catch eyes with

Pilar, and while her smile was kind, there was a certain authority to it that Pilar wasn't used to seeing. "We'll stop them. I promise."

Pilar cheered up a bit hearing that. Zoe hadn't really said anything that Pilar hadn't already told herself, and yet, hearing her say it reaffirmed it. *We'll stop them*, Pilar repeated to herself.

Madri wandered in, making sure everyone knew she was exhausted. "What a night," she exclaimed before she crashed on the floor not too far from Pilar, her cup of hot tea in hand. "Yo, this place is spacious as hell! Gotta say, at least you got a spot with a lot of room now, right?"

Pilar shook her head, but still smiled at her. "Such a poet you are. And yeah, it's roomy."

"How many people are gonna be staying here?"

"Just me, Zoe and Seth as far as I know. Probably Bianca, too."

"Full house, huh?" Madri took a rather loud slurp of tea, and exhaled. "Okay, wow. That was way hotter than I thought."

"Madri, it's got steam literally pouring out of the cup. It looks like a damn sauna. What exactly were you expecting?"

Madri laughed. "I expected it to not burn the roof of my mouth, thank you very much for asking!"

Zoe's eyes wandered to Pilar, and once their glances met, they both looked to Madri again, utterly perplexed. "But . . . you made the tea."

"Yeah, well, you know . . . I wasn't really paying attention when I poured it and stuff. So much on my mind after last night I just, you know, made some tea." Despite her previous complaint, she sipped again, pursing her lips more this time as though it would somehow cool the tea before it reached her tongue.

"This girl," Zoe mumbled as she looked to Pilar, trying to hold in a laugh.

Pilar didn't bother to hold it in. She just laughed at that point. "You aren't even careful about the tea you make for yourself, and you're bugging me about wearing high-grade, sophisticated, computerized battle armor."

"Well, wearing battle armor isn't pouring tea now, is it?" Madri looked to them both, recognizing the incredulous looks they were returning. "Oh my God, I swear if either of you says something ridiculously stupid like comparing it to making tea and how making tea properly will mean I'm ready to wear high-powered armor, I swear . . ."

Their camaraderie was interrupted by the return of agents Swords and Rose. "I take it you girls are doing a little better now," Swords asked as he pulled his shades back to the top of his silver hair.

"Oh, we're fine now! Just needed some showers and warm liquids," Madri raised her cup up as if Swords had no idea what a cup was.

"Thanks, Madri, you were definitely my biggest concern," he answered as wryly as humanly possible.

"We're okay, considering," Pilar added. "I can't really say we're fine. A lot on my mind, anyway."

"Same," Zoe added. "I just . . . I need a few days."

"Pretty reasonable, considering," Agent Rose added. "I'd also suggest staying away from the television, or at least the news for a couple days."

Zoe sunk in her seat, hearing that. "Reports running all day long about the apartment attack?"

"Not to mention the destruction Leech caused downtown." Rose picked up the remote from the love seat, and clicked the power button. Without even having to change a channel, the first thing that appeared was the remains of the destroyed apartments. The headline clearly read: "70 Dead, 34 Seriously Injured in Rosevilla Apartment Attacks."

After a moment of watching it, Rose turned off the television again. "It's running on every local station, and some national ones. Media is referring to it as a terrorist attack, or a terrorist mishap."

All three girls looked to each other. Pilar quickly found the sunrise easier to look at. Zoe and Madri seemed to agree.

"It won't happen again." Pilar spat the phrase with a quiet, firm anger. Her fervor had permeated her face. That anger waned when Pilar caught sight of Bianca exiting Seth's temporary room, once again cleaning her hands of dried blood.

"How is he?" Pilar didn't even realize until she'd said it just how desperate she sounded, and how selfish it probably appeared.

Still, Bianca comforted her. "He's going to be fine. But I can only do so much for him here. By tonight, I'd like to get him to the hospital. Agent Rose, I'm sure you can spare a few agents to make sure the hospital isn't attacked, at least."

Rose gave Bianca a slight, but confident nod. "Aegis agents are usually around St. Anne's anyway. They hired us on as a security consultant years ago."

"Good. I can give my new boss a believable cover story to buy Seth some time there, and we can figure out the insurance issues later. But for now, he's stable."

"I don't suppose he's awake, huh?" Pilar tried to keep her smile reserved, but hearing that he was okay . . .

"Not now, no. I'm sure he wouldn't mind having his little sister in there for a bit, though, even if he's asleep." Bianca gave Pilar the warmest smile that Pilar could ever remember seeing.

Pilar smiled back, and made her way into Seth's room. Seeing all the bandages and blood . . . he didn't look "okay," no matter what Bianca had said. Pilar could hear him wheezing as he breathed. She could see all the wounds he'd suffered, all the bruises, his right arm wrapped in a sling . . .

Pilar kneeled at the side of Seth's bed and Bianca put a hand on her shoulder. "It looks worse than it is. I know that's not saying much considering how bad it looks, but . . . Seth will be okay."

"Bianca?"

"Yes?"

"I'm sorry for how I acted. You know, when you first came back."

"There's no need for that. Especially not now. But it is nice to know you're capable of it."

If it had been anyone else, that would have cut deep. But after what they'd been through, and especially after that night,

Bianca had earned the right to give Pilar that one, whether she was joking or deadly serious.

"Yeah. I guess I'm capable of it, sometimes."

". . . That's . . . a good thing."

Pilar's eyes lit up hearing her brother say that. "You're awake!"

"You're supposed to be resting—oh, for God's sakes why do I even say it?" Bianca ran a hand through her hair. "Just don't overdo it, okay? You have a lot of healing ahead of you."

"I know. I know . . . Going back to sleep. Just wanted to say . . ." Seth looked at Pilar, smiling as best he could.

"What? What is it?" Pilar grasped his hand.

He winked at her. Of all things, he had the nerve to wink at her. "You're not . . . getting out of class next week."

"What?"

His smile widened. "Tuesday . . . is History at eight . . . English at noon . . . Wednesday is Calc at four . . . You know the rest. I'm too wasted to . . . uh . . . remember it right now."

She nearly burst into tears right then. "Just rest, you big dope," she managed to get out.

38

The small, black worm at his feet was insignificant. Yet, he still took the time to pick it up with his fingers, examining the struggling little leech.

"You don't seem very thrilled." Widow approached Mantis's perch, arms folded and all her eyes focused on what he held in his grasp. "Considering your plan worked without even a slight flaw, I'm surprised."

"There was a flaw, Widow." He turned to face her, revealing the leech now in his palm. "Converting Leech into that unhinged beast wasn't hard. He was already part of the way there, anyhow."

"Then what in the world has your mood so terrible?"

Mantis looked to the sunrise as it washed over the desolate cityscape before him. He'd become quite used to the wasteland that was District 99, having lived amongst the rubble for years now under his current guise. His perch was the remains of an old office building, one of the taller pieces of ruins that remained after the battle over a dozen years before that had leveled the district.

He played a bit more with the leech in his palm. "He was supposed to succeed in killing Bug, not helping her find the weapon she needed to be a bigger pain."

"Well, even with his powers enhanced, he was nothing more than a useless mutt, after all." She rested her arms around his shoulders, leaning on his back. "That doesn't change what we plan to do, does it?"

"No."

"Good. Because I grow more and more weary of listening to that grumpy old man boss us about as though we owe him our lives."

"Have you kept up the dummy network as well?"

She held her wrist out, showing Mantis the glowing bracelet that rested upon it. "He and the Core still believe we are connected and obedient as always."

Mantis turned to her, giving her a childish smile. "This is why you're the best!"

"There is another problem, however."

"Oh?"

"Centipede and Scorpion. Who knows where their loyalties truly lie, if they aren't completely lost in the Core's embrace."

Mantis could see the frustration welling up on her face. As beautiful as she was, anger and frustration always brought out the worst in her Indigo deformities.

"They'll either side with us or fall. Simple as that."

"There's one other problem."

"Oh?"

"His daughter." Widow smiled. "Though once she's been completely transformed, we can likely turn her before she's fully matured."

Mantis nodded. "How fitting that would be, to have his own daughter turned against him and be his undoing."

"Perhaps we can manage to kill his other daughter and lay her corpse before him as well."

Mantis scratched his cheek with his free hand, and still observed the leech with his other. "I'd rather she see her sister first. Actually, I'd rather we turn her, too. But I doubt that would be easy to accomplish with those suits around. But . . ."

His eyes locked onto the leech that wriggled about, trying its best to suck upon his blood. Slowly, it began to writhe in pain. Smoke began to rise from its body. It erupted into flames, and after a few more seconds of agony, Mantis's entire hand was engulfed in a bronze-red fire. He smashed his hand closed, and with barely any concentration at all, the fire dispersed, replaced by an icy black mist that erupted from his palm.

"Hyde still believes that we failed, and that the boy's power is no more." Widow's grin matched Mantis's delight. "We're at a distinct advantage."

"The mass experiment he's planning . . . that will be our best opportunity. Let him and his forces do all the work for us."

Widow nodded, then stood. "Come on. Time to go tell our beautiful lie."

Mantis stood as well, following her from his perch as he chewed upon the frozen remains of the bug.

39

Seth wasn't sure why he hadn't expected to see Pilar there.

Maybe it was because the last time she'd gone to the hospital as a visitor, it was the last time they'd seen their mother alive. He figured that was the cause of her irrational hatred of hospitals to begin with.

He didn't want her to see him so weak, either.

A small part of him, however, still worried that even after all that, their relationship wasn't fully repaired, nor would it be. Even with everything that had happened, he still held a lot of anger towards their father, Pilar held a lot of angst in her about their mother, and they could not agree whether their dad was alive or dead.

When Pilar embraced him as he sat upright in bed, he could at least eliminate the thought she hated him.

Still, he felt as though there was too much he'd done wrong.

His room was on the opposite wing Pilar's had recently been on, so there was far less light pouring through the blinds. The fact it was raining outside added to the darkened room, and he refused to have any lights on aside from a couple low-watt bulbs on the counter.

It was still reasonably light, of course. But he much preferred the subdued natural light of the outside world to those blinding full-strength fluorescent lights.

Come to think of it . . . guess I hate hospitals, too.

"You look really surprised to see me." Pilar noticed exactly the reaction he was trying to hide.

Seeing that, there was no use lying. "Kinda am. You hate hospitals."

"That hasn't changed. But you really think I'm so coldhearted that I'd just use that as an excuse to not make sure you were okay?" He was taken off guard by the genuine smile she gave as she said that. Her eyes even watered a bit. She really was still worried.

He patted her head. "I'm fine, sis. A couple minor injuries. Nothing to worry about. Couple of days rest and I'll be back at home. Well, the loft now. Technically home."

Bianca's little laugh was beyond snide. "Minor injuries? Multiple broken ribs, torn ankle ligaments, damaged knees, dozens of severe bruises and lacerations, and a concussion. You'll be lucky if you're let out in a month."

Seth looked to Pilar, smirking. "And let me introduce you to our good friend, Captain Killjoy."

"Oh, thanks, Seth! All I'm trying to do is keep you alive." Bianca was at his side, leaning on the bed. "So be thankful."

"I am thankful. You're still a killjoy, though."

Bianca shook her head, then started towards the door. "I'm going to make some rounds. Still too new here to just do as I please."

As she walked out of the room, Seth yelled after her. "Could you bring me another one of those bagels?"

Bianca nodded to him, then closed the door gently behind her.

Seth looked to his little sister, who sat there with a devilish smirk. "So you're clearly better."

"Actually, there's a li'l more to it than that." Seth lifted his left hand, and held it upright. "I don't know whether it's good or bad, but . . ."

"Your powers are completely gone," Pilar finished his sentence.

Somehow that got Seth to laugh a bit to himself. *Not exactly.* A flare of red light burst from his hand, and soon it was enveloped in blue fire again. After a moment of letting the flame flicker about, he closed his palm, and the flames themselves crystallized, leaving a humming cloud around his hand.

Pilar's mouth was completely agape. "That's. . . that doesn't make sense."

Seth figured that Pilar probably didn't realize she was leaning on his bed, glaring at his hand as if it were another sample of that Indigo mess. She was utterly amazed at what she was seeing, that was certain.

"Seth, how? I thought they drained it from you? And I thought you were supposed to lose it over time?"

"Bianca may've found an answer that I wasn't aware of. But she can't narrow it down yet." He waved his hand about, and the beautiful display he'd created dissipated like steam. "But what's important here, is that this means that Dad's theory about my power was completely wrong, from start to finish."

His irritation peaked as Pilar was examining his hand as though it were some lab rat. When he snatched his hand back with a scowl, she sunk back in her seat. "Sorry. Can't help it. Lab habit. That was probably a little creepy."

"Yeah, little bit creepy." He knew she meant well, though. And honestly, it wasn't like he didn't want to hear whatever feedback she could offer. She could just stand to do so in a less creepy manner.

He put his mind back on task rather quickly. "This makes things a little harder than I thought."

"You figured they'd be done with you," Pilar replied.

"Yeah. Mantis got what he wanted, I lived, and my power was gone. There was no need for them to chase me down again. Of course, on the other hand, that meant I couldn't help keep you safe either. Kind of a crummy trade." He glared down at his hands again. "At least now I can manage that much."

"You really can't let go of the 'big brother has to protect little sister' thing, can you?" She leaned back in her seat, arms folded, a smile permeating her face. "I've got you covered. Trust me on this. I'll make sure our defenses are so tight they won't even get to see your face before they're blown apart. And once I find Dad, we can get go after Hyde and end his scheme."

There was no way that conversation was happening. How could Seth argue with her right then? He knew she wasn't letting the point of "protecting" him change, but he was infuriated that she still clung to the unrealistic idea that their father was alive.

At the same time, could he really take that away from her? He knew some of the truth. Not all of it, but enough to know that whatever once was of their parents, no longer existed.

That was especially true in the case of their father.

He couldn't tell her how he knew, though. He couldn't tell her why he knew, why he was so sure. It ate at every part of him to keep quiet.

Then again, maybe that was a part of it.

Maybe there was some part of him that wished, that prayed, that hoped beyond all else in the world, that their father was somehow alive. That somehow, Seth's kid sister could prove him and everything he thought he knew, wrong. After all, he didn't have any physical evidence. She was the last one to have seen Dad actually living, breathing, and in one piece. But no matter how hard anyone pried, Pilar could not remember what she'd seen of him in those last three days.

She just knew that nightmare. That one dream that woke both of them in the middle of the night and usually ended with her screaming, or lying on the floor, groaning about falling out of bed again.

It wasn't as if she even had a theory to begin with! It was just this idea that "he's alive, he has to be" that she continued on with. It took everything within him to keep Seth's sense of logic from taking over. *I have to leave it to her to figure out the truth.*

The truth that he couldn't get rid of, the one guilt that ate away at him more than anything else, was that he had to watch his little sister stress about finding their father, when Seth himself could not care any less than he did. He had to let that grudge go, somehow. Maybe that was part of what compelled him to interfere. But, she was old enough, and at the end of the day, he couldn't stop her. He wasn't her father.

"Seth."

He looked to his sister as she approached. "Yup, that'd be me."

Once she was at his side, she thumped his forehead as hard as she could.

"The hell?"

"Don't do anything that stupid again, alright?"

He started to snap at her for doing that, but before he could even react, he could see her eyes had reddened, and her breathing was troubled. She cleared her throat. She stood stiff, yet a bit of trembling in her hands could not be stopped. "The next time me or Bianca has to hold you together to make sure your body doesn't come apart at the seams, I'm going to kill you myself for being an idiot."

"Well, that was unnecessarily dark." He scratched his cheek a bit, flicking the growth of hair that had started to form a beard. "I remember being on the opposite side of this a few weeks ago. Kinda weird having to take my own advice."

"We'll both take that advice. Fair?"

She embraced him suddenly, then nodded to him before she began to make her way out of the room. "Rest. I can handle things fine on my own."

As they left, Madri peeked her head back in, grinning so happily at him that he figured she was just trying to be as much of a cartoon character as she could within her human capabilities. "Don't worry, I'll help keep her safe! Agent Madri Mars, official protector of your little sister!"

"Just . . . keep her safe. And try to act normal about it?"

"You got it, coach!" She punctuated her declaration with a firm salute. As the door slammed behind her, Seth rolled his eyes.

"'Coach'?"

40

Pilar finished showering after yet another beating at Zoe's terrifically skilled hands. Zoe continually assured Pilar that she was "really improving" and how excited she was to see it.

Pilar, of course, didn't see this awe-inspiring improvement.

She made her way to the elevator in the back of the loft, hidden away in the wall like some sort of hidden door in a haunted house. Of course, that was for good reason.

In the center of the door, completely hidden underneath the cover, was a PPRD, similar to the device that was outside the lab. She placed her palm over that area, and it was scanned fairly easily. Once it recognized her, the door to the elevator slid open.

It was odd for her, going into the lab that way. She'd gotten used to the front entrance after so many years. That front entrance still functioned for emergency use, but to her, it felt better to leave that path locked until it was absolutely necessary.

Zoe had already beaten her down there. When she thought about it a bit further, Zoe was beating her a lot that day, and in many different ways to boot. In any case, she was there looking at various news stories alongside Bianca.

"This new search program is phenomenal, love! I've never seen anything like it!" Bianca was enjoying the upgraded interface of Andromeda. Pilar had managed to make the entire display appear as a three-dimensional holograph, with touch functions incorporated. As such, the glowing blue globe of text and icons were like a sort-of virtual reality desktop.

"She's having too much fun with that." Zoe sat down beside Bianca, her arms folded as she watched the screen for any news. "Any word from Agent Rose since last week? Or from Aegis at all?"

Pilar shook her head a bit. "Nothing yet. Not that I'm really excited about meeting with them. At the very least, our battle suits are up and running again." She took a few steps forward, stopping right before the containment tubes that housed their suits. She leaned forward a bit, then tapped the container that held her suit within its emerald light.

"Yeah. I'm not trusting them either." Zoe folded her arms. "But I can't think of why they'd want to meet with us other than trapping us."

"I don't suppose you two are returning to school anytime soon?" Bianca peeked back to them, a sly smile on her face.

"Not really sure. Right now we're still laying low." Pilar looked to Zoe. "Your sister and father are okay with you living here for a while?"

"I'm certain they are. There's not much they could argue after seeing what happened."

Just as she spoke those words, Agent Rose stepped out of the elevator chamber, in his usual black suit with black tie. The look he had on his face was a dry, cold, serious stare. Even for Agent Rose, he seemed unnatural.

Right behind him was Agent Swords, who looked as serious as ever. Pilar wasn't sure he could actually act any other way.

"Looks like it's time for our meeting." Pilar folded her arms, giving Agent Rose a bit of a stare. "I take it we're going to see her now?"

A hand clasped her shoulder, and she was taken so off guard that she couldn't even flinch. She was utterly petrified. Pilar's heart nearly burst out of her chest when she heard an unfamiliar voice from behind her.

"No need for that. I brought the meeting to you."

The caramel-skinned woman before them had streaked, platinum blonde hair, and was dressed in a loose-fitting navy blue blouse with the top two buttons undone. She wore a matching skirt as well, and a large, open, white lab coat over it all. She looked disheveled, and yet somehow managed to still seem professional.

The woman walked right pass Pilar, patting her shoulder. She made her way to the nearest inspection table, flailed her long lab coat out, then sat down, legs crossed and hands on her knee.

"So, I see you're all here. This is good. Saves me the trouble."

Oddly enough, after a moment of sitting there and looking Pilar over, the director removed her shoes, letting her stocking-covered feet get some relief from the black pumps she wore.

"Wow. Seeing you in person after all these years? Yeah, you are absolutely their kid." She looked to Agent Rose, then back to Pilar. "Except the hair. Pretty sure it was black. Emm and Bee didn't have pink hair that I know of."

None of that was of interest to Pilar, of course.

"How . . . ?" Pilar looked all about the lab, then looked to Bianca, then Zoe, then to Agent Rose, and finally, examined every bit of the ceiling. "The hell? How? How did you get in?"

The director raised her hand, and pointed to her palm.

"No way in hell," Pilar spat. "My father would not let someone this high up in Aegis set foot in—"

"Yo, Gil," the director yelled above Pilar's protest. "Please tell me there's still something good to drink down here!"

Gilgamesh, who was on the far side of the enormous lab, recognized her voice and answered without hesitation. "No, I am afraid we are limited only to non-alcoholic beverages at the moment, Miss Delacruz."

"Miss Delacruz?" Pilar looked to Gilgamesh, eyes erupting with shock, voice filled with confused rage. "You're on a last-name basis with this woman?"

"Ah. Good point." The director cleared her throat. "You don't have to be formal Gil!"

"Yes, my apologies, Angela." Gilgamesh bowed, then returned to his maintenance task as if it were all normal.

Pilar found the nearest chair and just . . . sat. She was defeated. The entire time, Aegis had had this much control of her life, and she'd been completely ignorant of it. Of course the director could come and go as she pleased. She was basically paying for the place, anyway. Why should Pilar have even been surprised by this?

"Calm down. Me knowing the ins and outs of this place is not the end of your world." Delacruz leaned against the table behind her. "Just means you aren't as aware of how the rest of the world works."

"Can you, at the very least, explain how you got in here?" Bianca still sat at the Andromeda station, trying to process just what had happened, herself. "I've been here most of the day and didn't even see you pull up."

"Dock," Delacruz answered. "There's a northern entrance that comes straight off the lake. Access there is amazingly restricted. I'm probably one of four people who know about it."

Pilar rubbed her forehead. "I knew about it. I would've never imagined you knew about it."

"Can I just rock your little world a bit more, then? I feel it's necessary to get you to understand things a bit better."

Pilar waved her arms in surrender. "By all means, put me to further shame."

"You are being surprisingly overdramatic right now."

"You just proved my security sucks complete ass. You, the director of the company I thought I was at least half a step ahead of, walked right in, no problem. Yes, I'm a little overdramatic about that."

The director was smiling like a kid who'd just one-upped a bully. "Well, let me calm you down a little. Your security doesn't suck. I just happen to be one of the people that helped build it."

"What on earth are you talking about now?"

"Your parents, Abel, and I? We were pretty tight knit. I've probably spent more time in this lab than you've spent, well, being alive." She looked to Agent Rose. "I just aged myself, didn't I?"

"Wouldn't be the first time, Director."

Delacruz looked to Agent Rose and gave him a smug laugh. "Look at you! Being all professional!"

"One of us has to." He folded his arms. "Come on. You've had your fun, Angela. Kid's been through a lot. Really think she needs this, too?"

Delacruz shrugged. "All right then. I'll play fair. Guess that was a bit much if you're complaining about it. But, I'm sure Pilar understands more than anyone else. It's not often we get chances like that to show off, right?"

Pilar really didn't want to agree with this woman on anything, but she was absolutely right. Still . . . "How would you know?"

"You've inherited your dad's genius," Delacruz waved her hand about the air, gesturing to all the equipment in the lab. "But, you also inherited your mother's ego. All of her ego."

"Are you say—"

"I mean that in a good way, before you get riled up. Your mother was my closest friend next to Emmanuel. Her confidence was a positive. Usually." She looked to Andromeda, rubbing her chin as she observed it. "Good to see Andromeda up and running again. Haven't seen that thing in years."

"Alright, so what do you actually want, Director? You needed me to wave a white flag and fork all my stuff over to Aegis? Or are you here to gloat?"

"You've misunderstood something." Delacruz folded her arms, still casually leaning back in her chair. "'I', as in 'Angela Delacruz,' know about this lab and all its intricacies. Aegis knows jack about it. And as far as anyone in the city knows? It's just some old relic of a place. Not even on the housing market."

Pilar's scowl tightened as she listened to more of this woman's weird reasoning. She felt like her brow might fold in on itself as she glared Delacruz down. "You're the director of Aegis. Therefore for, by logical extension, Aegis knows about it. Because you are Aegis."

"Do you always think that black and white?" One of the service robots happened to roll up to Delacruz's side, and she offered her index finger. It willingly shook it, then went back about its task. "I'm the director, yes. They don't know everything I know because frankly, I don't need them to know. This place is one of the things I'd die before telling the other directors about."

"Other directors?" Even after all Pilar's research, this was the first she'd heard of anything like that.

"I sit on a board. Actually, amongst the directors of the company I have the least pull, since I technically inherited the position. The rest of Aegis doesn't really like me, outside of my own division. Which is ironic, considering I'm the public face of the company. But I'll save my bitching for another time." She looked to her watch. "Guess I'd better get to business. I don't get back in time, they're going to get more curious than I'd like them to be."

Pilar wasn't sure she was there mentally. She looked to Zoe, who seemed just as shocked, trying to understand just what was happening. "Okay then, fine. What exactly do you want?"

"To hire you. Well, more specifically, to hire your team."

Pilar looked to Zoe, then to Rose. "Is she for real?"

Pilar found herself even more surprised by Rose's reaction. He placed his hands in his pockets, turned to Delacruz, then back to Pilar once more.

"Told you she'd hate it," Rose said to Delacruz, smirking. It was obvious that he'd known this was going to happen from the start.

"Oh gee golly, ya think?" Pilar snapped.

Delacruz barely had a reaction, if any. She just stared Pilar down, her confidence unwavering and her lips not forming anything other than her words. Not even a glimpse of a smile crossed her face now. "I'd like to bring you two in as contractors. That simple enough for you?"

"Not gonna happen," Zoe answered in Pilar's stead.

Delacruz's tone still didn't waver. "You need more evidence of what's going on at Aegis to help your father's abandoned case. Am I right?" Both Pilar and Zoe glared with widened eyes when Delacruz said this. "And you. You need to find out what happened to your parents right?"

"I'm well aware of what happened to my mother." Pilar did her best not to sound as though she was even slightly interested, but . . . what was she getting at?

"You think you know what happened to your mother."

Delacruz certainly had Pilar's curiosity peaked, hearing that. She'd given such a definitive answer, she had to know something.

"I'm listening."

"I'm not saying I know anything about it, other than it makes no sense. She should have recovered from that illness. She had recovered. And then, just like that? Dead. That can't satisfy you any more than it does me." She took a peek at Agent Rose, then continued. "And you're the only one who has a clue to what happened to your father. By the way, that whole bit with the news years ago? Shaming him and all that? Nothing to do with me."

"You're telling me Aegis had nothing to do with—"

"I said the news coverage had nothing to do with me. Not Aegis." Delacruz sat back, then her eyes focused right into Pilar's own. "Which brings me back to my earlier point. Truth is? I'm in the same boat as you."

"Oh?"

"You lost your parents within two years of each other, and you have no idea how either of them really died. I lost those same two people, and they were closer to me than my own family. The fact I'm sitting here should prove that. So now you get why I showed off a little."

Pilar didn't say anything, but when she looked to Zoe, she wondered if she had the same thought: She did all that showing off just to prove her connection to Pilar's parents.

"Sands was overprotective of everything. Only people he allowed in this lab have gotten in this lab, haven't they? Bianca? Your brother? Rose?" Delacruz pointed to Zoe. "Granted, she's the exception, but that's your doing."

"This is all quite adorable." Pilar realized, right then, that she was dealing with someone who had far more power in her world than she could ever fathom. She had information Pilar needed, she knew Pilar's secrets, and she knew things about her parents that Pilar probably couldn't remember if she tried. "But if you've got all this, what do you need from me?"

"That's the hard part. I can't really investigate things on my own. Looks suspicious. And I can't afford to be displaced or voted out of my position. A lot of good people, who don't even know it, would be in danger if my theory is right."

"Yeah well, that's not shocking," Zoe added.

"So, I'll give you things to investigate via my agents. As far as school, you'll also only take online classes until we can confirm the Cloaks are no longer a threat. You'll need to be out of school while we find a way to neutralize them. Last thing we need is them parading through another section of the city and killing off the masses again."

Pilar looked to Zoe, who didn't seem to disagree with that. *It's logical*, Pilar then thought, *considering what happened the last time we were some place they knew of.*

"Go on."

"You will still continue your activities in those battle suits at night. And I'll make sure the high-level agents, namely those in this room, work with you."

"You want us to investigate your company's failings, behind even your own back." Pilar folded her arms. "Isn't this something the government usually does? Or even the RCPD?"

"Yeah. Except . . ." Delacruz looked to Rose again. "Do I really need to tell them this?"

Rose nodded. "Think it's time we told them what's happening."

"Of course you do," she answered. And for the first time since she'd been there, her iron exterior slipped into a regretful, pained smile. "The other seven members of the board may also have plants in those places. I don't play that dirty, but that also puts me at a distinct disadvantage when it comes to who I can ask for help. And even then? RCPD's relationship with us is tepid at best. Remember, we couldn't even interfere during the club attack, and that's practically what the city contracted us for."

Zoe stepped forward a bit more, now standing right next to Pilar. "So then, they already know about the Cloaks . . .RCPD, city officials, they already know about the attacks."

"They know of them at a base level. Not the details. Though with the last attack I imagine they're going to want to know more beyond that. And of course, politically, they want things to be talking points for their approval ratings. Sounds good to tell the people on the island that they stomped out a terrorist experiment gone mad."

Pilar had to admit, she wasn't wrong there.

"Furthermore," Delacruz looked to Rose for a moment before continuing on. "I don't know which of my own lower-ranked agents they have control over."

"Your fellow directors are spying on you." Zoe peeked over at Agent Swords. "And that's saying something, considering they could just as easily kick you out anyway."

"Sharp."

"It's what I do." Zoe didn't take the compliment well, still standing firm and not cracking even a slight smile. "Sounds like they still want you as the face of the company until they work on another plan."

"And we have no idea what that plan is," Pilar added. "But my guess? It's related to Indigo."

"Indigo, and your battle suits." Delacruz sat forward. "But right now, it's still up for debate what their actual goal is. Only thing I do know is their reaction to everything happening right now, including our agents, doesn't speak to people who give a damn about the value of human life."

"They sound like the Cloaks," Zoe concluded.

Pilar remembered that much as well. The way Widow spoke of the people in the apartment, them, and the Aegis agents . . .

Unevolved beasts.

"I can't directly order anyone to investigate outside of my top agents, and even they are restricted. That's also why you two are the perfect choices for this. You've got nothing to lose. You're about as neutral a party as I can get."

"Good points." Zoe grasped her chin. "You're taking a big risk, trusting us to investigate your company for you, giving us free data that could be used to shut Aegis down completely. After all, we still could be coerced by the same execs to betray you, right?" Before she even realized it, Zoe began slowly pacing about. "Or we could take what we find out and expose the company ourselves. Or we could destroy everything we get our hands on to purposely cripple you."

Delacruz tapped her forehead, then looked to Pilar. "She always ramble on with theories like that?"

Pilar was still despondent. "It's what she does."

"How nice of you." Zoe smirked at her partner. "I say we do it."

Pilar had to rethink her strategy at that point. After all, this was too good of an opportunity to pass up. This was her chance to investigate them right at their epicenter; investigate her father's disappearance, watch the Cloaks, and at the first sign of trouble, or anything she didn't like, or even if she didn't like the coffee in her lab that one day, she could blow the whole company wide open.

Which begged the question . . .

"You sure you want to hire us? Seems extremely counterproductive for you."

"Oh, but I get the best reward of all." Delacruz didn't bat an eye. Her smile was absolutely devious. "This is also an easy way for me to openly keep an eye on you, and make sure you don't get yourselves killed, or do something obscenely stupid. You know, rather than having to spy on you like another set of enemies."

"And you care because?"

"Because if anything, you're my responsibility." Delacruz sat back once more in her seat. "Things are going to get very, very messy from here on out, which is saying a lot, considering. Especially with the Cloaks running around and trying to cripple not only us, but you. I'm sure you saw the slaughter in the Shopping District."

Pilar shot a worried glance over to Zoe, who returned with one of her own. "We'd rather forget that night."

"So would I. So imagine my elation to hear that they leveled an apartment complex simply looking for Seth. They found where you both live. Then they killed almost a hundred innocent people of all ages just to draw you out into the open and try to kill your brother."

There was only so much of Pilar's anger and frustration from that night she could hold in. Bringing it up right then was not something she wanted, at all. It was a vulnerability, something that could make her decision more rash.

Pilar knew that was exactly why Delacruz had brought it up.

Pilar couldn't react on emotion. But the more she thought about it, her whole mission was already driven by it. She wanted to find out what happened to her father, and why Aegis tried to bury him. She needed to find a way to stop the Cloaks and destroy Hyde before more lives were taken. And she still had no idea what they were even after, other than her brother, and some weird revenge fetish for Aegis agents. And at that point and time . . .

"Fine," Pilar replied. "But let's get one thing straight, right now."

"Oh, by all means," Delacruz said almost chucking as if listening to a baby speaking gibberish.

"You are not my boss. I am not here to be your favorite employee. Name-dropping my parents doesn't suddenly warrant my full trust in you. Got it?"

Delacruz glared at Agent Rose as though she might throw her chair at the girl. And yet, he just casually shrugged back. "You knew what to expect, Angela."

Delacruz stood. "Fine. I can see this is going to be a pleasant experience. That said, we need to—"

The elevator door opened behind them, and Madri Mars, who was actually dressed in much more casual attire, emerged. Surprisingly, the pink hoodie fit far more than her usual work wardrobe. In her grasp was a large black duffle bag and a red backpack, both filled to the brim.

Before any of them could react, Madri dropped her belongings on the floor and ran to Pilar and Zoe, hugging them like a happy little kid. "Roomies!"

Pilar's eyes rolled hard and fast to Delacruz. "Explain."

Agent Swords had arrived with Madri, and walked to Delacruz's side. "You didn't tell them yet, I take it."

"I was getting there," Delacruz answered. "So, uh, yes. Madri will be staying with you and working alongside you to ensure you are safe, and assisting you if and when anything Cloak-related occurs. Seeing as the three of you are already familiar, having her stay at Emm's old lab with you makes the most sense. So, in her words," Delacruz cleared her throat, then mocked Madri's excitement, "'roomies!'"

"Ten minutes in, and I absolutely despise you. That's a new record." Pilar moaned.

Despite that, Madri still clung to Pilar. "Aww c'mon, it'll be great! Now we can get to know each other and hang out and watch TV shows and stuff and discuss *Super Sentai* and—"

"Wait." Zoe's eyes narrowed as she observed Madri. "'*Super Sentai*'? As in?"

"*Gorgon Zola Nine?*"

Zoe took a moment, then pulled Pilar to the side.

"What now?" Pilar was getting tired of getting dragged places by other people, whether by command or by unintentional force.

Zoe was as stoic as Pilar had ever seen her. "Anybody who knows about that isn't all bad."

"Fine, you two can share a damn room." Pilar looked back to Delacruz and almost moaned her next question. "Is there anything else you want to just inject into my life real quick? I'm having a severe shortage of crap to deal with."

"Hey! I am not crap to deal with!" Madri huffed. "The nerve! Just because I don't have a broom up my butt doesn't mean—"

"Ladies." Swords shot out. They were all surprised to hear him suddenly interject. "We're here on business."

"It's fine," Delacruz replied, chuckling. "They're kids. I don't exactly expect them to be buttoned down and all business like us."

"Then the least they could do is keep this noise to themselves for a few minutes so we can get this done." Swords looked at all three of them as though they were kindergarten students. "Stop wasting time."

"Robble robble robble I do say you're all too noisy robble robble robble stop wasting time," Madri mocked him under her breath. "God. I'm just glad to have people my age to deal with for once, you old curmudgeon."

Pilar and Zoe really didn't want to laugh at that. Pilar was at least able to contain her laughter by curling her lips as tight as she could. Zoe nearly blew her nose. Even Rose had to rub his head to hide his laughter at his coworker. Delacruz had to fake clearing her throat just to keep from laughing at that herself.

"Madriella Mars will be my liaison going forward," Delacruz eventually continued, "she's your roommate and extra set of hands."

"Wait, I thought that was Agent Rose?"

"Agent Rose is absolutely terrible at looking inconspicuous," Delacruz answered. "Besides that, Madri obviously will blend in quite a bit better whenever you have to be seen."

"I am not terrible at being inconspicuous," Rose protested. Literally no one backed him up. Silence enveloped the room.

Delacruz coughed again before moving on. "That aside, I need him for other matters. He's one of the most known agents in the division, so having him run interference constantly is starting to hit his reputation. Can't have that."

Rose gave a nod. "I'll still be around, but much of Aegis's own security relies on me. Lot of my peers getting too curious."

Delacruz gave a satisfied breath, leaning back in her seat once more. "So, there it is. Now you get how this all sets up, right?"

Pilar still wasn't terribly comfortable with any of this. But, just as Zoe had pointed out, it all still worked to their advantage. And truthfully, if it meant that there was one less side she had to watch out for, she could make worse choices.

"I understand."

Delacruz stretched and yawned loudly, seemingly not caring a bit about how professional she appeared anymore. "Well, I'm glad that's done."

"Director."

"Yes, Pilar?"

"One more rule. Please announce when you're coming by. If you sneak in here like that, I can't promise that the security measures won't be less friendly next time." Satisfied with her answer, she stood there, arms folded and a smile on her face.

Delacruz was already making her way to the dock exit. "Oh, go right ahead. I'll just override that. Or my intern will. Someone will."

Pilar collapsed back into her seat. "Please, just . . . leave. I need to rethink all my life choices right now."

"You are going to be a joy to work with." And just as suddenly as she'd snuck in, the director left.

Madri was quick to jump to Pilar's side, happily sharing a space Pilar would rather keep to herself, and even bumping into Zoe as she squirmed her way between them. "So! Roomies! What are we doing first? Movies? Games?"

Zoe just shook her head at the girl's display of hyperactive wonder. "Not even going to unpack before you go all hyper, are you?"

Pilar didn't seem phased by Madri's act even a slight bit. "Shower," she sighed back. "I'm going to go shower. Not a two-person event."

"Well, technically that's not true. Also, didn't you just shower? Did meeting with the boss lady really make you feel *that* dirty?"

Pilar paused mid-stride. "Oh my God, I am going to kill you before the day ends." Pilar got up from her seat and marched her way to the elevator. "All of you do whatever you want. Just don't break anything."

Agent Rose placed a hand on her shoulder to stop her as she marched by.

"What?"

"Sorry about all this. I know it's inconvenient. And I know the boss lady can be, well, immature. But trust me on this. She means well. We all do."

Somehow, hearing him say that calmed Pilar down a bit. And she remembered why this was all happening to begin with. "It's okay. I know. Thanks, Rose."

"Don't mention it. We'll get out of your hair and let Madri settle in."

"You can't take her with you?" Pilar joked, peeking back at Madri to make sure she'd heard that.

"No, they can't," Madri yelled back.

Pilar loosed a bit of a grunt before making her way to the elevator. This would probably be as terribly annoying as she thought.

41

Sunset had become her favorite time of day.

She sat on the balcony, looking out across the lake as the sun sank into it, the skies becoming a mix of orange, purple, and a dark-blue haze. Clouds were rolling in from the east, creating a living painting right before her eyes.

Just like the sunrise after that night of terror, she appreciated this moment more than she ever could have weeks ago.

Still, she worried now where everything would lead. Did she really want the answers that lay ahead of her? Something in her heart felt off. It felt as though a part of her path had become forbidden.

But she couldn't sit and wait for her to be allowed to follow it. She needed to move onward. She needed to unravel everything.

The truth of her father's whereabouts was trapped within that knot, after all. Much like that nightmare, he was lost deep within that darkness. She was the only one who could free him.

And freeing him would free her.

She looked to the opening sliding door, and watched as Zoe sat on the ground next to her without bothering to ask if she could.

Pilar didn't mind this time, though.

"You okay?" Zoe asked of her.

"I guess. I mean, I'm not, not okay. But, okay seems strong."

Zoe was utterly confused, and her eyes showed as much.

Pilar got a bit of a laugh out of that. "I'm fine, considering how this afternoon went."

Zoe sighed. "Yeah. I can relate, considering the call I just had."

"Talking to your dad?"

Zoe nodded. "He's . . . not happy. I can't blame him. I mean, I really can't blame him. Or my sister."

"They at least understand why you're staying here, right?"

Zoe smirked, staring at the horizon herself. "My dad does. Tessa? Not so much. And she wants me to never wear the suit again."

"You know, you don't really have—"

"Don't even." Zoe's smirk was still there, but the way she said that was far from joking. "We're in this mess together now. Partners in crime. Or something like that."

"I get that. But, it's just . . . I don't want to be the reason you and your family fall apart or anything. I know you want the evidence and you're trying to solve this, but . . ." Pilar looked to Zoe again, realizing what she was saying. "Is it really that important?"

"If this was still just about getting evidence, I wouldn't still be here, and I wouldn't be training you. I wouldn't have sat in the lab working on battle armor and trying to understand techno-garble I never studied, and will probably never use again. And to be honest?"

"You wouldn't have asked to be partners in all this to begin with." Pilar smiled. Hearing that, even if it was the third time she'd heard it, put her a bit more at ease.

"See? You do get it. Eventually." Zoe shoved her a bit. "We may have had our reasons to team up, but that was just a means to an end."

"I know."

"So don't even suggest that, okay? We're friends. Considering what we've been through the past few days? We're probably as close as friends can get."

It wasn't as though Pilar didn't know that or didn't agree. Still, it was hard for her to accept. Why? Why was it so hard for her to just accept that?

"We're still going to have to get used to the third wheel in there, though." Zoe pointed back inside the loft. "She's a little hyper, but she's not bad or anything."

Pilar snickered a little. As much as Madri annoyed her, she was pretty harmless. And she couldn't be too upset with someone who had helped keep her safe even when she didn't have the weaponry to do so.

"She's not going to be as helpful without armor," Pilar said.

"Uh, let's . . . not be too hasty on that. Nothing against her or anything, but she was having some real struggles with Andromeda earlier."

"Struggles?"

"Don't worry, it's fine. Rose was still here and fixed it before you got out of the shower."

Pilar should have been angry. Normally she would be. But, for some reason, she just shook her head at it all. "You know what? Yeah, I don't even want to know."

The glass balcony door slammed open at light speed, and Madri poked out of it to glare at them.

"Um, hi," Zoe uttered. "Can we help you?"

"Geez, you two holdin' a group meeting without me?"

"Personal conversation," Pilar answered, slowly getting to her feet. "We're done now, anyway."

"Sweet! Recreation time, right?"

Pilar looked to Zoe. When all she got was a confused shrug, she scratched her head. "Recreation time?"

"*GZ Nine* is about to start! Figured you two would wanna watch it with an expert on the show!"

Zoe yawned. "Sure, I'll watch, I need to catch up on it anyway. I think Pilar said she has work to do, though."

Pilar was shocked to hear that, especially considering she actually didn't have immediate work to do. She realized then that Zoe was giving her an out.

Pilar looked to Zoe and Madri, realizing the irony of the moment. She was standing there with the first person she'd tested her suit on, and the first person to crack her identity. And they were her roommates.

After a deep breath, she walked inside. Before either of them could ask, she was lying across the couch.

"This better be worth my time."

They were both shocked to see her lie down to watch TV, but didn't hesitate to sit on the floor in front of the couch. Madri started rattling on about the show, with Zoe chiming in on the rare occasions Madri would bother to stop talking. And all the while, Pilar lay there, somewhat mesmerized by it all.

Somehow, it all felt normal.

ACKNOWLEDGEMENTS

First and foremost, thank you to my Aunt, Lillie Plummer, who has quite frankly inspired me my whole life, and has kept me going at every step of the way. If not for her, I would have likely given up and jumped off this path a long time ago.

Infinite thanks to my parents, Cicero and Phyllis, and to my little sister, DeCarla, who gave me strength when I lacked it, who encouraged me to keep going, and who often listened to me whine about life for hours on end without hanging up the phone.

Many, many thanks and love to my grandmother, whose strength is only matched by her kindness, and whose encouragement pushed me onward. "Keep your eyes on the prize" – she makes sure to this day to tell me those words whenever we talk.

Much appreciation and thanks to fellow writer David Alderman, my good friend and the person I've bounced more than a million ideas off of since we met in that call center classroom thirteen years ago.

Another big thank you to Jeremiah Smith, who took the time not only to read multiple drafts but followed that up with an in-depth edit that really put this story on the right track.

Last but certainly not least, thanks to you, who holds a copy of this book in your hands. Thank you for taking the time to read my work.

ABOUT THE AUTHOR

Originally from Southfield, MI, Jelani-Akin Parham moved to Phoenix, AZ in 2005 to pursue an education and career in the creative realm. From the early days of middle school till now, he's been fascinated with stories of sword masters, superheroes, mythical monsters and exploring foreign worlds. He was so enthralled by these things in fact, that he acquired a BFA in Media Arts and a MFA in Creative Writing to help him show how awesome they are.

When he's not writing crazy adventures and building worlds or working as an illustrator, he can be found playing competitive fighting games, recording content for his YouTube channel, or composing music. His work can be found on *www.jelani-akin.com.*

www.ingramcontent.com/pod-product-compliance
Lightning Source LLC
Chambersburg PA
CBHW071814200626
46813CB00021B/2602